I0717269

UNDER A COVERED SKY

UNDER A COVERED SKY

LAWRENCE SIMPSON

LawrenceSimpsonWrites Publishing
Copyright © 2023 by Lawrence Simpson
All rights reserved.

ISBN: 978-1-953265-04-3

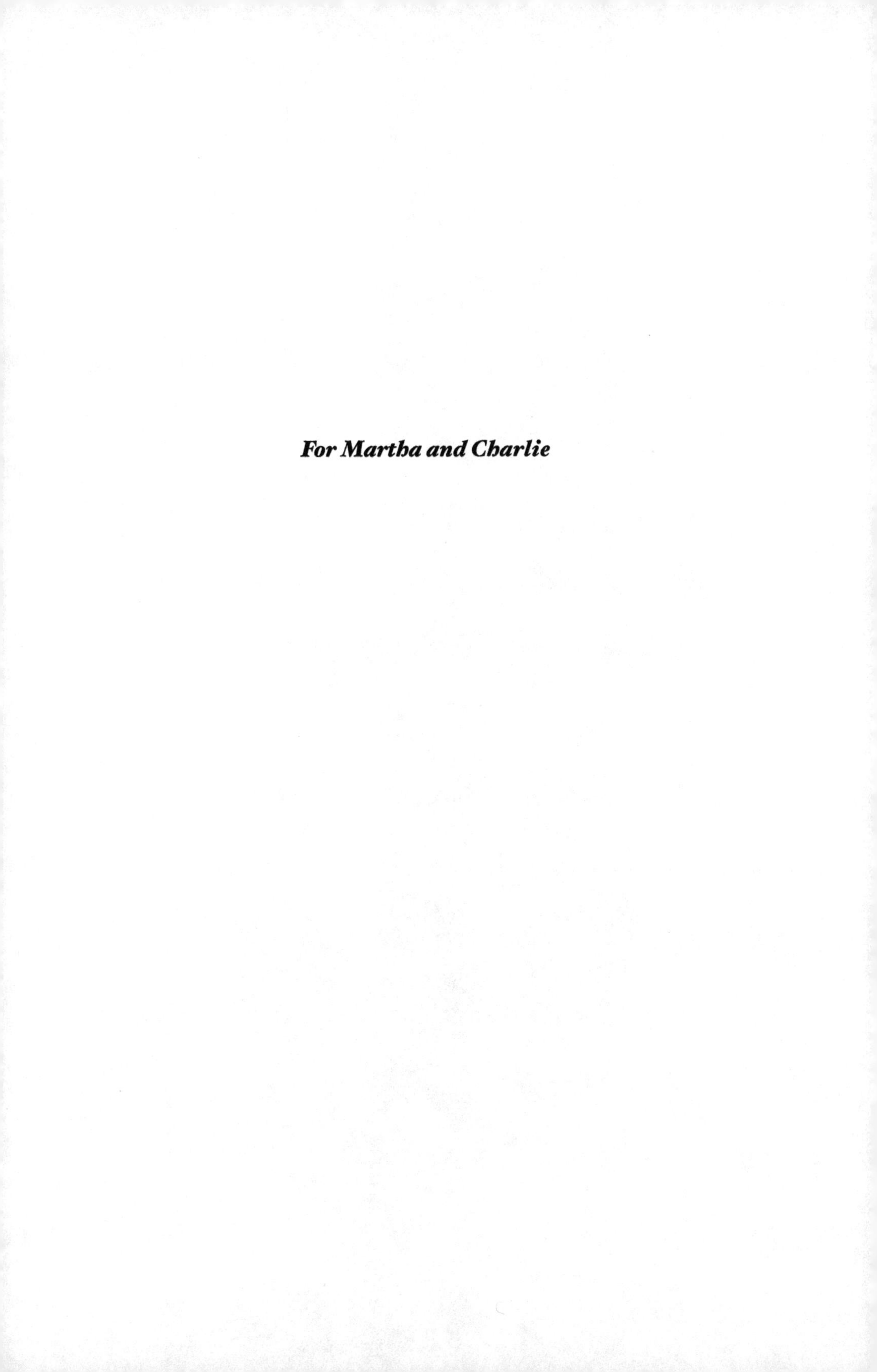

For Martha and Charlie

*"**While the world picks at imperfection, the universe whispers of miracles to those who listen with a willing heart.**"*

- excerpt from The Reverend Father Francisco Romero's first homily on becoming pastor of Our Blessed Mother Church

LAWRENCE SIMPSON

UNDER A COVERED Sky

CHAPTER ONE

Zeke Adams shook the ocean water from his blond hair and carried his carbon fiber surfboard under his right arm as he walked in from the tide line. He'd grown up in California and couldn't remember not surfing. He still enjoyed the early morning swells.

Strong of limb, well proportioned, and brimming with the fullness of youth, quiet mornings in the ocean served as his church. If there was a deity, he felt closer here than anywhere else, and just like this morning, his concerns disappeared in the push and pull of the waves.

He looked at the ocean again before starting the walk up the beach toward his used Subaru hatchback, which he had parked along Pacific Coast Highway. Palm trees fluttered in the breeze by the road, and he could just see the hills beyond. Other than a few surfers and one or two beachcombers, it was quiet this early on a Sunday. He loved living near the ocean and promised himself again that he always would.

He thought of his parents and their most recent argument. Splitsville for sure. He was surprised they lasted as long as they did. Almost all of his friends' parents were divorced. He shrugged his shoulders. He was almost out on his own, but his sister was only fourteen. Danielle was still wrapped up in herself, and she would take it hard. He didn't know what to do about that.

A thrumming noise along the road caught his attention. Sheets of birds sprang from the trees and took flight. There were cormorants, willets, herons, pelicans, and more, well, all of them, and just as he realized something had spooked them, he felt the sand shift beneath his feet. The hills convulsed in a dust cloud beyond the trees, and the morning sunlight shimmered against unwilling concrete, stucco, glass, adobe, and clay-tiled houses vying for prominence in the rapidly growing roller coaster that was once stable ground.

Zeke was no stranger to earthquakes, and like most Californians, he imagined himself an expert, but this was beyond anything he had ever experienced. Bitter fear clung to the back of his throat, making it hard for him to swallow. He dropped his board, but it still anchored him to his spot in the sand by his ankle strap. At least that's what he told himself. He would never admit he was too frightened to move, not in the moments to come. He saw the dust wave move toward him, and he dropped to his hands and knees with his head down. The bone bead necklace around his neck nearly touched the shifting sand. The initial cloud passed over him, and he picked up his board, thinking maybe he should retreat to the safety of the waves. He stumbled back and back while looking at the chaos ahead of him. Surely, it would end soon.

Please let it end soon.

He tried not to think of the people beyond the hills in the streets and houses.

Oh dear God, Dani.

She was probably sleeping in her bed when it started. His insides churned at that thought, and adrenaline quivered his muscles in his mushy disbelief. He moved in slow-motion as the shore under his feet seethed to quicksand. The hills gnashed and groaned as house after house surrendered and crashed in a domino-dance along the highway, easing away to the intermittent collapse of leaning partitions punctuated by random screams smothered to silence.

Even as Zeke choked back tears of relief that it might be finished, vibrations churned through his feet and ankles in the damp sand, and he realized he wasn't standing in salt water. He looked over his shoulder, and the fishing pier undulated like a sea snake trying to make it back into the surf, which had receded beyond the outlying sandbar farther than he had ever seen at low tide. The shuddering at his feet traveled through his backbone to his skull and banged the ossicles in his ears like the drums of something soon to claim vengeance.

Zeke squinted through smoke and haze and saw a shadow on the ocean horizon. He blinked, and the shadow loomed larger. The surfboard fell away, and his feet rooted in the sand like living driftwood as memories flooded his eyes, teasing his parched throat.

"Why God, why?"

He mouthed the words around a globule of acidic bile. He had seen videos on the Internet and knew he should run, but it was useless. It was too late for him and much too late for the stunned survivors at the beach or those at home like his sister.

The grinding roar of a dozen locomotives bore down on him, and he thought of the surfboard at his feet. It was impossible. Even if he were a mile out, he would never be able to ride the wave looming several hundred feet over his head. He could see the crest forming, and his experienced surfer's brain processed the break. It wouldn't be long now.

He thought of Dani again and wished he could tell her he loved her one more time, even if she shrugged him off and called him a jerk face. He thought of Mom and Dad. Each had tried in their own flawed way but had grown tired. They were only human, and he loved them both even in their failure.

He woke up this morning worried about finishing his senior year of high school and the next step beyond that. He wished he could see Candace walk down the halls one more time. She had more grace in a simple stroll than he would ever possess.

He saw the birds flying higher and higher, looking for a hold to light-and-rest, but there was no safe place. To stay in one spot too long merely invited disaster. They had the right idea. Move along when the time seems right. That's what he would do. He would move along, and wherever it was, he hoped he would see his sister and mother and father, and even his aunt, the one who always disapproved of his relaxed outlook on life. Yes, even her.

And then it was upon him.

❖

Parishioners and guests gathered at Our Blessed Mother Church for Sunday morning Mass. Renovated three years ago, the one-hundred-year-old church gleamed like the year of its founding. White columns separated dark-stained wood pews angled in four sections, and those in attendance faced the sanctuary with its white marble altar. A gilded reredos reached twenty feet in custom stonework to a ring of stained-glass-windows illuminating radiating chapels overlooking the congregation. Sunlight filtered through the windows leaving jewel colored hues scattered about the interior of the church.

Maria Valentina Perez sat in a pew in the left front third of the nave dressed in a white long-sleeved shirt, a navy vest and skirt, and a short white chapel veil. She monitored Sofia, who watched with rapt attention. The little girl sat beside Maria with her rolling walker just to the left in an indented area reserved for wheelchairs. After leaving the convent with Mother Mary Margaret's consent, Maria had cared for Sofia for the last three weeks at the request of the archbishop.

Already nervous, Maria hadn't known what to expect when Father Romero introduced the little girl to her as a foundling with unknown history. Sofia had approached haltingly on her walker, which cradled her left arm and side, and regarded Maria intently with clear blue eyes framing a young girl's lopsided smile filled with white teeth. Sofia had the same look on her face now as faithful parishioners brought the gifts up to the front of church and placed them in the priest's hands.

Father Romero addressed those present.

"May the Lord accept this sacrifice at your hands, for the praise and glory of His name, for our good, and the good of all His Holy Church," he said, holding his hands out as the congregation stood.

Sofia insisted on standing when everyone else stood, even though it was an ordeal for her to change positions with her walker. She made the sign of the cross at the image of our crucified savior with her functioning right hand.

Once again, Maria felt her indecision and questions fade away before the faith of this little girl, abandoned by those who brought her here. Sofia could tell them nothing. Somewhere, someone had a record of this little one, but for the time being, she lived at the rectory.

They were sitting after the offertory when a disheveled man shuffled up the aisle favoring his left leg. The stranger flopped into a space on the pew in front of them, his threadbare coat and scarf drooping from his bony frame. He turned around and smiled at Sofia with dingy yellow teeth, and she grinned back at him.

Maria had seen the little girl smile at Father Romero or her, but otherwise, Sofia kept a reserved, shy tilt of her mouth for other people. She seemed enthralled with the unknown man and reached over with her good hand to tug at Maria and point to him. Sofia's eyes glowed, but Maria saw only rags, whiskers, and poor hygiene. The people in the pew in front of them had inched away creating a bubble of space around the ragged visitor.

Maria tried to focus on her prayers while paying attention to Sofia, who watched the stranger intently. They stood for Communion, and Maria helped Sofia into the aisle where they haltingly walked around the pews and joined the line for the Eucharist in the center aisle. At first, Maria had no idea if Sofia understood the Sacrament of Communion, but over the last three weeks, the determined little girl had insisted on fully participating. Sofia tried as hard as she could, but with her disability, they would be near the end of the queue for the living host. She labored with her walker and found her way in front of Father Romero, who placed the body of Christ on her tongue and put his hand on her head in blessing.

Maria followed Sofia in receiving Communion, and they made their way toward their seats. Sofia had mastered the maneuvers to get back into the pew by now, and Maria patiently prepared to help. They slowly shuffled under the statue of the Blessed Mother and turned at the corner of the pews into the aisle when it happened.

Sofia stumbled and fell forward, her walker pushed off to the right, and Maria tried to react in time. Sofia was going to take a hard fall on her left side. There would be injury and a trip to the hospital and questions that no one could answer.

Suddenly, the stranger appeared and caught Sofia before she hit the floor. Maria exhaled, grateful that the man kept her charge from harm. The unkempt visitor held Sofia without moving. He spoke to her, and Maria couldn't hear what he said. At first she told herself that the man was getting his balance after his inhumanly quick response, but he didn't let the little girl go. Sofia looked so frail in his grasp, but her eyes sparkled with a splendor brighter than the windows above the alter, soaking up every question and doubt, and Maria hesitated.

The closest parishioners had reflexively reached out for Sofia, and now, they waited with hands outstretched in silent witness to her arrested fall and her rescuer, who remained on his knees and murmured soft words that sounded like music to every surrounding heart. When the stranger kissed Sofia on her forehead, the concern from the surrounding parishioners changed to righteous consternation and then to amazement as the stranger and Sofia huddled together. Portent filled the air about the hushed onlookers as a soft glow bathed both Sofia and the stranger and surged to blinding brightness.

Maria blinked her eyes several times to find Sofia splayed on the carpet between the pews while the bedraggled stranger glided up the aisle past stunned witnesses and through the doors opening to the narthex.

Maria knelt and touched Sofia on her forehead, and she didn't respond. Maria prepared to pick her up, but the little girl opened her blue eyes and smiled. Sofia raised her right hand to touch Maria's face, and then, she raised her left hand and touched her own face. She extended her left arm and looked at her fingers, wiggling each one at first and then all together.

An indelible silence enveloped the congregation as more in attendance realized something had happened and strained to see. Sofia reached down and placed her hands flat on the carpeted aisle and bunched both legs beneath her. She reached out her hands to Maria, and inch by amazing inch, stood up on her own two legs, straight and beautiful. Her bright eyes darted about seeing stunned faces all around, and her walker lay on the carpeted aisle floor.

Someone called out, "She's standing on her own!"

"But she was crippled," said another in an excited and confused voice.

"It's a miracle!" exclaimed another.

"Praise God!" said several parishioners at the same time.

Father Romero came down from the altar and stared up the aisle toward the narthex as if searching for understanding, and then he reached out to hug Maria and Sofia. After assuring himself that they were all right, he led both of them back to the altar and raised his hands for quiet. All the murmuring congregation could see Sofia now, and the excitement in the church swayed and teemed, electric and palpable.

"What we have seen is for us," said Father Romero. "Let us celebrate in song."

The parish priest launched into a familiar hymn about grace and miracles, and the congregation joined him, singing from their hearts, their voices hoarse in their excitement. Maria thought the roof would bounce off the church, and she found herself singing just as loudly while Sofia beamed at her with the face of an angel.

Father Romero gave the benediction, and the crowd gathered around little Sofia in front of the altar. Parishioners took pictures and video with their cell phones to spread the news, and Maria found it difficult to hold on to Sofia as the crowd jostled in their excitement to touch or talk with the little girl.

Maria felt a hand on her shoulder, and Father Romero led both of them back to the sacristy and enjoined them to wait for him. The pastor stepped back out and spoke to the deacon who began to recite a litany prayer. Many of the parishioners joined in while Father Romero brought out the Host for adoration for one hour, and the deacon made the announcement. Most of the crowd quieted out of respect in the presence of our Lord, but some could not contain themselves and fled to the narthex, where a growing din of excitement prevailed.

In the sacristy, Father Romero shook his head in wonder at a rosy-cheeked Sofia defying everything mundane. She was a living confirmation of the healing power of God, and he only had a brief time before the rest of the world would beat a path to his door seeking the little girl.

Maria seemed to intuit the same, even as she held Sofia in disbelief.

"Father, we have to get her away from here," she said. "You know that."

Father Romero thought furiously. Maria was right, but who did he know? There had to be somebody. He couldn't let this miracle of God, this sweet little girl, face the coming onslaught until they had time to prepare, time to think. Did she not still need sanctuary? And then he had a thought. There was somebody. He had become a bit lost, but he was a good man, and best of all, no one would suspect him of harboring this little one. Father Romero might have to twist the man's arm, but he felt confident in his ability to guilt with the best of them.

"I have an idea," said Father Romero. "I need to make a phone call."

CHAPTER TWO

Mark Lawson drove along the two-lane highway. The asphalt flowed under the tires, and his headlights reached for the tree-lined curve ahead. Maddie was by his side, and Faith sat in the rear seat. At seven years old, their daughter was beyond a booster seat and very proud of that fact. They had spent the day at the lake. Happy and tired, they were on the way back home, and once again Mark gave thanks that a woman as beautiful and warm as Madelyn thought him worthy. He concentrated on the road ahead and kept his speed down for safety. A flash of light in his driver's side mirror made him look over his shoulder to see a sneering black shadow far too close.

Mark turned the wheel and veered right. The right front tire crunched deeply into the gravel beside the two-lane road and pulled their vehicle into a skid. He turned the wheel, trying to stop the inevitable, and the roof of their car rang off the pavement as they rolled.

The ringing kept on until he opened his eyes with his hands in the air in front of him, twisting an imaginary steering wheel in a failed attempt to prevent what had already occurred. Groggy from lack of sleep and regretting his late-night binge with a vodka bottle, he flailed out to pick up his cell phone on the table beside the couch.

"What?" he said. "This had better be important."

There was no answer. He shook his head to clear his vision and regretted it as the pounding between his temples intensified. The ringing continued. It was the doorbell. He slowly got up and shuffled to the front door.

"Hold on. Okay, who is it?"

Mark opened the door, and late morning sunlight dazzled his eyes.

"Oh, good morning, Gene." Mark looked at his watch. "Shouldn't you be in church about now?"

Dean Gene Randall walked in and stood inside the door, which Mark closed very softly in deference to his headache. Standing there in his rumpled clothes from the night before, Mark knew he made a sad sight, but he didn't care at the moment.

"Mark," said Dean Randall. "I'm sorry to bother you on Sunday, but something has happened."

The dean had his hands clasped together in front of him.

His boss wasn't wearing a hat, or Mark would have thought something about hat in hand, but that really should be me, he thought. He waited for the dean to continue.

"I received a call from the archbishop about thirty minutes ago," said Dean Randall. "Something inexplicable happened at Our Blessed Mother Church this morning. People are calling it a miracle."

Mark sat down and shook his head to clear his thoughts. His transition from his previous life as a detective to teaching at the college level would have been a good fit for his family. He could understand why the dean might have sought him out for an opinion. His master's thesis had centered on the thread of the miraculous from Jesus through the written history of the apostles.

His insides churned, and he pressed his hand against his abdomen. He had grown up as a Roman Catholic and, like so many, took the stories on faith, but since the accident, the miraculous no longer seemed possible to him.

"That is very interesting," he said. "But why come and see me early on a Sunday?"

"The archbishop asked me if you would be interested in interviewing the people involved today while it is fresh in everybody's memory."

Gene swiped at the floor with the toe of his shoe.

He looked up and said, "I told him you would be glad to get involved."

Mark gathered himself upright and clenched his hands until his knuckles whitened. His tongue chased syllables past his teeth before he could stop.

"It's like that, is it?" he asked.

Gene held up his hands in supplication.

"The archbishop really needs our help," said the dean. "We need you, and this is your area of expertise. Apparently a little girl is involved."

Mark reached out to the couch to steady himself and glanced at the mantle over the fireplace, but the photographs were no longer there. He had moved them months ago when he couldn't look at their faces any longer without collapsing. Planning for life after the police department, Maddie had encouraged him to continue his education and pursue teaching, and in the two years since the accident, he had endured each day, sometimes on his hands and knees, shuffling from one task to another. However, in the last few months, he had iterated between happy memories like a rusting robot robbed of crucial programming, frozen forever in the moment he lost his world.

"How old?" he asked.

"I'm told she is close to the same age as your daughter would be now," said Dean Randall, handing Mark a folded piece of scribbled notepaper. "I know that might be painful for you. I wouldn't ask, but we are a catholic university, and the archbishop is asking, and well, it's been months, Mark. There's been talk. The teaching assistants can't carry the burden any longer, and the students are complaining. We really need you to step up on this one, and I think it could be good for you."

Dean Randall had the grace to look regretful, but Mark could tell he was serious.

"And if I don't?"

Mark let his voice hang in the air. He knew what Gene would say.

"I don't want it to come to that," said the dean. "I know you don't either."

The dean had been kind to him, but he was in a bind, and so was Mark.

"Okay, I can be at the church in about an hour," said Mark. "Will that be sufficient?"

"That's great," said the dean. "I'll let Father Romero know to expect you."

Dean Randall was kind enough to close the door softly as he left.

Oh great, thought Mark. After getting out of the hospital, he'd counseled with his parish priest for months. He was more comfortable in that setting than a professional psychologist's office.

Father Romero had repeatedly reminded Mark that accidents were without fault. They were driving at night, and it happened. He didn't need to hold that burden to himself. And for more than a year, Mark had managed by focusing on his work, but lately, he couldn't seem to find the will to read or talk on the phone. The pain from his injuries had faded, but the embers of grief in his chest had gradually replaced lung tissue until he couldn't breathe, let alone leave the house to teach.

He had ceased counseling with Father Romero and eventually stopped going to church. He could yell bitterly that he was angry at God for letting it happen, but what he could not tell Father Romero, what he could only admit in the middle of the night after anesthetizing himself with an appropriate amount of vodka, was that he was angry with himself because he knew it was his fault.

Madelyn had chosen him, something her parents had been hesitant about, and Mark had agreed with them. He had been a young police officer stumbling around most of the time, but she had seen something in him, character and ambition he didn't know were there himself. With her influence, he found his footing and finished his master's degree one class at a time. As he gained in experience and education, he earned a detective slot just in time for their first child, Faith. Maddie had taken some time off to care for the baby, and Mark had worked hard. Life had been good.

He rested his hands on the top of the couch to steady himself. The ghosts from last night had retreated from the room along with the photographs, confirming his doubt that anything good in this life could last. Shaking his head, he showered, dressed, and headed for the church.

❖

The ground tremor woke Cardinal Ronaldo Ricci from a troubled nap. Recurring dreams had disturbed his sleep for the last three days, and he had fallen asleep at his desk. He washed his tired face and watched the local afternoon news cut in about a low-level earthquake. He dressed in his cassock, prepared his thoughts, and left his quarters. He had lived with a secret for the last twenty years, and many days he imagined that his heart persistently pumped each day only to prove him wrong. At least, he had hoped that was the case.

He longed for his early years as a priest serving a parish. His life seemed simple then, unlike this moment which found him walking toward the papal apartments. As he approached the secretary's desk, a middle-aged cleric turned from his reading.

"Good Morning, Your Eminence," said Monsignor Esposito. "You look troubled. Is something wrong?"

Esposito naturally wanted to protect the pontiff. The monsignor was a good man of service, and Ronaldo did not want to tell him anything less than the truth, but briefing the pontiff's assistant wasn't his decision to make.

"I am troubled, Monsignor," said Ronaldo. "I confess myself quite constrained, but I am here at the order of His Holiness."

Not quite true, but not a lie either, he thought.

"Without appointment, Your Eminence?" asked Esposito. "He is sleeping. You know he is still weak?"

Esposito didn't want to wake the pope unless absolutely necessary. The pontiff had only recently suffered a bout of pneumonia. None of them wanted to admit it, but anyone could see Anastasi's health declining. Undisturbed sleep at night and an afternoon nap had proven very important for the pontiff's health.

"I understand, brother," said Ronaldo. "I would not trouble him, but this is truly important. I would share details with you, but they are not mine to share."

Ronaldo waited. He had said what he could, and hopefully it would be enough.

Monsignor Esposito wavered, likely considering many factors including Cardinal Ricci's favored position with Pope Anastasi.

"Very well," said Esposito. "Let me attend the pontiff."

Esposito turned and waved at the two bodyguards standing at either side of the papal apartment. Unlike the ceremonial guards at the public exterior entrances, these Swiss soldiers wore dark suits and carried concealed modern weapons, presenting a formidable defense against any attack.

Shortly, Monsignor Esposito returned and signaled for Cardinal Ricci to follow. Entering the papal chambers, Ronaldo took a standing position and waited. Twenty minutes later, Pope Anastasi entered, his face still damp. Monsignor Esposito retired, and they were alone.

Ronaldo stepped forward, bent to one knee, and kissed the pontiff's papal ring. Anastasi smiled at him and waited for him to proceed.

"I am certain it has begun," said Ronaldo.

"I see," said Anastasi.

The pontiff gestured to one of two comfortable chairs, and they conversed.

Not long after, Ronaldo departed from the papal apartments with a thank you to Monsignor Esposito. He moved at his most efficient gate, each stride long enough to press forward without losing his balance. Anastasi had given him explicit instructions, and he must not delay.

The afternoon waned, but Ronaldo walked in a direct line to the Via dell'Aquilone and turned to find the Pontifical Academy of Sciences. The ornate portico entryway led to a marble and stone entrance. It was important to search in the right direction for confirmation, and he felt sure someone had already called an urgent request to assist him. Ronaldo was certain that the prophecy was at hand, but Anastasi had asked for as much evidence as possible.

Stepping inside the scientific academy always brought a sense of wonder. The list of members of the academy were some of the greatest names in the history of science starting with its first president, Galileo Galilei, but with the dread of conviction weighing on his soul, Ronaldo had no time to marvel. Father in Heaven, he prayed to be strong enough. How could they see their way through the coming trial without faith?

He knew the way to the administrative offices from previous visits and found his target sitting at his desk shuffling through several papers interspersed with diagrams and mathematical equations.

Professor Ernst Raoul Bernard looked up, frowning at the intrusion.

"Cardinal, I see you have taken advantage of your office once again," said the professor.

Professor Bernard tolerated other people poorly. There was talk about how someone with his disposition, especially an avowed agnostic, maintained his position, but Ronaldo knew Professor Bernard to be one of the finest scientific minds in the world and one of the few men the pontiff might trust with the information he now carried.

"Professor. I am sorry to disturb you, but it is urgent," said Ronaldo. "Pope Anastasi requests your assistance."

"So I was told. Well, then proceed," said the professor. "I am at the pontiff's service."

Professor Bernard gestured to a chair across from his desk, and Ronaldo disposed himself to sit, all the while forcing himself to calm down. It was important that he convince the professor of his sincerity, and over the next half hour, he shared the secret he had carried for twenty years. Afterward, Professor Bernard leaned back in his desk chair and regarded Cardinal Ricci with skepticism.

"And Anastasi believes this?" he asked. "What would he have me do about it?"

"Professor, I know this is difficult," said Ronaldo.

"Difficult is an understatement," said the professor. "Do you have any evidence to support this assertion that sounds more like a fairy tale than reality? Really, Cardinal Ricci, the pontiff believes this?"

"Yes, he does, Professor," he said. "He is convinced, just as I am."

Ronaldo sat in his seat calmly. He could do no more. Professor Bernard would either believe him or not.

"Why?"

The professor's one word question spat out just shy of contempt.

Ronaldo knew Professor Bernard cared not for conjecture or speculation and put no faith in anything he couldn't scientifically prove through experimentation.

"Because he had the same warning visions," said Ronaldo. "in the beginning and today, just as I did, exactly the same."

Professor Bernard stared at him blankly for a moment. Shrugging his shoulders, he picked up the telephone and began working the problem. He had the pope's requested task and enough uncertainty to proceed. Once on a scientific quest, Professor Ernst Raoul Bernard suffered little regard for anything or anyone else.

In a flash of insight, Ronaldo understood why the pontiff had installed Professor Bernard as the director of the academy. The professor would be unswayed in his pursuit of truth, and that is all anyone could ask.

Slowly, Ronaldo emptied his seat and walked out of the scientist's office. His heart hammered in his chest. Since first exposed to this prophecy, he had prayed he would not live to see it confirmed as real, and yet somehow, he always knew he would. His face showed no tears as he focused on his duty, but he wept within for the world and the chaos to come.

CHAPTER THREE

Colonel Ari ben Eitan stepped between puddles in the graveled parking lot and climbed the wooden stairs to a mobile air defense headquarters. The ten-by-fifteen meter modular structure housed rows of tables staffed on both sides by technicians at consoles linked via computer to various radar, communication, and air defense missile sites. Overhead fluorescent lights outlined the technicians and soldiers in an artificial white glow. Cooled air bathed the consoles and the men and women who operated them, but the heat from the electrical equipment and the palpable tension in the room helped it feel warmer.

Ari commanded the Israeli Air Defense squadrons ringing Israel to the north and east, and his mission involved intercepting enemy missile and artillery attacks before they could impact Israeli citizens. He had been called in early and late to duty many times, but one look at the current intelligence map made him feel like something ice-cold had seeped into his bowels.

"How bad is it?" he asked.

The new Iranian government had promised moderation, but had proven even more militant. For months, Ari and others in his command had suspected that the unusual activity along the borders to the east represented preparation for an offensive.

Where the day before there had been nothing tangible, there now appeared row upon row of military vehicles staging in northern Iran and crossing the border into Iraq while advance troops raced toward the Tigris and Euphrates rivers. It seemed that Iran was about to make good on their pledge to destroy Israel and had convinced other governments in the region to join their efforts or at least not to get in the way.

"Sir, we have movement," said a specialist. "Unidentified radar tracks in the eastern sky suggest aircraft, possibly enemy reconnaissance, and it looks like their advance detachments are carrying materials for a river crossing."

Lieutenant Noem handed Ari a cup of strong tea, which was a blessing.

"They have never tried to cross the rivers before," said Lieutenant Noem. "It is the shortest route to us, but do they have the bridging equipment for a force that large?"

Ari and the other general staff had considered the northern approach from Iran across Iraq, especially in the power vacuum after the previous dictator had been put down, but the rivers were formidable water obstacles to armor. It would be dark in a few hours, and only the unexpected break in the weather had allowed satellite reconnaissance observation to pick up the troop concentrations.

Lieutenant Noem said, "We estimate two hundred and fifty thousand troops supporting four armored divisions, sir. This is no exercise."

"Agreed."

Ari said nothing further as there was little else to say. That was a significant portion of the Iranian ground troops. What other nations were involved in this pre-invasion staging? Israel had no shortage of enemies.

"Organize what you have in writing for me," said Ari. "How is our air defense readiness?"

"We are nominal for all missile batteries," said Lieutenant Noem. "The new emplacements for David's Sling are in place and active. We are alerting all air defense squadrons."

Noem provided an updated list of observed potential enemy forces as he spoke, and Ari thought of the phone call he needed to share with his superior.

"Any communication from Washington?" asked Ari.

In the past, the intelligence services of the United States had often alerted Israel.

Noem shook his head.

"We have heard nothing from our allies."

Lieutenant Noem rolled his eyes to accent his statement, and Ari nodded. Most Israelis understood that the alliance with the United States had thinned over the last few years. Ari sighed. So many years to build up trust, and it was so easily damaged by changes in leadership. Of course, they are likely preoccupied with the disaster on their West Coast. He had heard of it on the international news via satellite radio during his drive to the command center.

"I need to update the defense minister," said Ari. "He will need details."

Ari considered their situation. With the forces being arrayed against them, Israel must strike. Defense had been the heart of Israel's military doctrine since inception, but sometimes, the best defense was a good offense, and one tactical strike in the center of that mass of troops could disrupt their plans entirely. He tried not to overthink what he considered, knowing it might save Israel but would make his country a pariah nation among the rest of the world.

A tremor beneath his feet rumbled to a continuous shaking, and a sharp jolt threw him to the floor. Debris fluttered from the ceiling, and one of the fluorescent lights swung free of its mounting brackets. The loud pop as a bulb shattered added to the confusion, and one table loaded with computer consoles crashed to the floor. Was it an attack? It had been hundreds of years since a major earthquake, but seismic faults crisscrossed Israel as part of the Sinai microplate.

Lieutenant Noem was on the phone immediately.

Shortly, he said, "Earthquake, sir. A large one centered in the mountains of Eastern Turkey."

Ari stood and gripped the console table in front of him like the pilot of a ship pitching at sea. He forced his voice to remain steady as he spoke.

"Contact our defense stations for any damage assessment," he said. "Tell them to double and triple check all systems for any damage. We will need them in the coming hours."

Noem nodded and said, "Yes, sir."

The lieutenant delegated responsibilities and started making phone calls.

Another officer told Ari that the defense minister was on the line for him. Ari sighed and picked up the phone. He gave his civilian boss the known facts and his assessment, and for a moment there was silence on the phone.

"Very well," said the defense minister. "Continue your preparations and keep me updated."

Ari couldn't explain the feeling that came over him at that moment. He felt like he was outside his body looking at all that was happening. He was proud of his country's heritage but couldn't remember the last time he went to temple. His shrine was his family at home, his wife Avigail and the children. All he wanted to do was keep them safe. He took a long breath in and out, despairing that this time he might fail.

❖

Donovan Giulanti waited in the library of his expansive home and tapped his finger on the leather arm of his favorite desk chair. So close, and now this. He turned down the volume from the local television news broadcast via the remote in his hand and heard footsteps outside in the hallway.

"Come in," he responded at the knock on the library door.

The door opened, and a black-haired, bronzed figure glided into the room with the grace of a panther as the door closed behind him. Donovan knew that his security had searched his visitor. He also knew that this man didn't need a weapon in hand to be lethal.

"Tomás," said Donovan. "Thank you for coming to see me."

The man nodded his head minutely to acknowledge the greeting and remained standing.

Donovan had talked with Tomás over the phone in the past, but this was their first face-to-face meeting. He was violating one of his rules by being in the same physical location as Tomás, but the man was an expert at avoiding surveillance, and he needed him for something important.

"I have a task for you," he began, and he saw Tomás give him his undivided interest. "We have found the girl."

Donovan glanced at the unfolding scene on the muted television set. Tomás watched briefly and raised his eyebrows.

"Yes, right under our nose," said Donovan. "Something unexpected has happened, but it changes nothing. I need her brought to me quietly by whatever means."

Tomás nodded his understanding.

Donovan considered for a moment. He had used Tomás before and learned that the man demanded honesty. Donovan needed to tread carefully.

"You've helped me in this matter so far," he said. "The man was of no help?"

Tomás brought his unblinking brown eyes back to Donovan and took his measure like a lion studying a herd.

"He knew nothing," said Tomás. "He will not interfere with your plans again."

Donovan nodded, satisfied.

"And the woman?" he asked. "Did you find her?"

Tomás averted his gaze for a moment before bringing his face back to Donovan.

"Yes," he said. "She was beyond questioning."

Donovan was seldom surprised. One didn't get to his position without planning for all eventualities.

"She killed herself?" he asked.

Tomás shrugged his shoulders and said, "She left a note."

He handed a piece of notepaper folded origami style in the shape of a crane to Donovan, who unfolded and read the run-on block print letters twice.

"There are no other copies of this?"

Tomás shook his head in confirmation.

Donovan tossed the note into the ashtray on his desk and lit it with the lighter he kept for his evening cigars. The torn and creased piece of lined paper consumed itself in yellow flickering flame leaving a black residue. He looked at Tomás.

"You read it?" he asked.

Tomás nodded and asked, "Will the girl be harmed?"

Donovan knew this was a critical moment. He needed Tomás and had utilized his skills in several sensitive situations. The man was a wizard, but Tomás lived by his own code and would not intentionally harm a child.

"Bring her to me alive and unharmed," said Donovan. "It is only in that way that she may help my son." He explained a bit further. "Help me find her, please."

He tried not to show his relief when he saw Tomás nod his head in acceptance. Donovan's most trusted men monitored the study whenever he had visitors, but he had no illusion that Tomás could be deterred from harming him if the slayer felt betrayed.

The discovery that the female courier had left the girl at a church had seemed a momentary complication until this morning. Now, with all the scrutiny, it would be difficult. More important was the matter of his wife, Vivian, and the way she would look at him if he failed.

"I need your skills," said Donovan.

"I live to serve," said Tomás.

Donovan heard the simple words from the man backed by his force of will and reaffirmed why he had involved Tomás yet again. Despite the assassin's cumbersome ethics, once committed, he never wavered. Tomás would retrieve the girl or die trying.

"You will find her at the church," said Donovan.

CHAPTER FOUR

Mark walked around the corner of Our Blessed Mother Church to people clustered on the grass and sidewalk talking and waving their hands toward the church and sharing their story of the wondrous event in a babble of excited voices to all who would listen.

A camera crew filmed an interview in the parking lot of the church, and two more television news trucks pulled up while he looked on. Flashing blue lights from different directions joined the crowd, and officers emerged from the cruisers and began the task of crowd control. Several people gathered around someone needing medical attention, and an ambulance arrived with flashing red lights and a pulsing siren, which further heightened the tension.

Mark had not been here in months, but he and his family had been parishioners at Our Blessed Mother Church. His steps faltered until he recognized an usher talking with a police officer beside an entry door of the church.

"Hi, David," he said.

David noticed him and said, "Mark! Hey, how are you?" He hesitated, not sure what else to say. "It's really great to see you."

The police officer next to them spoke into his radio and requested additional help for the growing crowd.

Mark said, "This is wild, huh?"

"Yeah, the news spread fast, and we were surrounded in no time," said David. "I mean we want people to come to Mass, but this . . . "

David waved his arm to encompass the expanding crush of people, many of whom seemed to have their own idea about what had occurred this morning.

Mark nodded at the police officer, who regarded him for a moment and turned his attention back to the crowd.

"David, I wonder if you can help me?" asked Mark. "I need to speak with Father Romero."

David looked left and right and answered in a hesitant voice.

"Father Romero asked us to keep everyone away for now," he said. "He and the deacon had us direct parishioners out after eucharistic adoration."

"I wouldn't ask right now if it wasn't important," said Mark.

David hesitated, probably realizing that he hadn't seen Mark anywhere around the church for months. Mark had worked with the archbishop's office in the past, and David probably knew he was a teacher at the catholic university, so his request was reasonable, but David wavered.

"Could you please check with Father Romero?" asked Mark. "It's important."

David nodded and let himself into the church. He returned a short time later and motioned for Mark to follow him. The crowd had grown, and Mark felt glad to step inside where the walls of the church insulated from some of the noise.

Father Romero waited inside the narthex.

"Mark, I am glad you are here," he said.

Mark greeted the old priest. After confession and extended counseling, Father Romero knew him as few other men did, and if ever there was anyone who knew what a lost cause he was, it was this humble priest standing before him.

"Hello, Father," he said. "The dean came by my house."

"I'm afraid that was my doing," said Father Romero. "As you can see, we've had something amazing happen this morning."

The pastor spoke in hushed tones, and Mark strained to hear him over the dull roar outside the church.

"And people are always afraid of anything different," said Mark.

He and Father Romero had discussed this in the past. The same human weakness had likely contributed to another man's death two thousand years ago.

Father Romero nodded and said, "Come with me."

He turned and led the way to the sacristy in the back of the church. Mark followed and found a woman in the white veil of a novice with her arms around a slender young girl, whom he guessed at around nine years of age.

"Mark, I would like to introduce you to Miss Maria Perez, and this young lady is Sofia," said Father Romero, enunciating his words carefully.

A pretty school-age girl looked at him with large blue eyes and long light brown hair that looked to have been brushed recently.

The young woman, Maria, appeared to be in her late twenties and of average height and slender build. Her features were plain, but her eyes were clear and honest, and there was something about her that made him want to look at her again.

Father Romero continued the introduction and mentioned something about healing.

"Hello to both of you," said Mark. He didn't know what else to say. He was the last person to know anything about healing.

"Maria is looking after Sofia here at the church," said Father Romero.

"What?" said Mark, looking back and forth between them. "So, where are her parents?"

"It's complicated," said Father Romero. "I first met Sofia three weeks ago." He explained briefly before adding. "Before then, we have no information. I have offered her sanctuary."

Maria held Sofia and watched closely.

Mark saw the modified walker leaning against the wall of the sacristy, and he could see that they were in earnest about what happened. He wasn't sure how to tell them he no longer believed in anything, let alone miracles. He couldn't countenance a God who let little girls die at the hands of their fathers in traffic accidents.

Father Romero stretched his hands out to rest on Sofia and Maria and prayed a blessing for travel and safekeeping for both of them.

"Mark is going to take you somewhere for now," he said.

Startled, Mark looked at his parish priest.

"Father, uh, I didn't get that," he said. "What exactly do you want me to do?"

Father Romero said, "We are not two hours from this morning, and people are clamoring to get to this little one. I can't allow them access to her, and Mark, before you say anything, you know better than most that if I surrender her to the authorities, they will place her with child services, and goodness knows what that will mean. No, I have committed to sanctuary for Sofia, but in this case, I don't know if I can keep her safe. If the courts get involved, they will force my hand. You know it to be true."

Mark had to admit that Father Romero was correct in his assessment. But what did that have to do with him?

"Father, I have been nowhere near a church for months."

Maria pursed her lips at that statement.

"I wonder if that was part of God's plan?" said Father Romero. "For now, you are the perfect man to shelter them. I pray that you will help us?"

Mark looked at Sofia. Her eyes reminded him of Faith, and he felt himself falling. She was not his child, but she needed him. Regardless of his feelings about God at the moment, he could not dishonor his daughter's memory. The archbishop and his parish priest had trapped him. He knew it, and he suspected Father Romero knew it too.

"Okay," he said. "What do I need to do?"

Maria looked more and more concerned as Father Romero further explained. She clearly wanted to protest but gently took Sofia in tow as Father Romero called David into the sacristy and asked him to set up for a statement outside the front of the church. David left to prepare, and the pastor turned back to face them.

"I will go and speak with the people gathered outside while you make your way," he said, placing his hand once more on Sofia's head in blessing before turning to leave.

Mark waited until the priest stepped through the doors at the front of the church. He took advantage of the distraction provided by Father Romero and led Maria and Sofia to a door in the back of the sacristy, which led to a connecting hallway and the parish office. Maria pulled back with a look of concern in her eyes.

"This is all too much too quickly," she said. "I have doubts."

She looked at Mark like she was trying to read his soul.

He cringed inside and hoped she couldn't actually do that.

"So do I," he said.

At that moment, they heard shouting and banging at the front of the church, and Mark sensed their time for escape slipping away. He reached hesitantly for Maria, and she let him wrap his hand around her cool and slender fingers. Gently, he led both of them through the door after him.

Emerging into the parish office, Mark hurried to the exit door in the opposite wall which opened to a covered walkway beside the modest one-and-a-half story rectory and prevented their discovery from the front of the church.

They walked along a small alley, careful to stay out of view of any stragglers, and turned up a residential street a block away. It looked deserted at the moment, but they wouldn't hear anyone following with the crescendo roar of the crowd behind them.

Mark hurried along the street and led the girls to his Jeep Commander parked at the corner. Amazingly, they almost made it to his SUV before an elderly lady living in an older home along the street stepped out on her porch and waved to them.

"Do you know what is happening at the church?" she asked. The old woman paused when she saw Sofia. "Is that really you, dear?"

She clutched her hands to her chest and made the sign of the cross.

Sofia didn't reply but looked up at Maria, who ushered her into the rear seat as soon as Mark unlocked the doors. Mark recognized the lady as a longtime parishioner of Our Blessed Mother Church. They had been spotted, and he tried to think what to do as he fumbled with his keys, suddenly nervous now that he was alone with Maria and Sofia. He couldn't breathe and felt a hand touch lightly on his shoulder.

"We should go," said Maria.

Mark started the Jeep and drove away. The elderly lady was still standing on her porch, but in his rear-view mirror, he saw a cell phone in her hand.

❖

Father Romero stood on a stepladder and addressed the crowd outside the front of Our Blessed Mother Church while David stayed close to guard against a fall.

"I feel blessed to see so many of you," said the pastor. "Today, our church has been host to the living power of God."

Several in the crowd asked him to speak up.

David adjusted the hastily assembled microphone for Father Romero, and the priest thanked him.

"I hope you can all hear me better now," said Father Romero, smiling. "Many of you have heard of the miracle witnessed today at our morning Mass. Some of you want to hear and speak with those involved, and you will, but I ask your indulgence for the sake of the child. She is overwhelmed and needs time to recover."

"Is that the official position of the Church?"

The question came from a news reporter trying to angle for position between the priest and her cameraman.

"It is what I believe," said Father Romero. "and what I have seen. That is all I can say at this moment."

Father Romero raised both hands with palms facing upwards to accent his statement.

"Where is Sofia?"

This question came from one parishioner standing at the front of the crowd.

"She is resting," he replied. "She has had a momentous day. We all have."

Father Romero seemed to want to end that line of questioning, but it was not to be.

"Wouldn't it be prudent to have her examined by competent medical specialists?" asked a voice from the crowd. "After all, she has had an extraordinary day, as you said."

The question came from a man named Paul Peterson. He stepped out of the crowd and faced off with Father Romero. Many recognized him. Paul Peterson's billboards echoed his message about town, and his podcasts on the Internet provided counter statements to religious views.

Father Romero hesitated to answer, and Paul quickly posed another question.

"We all want to know that she is all right," he said. "We want to understand what happened. Could we speak to her parents?"

Paul scanned the crowd before looking at the closest news camera, and he seized the opportunity to press his point.

"Each of us hopes this miracle is just what is claimed," said Paul. "I would hazard that each of us wants little Sofia to be healthy and well, but unfortunately, there have been sensationalist claims in the past that have bordered on fraud. I trust this is not one of those instances. If an all powerful God miraculously healed this little girl today, wouldn't she be fit enough to say hello? We only wish her well."

Paul's words seemed to float and simmer in the spring air, unsettling many in the crowd who murmured in agitated knots of flesh and marrow.

Tomás stood off to the side and made no move or spoken word to draw attention; however, his serene face hid his intense focus on the priest. Father Romero was holding something back. Tomás felt the energy in the crowd shift and threaten to pull him toward its vortex, and he resisted with all his discipline.

Tomás did not think of himself as good or bad. He recognized no such governance in himself and would not allow for it in others. He saw his services as needed but could only account for his actions if honorable. He tried not to kill unless required within the mission parameters set forth by his patron. He felt annoyed that Paul Peterson threatened to interfere, but making him disappear was not his mission. Donovan Giulanti had been very clear. Finding the girl was paramount, and his patron wanted to avoid publicity.

Tomás strongly suspected the priest to be the first step. Already, he sensed the hunt for the visiting stranger at the church would be fruitless. Not that he wouldn't try, but there was no recording of the man, and the witness statements in the crowd conflicted. There would be some who would claim responsibility, he felt certain, but he suspected the stranger who held the little girl would not be one to make himself known, or he would have done so already.

Paul Peterson continued in a focused tirade, and the crowd and press seemed to hang on his every word. The multitude edged closer to the doors of the church, and many seemed to have a glazed look to their eyes, as if some hypnotic spell had wrapped around their hearts like kudzu vine, choking off all reason. Father Romero stepped inside the church while Peterson continued speaking.

Tomás walked around the edge of the crowd and hurried to the door as an usher prepared to close it. While the door was still partly open, he placed a hand on the man's shoulder and pulled him backwards and down. Tomás felt pleased with his restraint as he stepped into the church narthex and quickly caught up with the priest.

"Pastor, may I have a word with you?"

Father Romero turned to face him.

"Yes," said the priest. "Do I know you?"

"No, but I need your assistance."

Tomás was pleased to see his plea trigger the priest's natural inclination to help.

"Everything is a bit unsettled at the moment," said Father Romero. "Is it something we can deal with at another time?"

"No, it must be today," said Tomás. "A life hangs in the balance. Please tell me what you saw this morning."

Tomás used his most sincere face. He knew he could be convincing when he needed to be. They could hear repeated yelling outside the church walls, and Father Romero seemed distracted. Tomás didn't have time for distraction, and he placed his hand on the priest's arm.

"Please, it is important."

The look on his face must have convinced the pastor, and the priest recounted what he saw that morning while they walked into the church and down the center aisle toward the altar.

"So, what about the man who held the girl?" asked Tomás. "People are saying he cured her. Do we know anything about him?"

Tomás needed to ask and expected no further information, but he was surprised at the priest's expression. Father Romero responded like a man certain of the truth, and Tomás had seen that same expression on his grandmother's face when she talked about faith.

"There was no trace seen of him after he walked through the doors to the narthex," said Father Romero. "The ushers did not see him enter or leave. I have told you what I and others saw as to his appearance, and that is all I can say."

Thumping and banging from the church doors heralded clamorous howls and sirens outside.

"Excuse me, my son," said the priest. "I must tend to an important matter."

Father Romero turned to make his way to the back of the church, and Tomás pulled him back around to face him. Something in his manner must have given away his intent.

"She's not here," said Father Romero.

Tomás expected that answer as the priest seemed too calm in the face of this chaos.

"Where did she go?" asked Tomás, taking hold of him again. "I must know, and you will tell me."

He didn't want to hurt this old man of God.

"I do not know," said Father Romero. "I sent her away, and I don't know where she has gone. That is the truth. Now, unhand me."

Tomás drew back his right hand to strike the priest but thought better of it. He needed a better answer than this priest dancing around the truth. He released Father Romero, who stumbled backwards over the steps leading up to the altar and fell. The priest struck his head and was still.

Tomás felt regret but not remorse. He had not intended to hurt the holy man, but things like this happened in his work. He walked to a side door and exited as he heard a crash at the front of the church.

The crowd overflowed into the church streaming up and down the aisles and between the pews. Feverish and angry, the mob searched here and there in a halting and disorganized effort, sometimes repeating their steps as if confused at their own actions. Some began throwing items about and pushing over pews. One threw a lit bundle of rags, and a banner blazed.

Police officers, looking the worst for their encounter, entered behind the frenzied crowd. One officer shouted commands over a bull-horn that went unheeded while another called on a radio for more backup.

Paul Peterson flowed in with the crowd and stared at Father Romero supine in front of the altar. The bedlam inside the church faded from his hearing as Paul witnessed the shadows in the corners come together and hover over the priest. Paul rubbed his eyes in the smoke from the burning banner, but the shadowy shape was still there. He pointed and called out, but no one else paid attention.

"Hey, you there," he called out.

The faceless figure looked at him, and Paul froze. He had seen that image long ago when no one believed him. He started moving forward to help the downed priest, and the wraith parted into billowing inky tendrils which caressed and lingered about individuals in the frenzied crowd leaving Paul Peterson to stand over an unresponsive Father Romero sprawled at the base of the altar.

CHAPTER FIVE

"Where are you taking us?" said Maria while double-checking Sofia's seat belt.

"Someplace we can figure this out," said Mark.

He looked both ways and made the turn toward his house out of habit. He still couldn't fathom how he ended up in this situation. He looked at Maria in the rear-view mirror. She had her arm around Sofia and looked conspicuous with her veil and miniature gold cross necklace atop her simple navy vest and white shirt.

"Do you have any other clothes or belongings?" he asked.

"No," she said. "We left suddenly, and there was no chance."

Maria's tone showed no patience with such an obvious question, but Mark liked to think out loud sometimes. It helped him process.

"It's just that we need to keep a low profile," he said.

In the mirror, he noticed Maria reach up to touch the veil covering her head, perhaps remembering that she wore it. Mark wasn't sure how much trouble he was in at the moment, but he was certain that a district attorney with a need for attention could make his life even more miserable. He smiled at Sofia in the rear-view mirror, and she twitched one corner of her mouth up shyly.

Mark turned into the parking lot of a branch of his bank and parked the Jeep. He remembered it was Sunday, and the bank was closed. He told Maria he wouldn't be long and exited. He approached the automated teller machine and withdrew twelve hundred dollars from his account using his bank card. The bills made his wallet bulge, but it wouldn't be enough for what he had in mind. He had some cash at home, but they couldn't go there. They had been seen leaving, and someone would figure out that the girls were with him. It would have to be the farm, he thought. Fortunately, he had some funds stashed there.

Although it took a few minutes longer than expected, he exited the ATM with his withdrawal divided up in several pockets and reviewed his plan while he approached his Jeep. There was no one inside. He looked around with a sinking feeling. He didn't notice the girls get out of his vehicle. Where did they go?

Getting in the Commander, he started it up, exited the bank parking lot, and paused at the corner. He did not see them, but across the street on the left, he saw a fast-food restaurant marked with its familiar sign. On a hunch, he drove into the parking lot, and Maria came out of the restaurant holding a white paper sack and the hand of a smiling Sofia. Mark realized Maria had removed her veil, and he exhaled. He hadn't realized how rigid his chest felt until he rolled down the window. He saw how happy Sofia felt, and he couldn't be upset.

"Hey, that's a good idea," he said. "Did you get enough for me?"

Sofia beamed and nodded, and Maria's face relaxed in a faint smile at his friendly greeting. Both of them climbed into the vehicle, and Mark told them his plan.

Maria stopped smiling. She said nothing at first, but Mark could tell she had reservations. Finally, she couldn't hold it in any longer.

"How long?" she asked.

"Honestly, I'm not sure," he said. "I'm worried that the lady on the porch recognized us, and I'm concerned that someone will figure out you are with me. If we stay at my house here in town, I'm afraid the authorities will knock on our door within the day. If we want to protect Sofia, we should go to a place where no one will look for us."

Maria put her lips together and didn't argue further. Mark had fueled up earlier in the week, so he pointed the Jeep in a southerly direction and tried to think of any pitfalls and complications. He soon had such a list in his head that he almost turned around. Fortunately, Maria handed him a cheeseburger, and he gave himself over to munching on the simple treat. He hadn't realized how hungry he was, and he thanked them both as he drove. Sofia didn't speak, but her face had big dimples when she smiled. It made him think of Faith.

Two hours later, at the outskirts of Bowling Green, he spied a sign for a discount supercenter. He had not made this drive in months, but he knew this was likely the last such store near their destination. He fueled the Commander and whipped down and around into the parking lot. They had been in the Jeep for over two hours, and it felt good to step outside and stretch.

Maria looked confused.

"Why are we stopping?" she asked.

"We need supplies, and the two of you need clothes and necessaries."

Mark stepped closer to Maria to shield his actions from others in the parking lot. He pulled out his wallet and handed her three hundred dollars in twenties.

"Just in case you need to pay separately, but I'd rather not get separated if possible," he said. He looked at Maria pointedly, and she had the good grace to blush. "You'll need a couple changes of clothes and some boots or sturdy shoes. I'll start in the grocery section, and we can meet inside."

After they entered the store, Maria and Mark agreed to meet at the junction between children's clothing and the main rear aisle of the store. The girls left to do their shopping and Mark started in on a grocery run. He had not been to the farm in nearly a year, and he figured he couldn't count on anything at this point. He had a neighbor who watched over the place, and Walter would have called if there were any trouble, but the cereal was probably stale by now.

The televisions in the electronics section all displayed the same scene from Our Blessed Mother Church earlier in the afternoon. The volume was muted, but there was video of the crowd and a photograph of Father Romero. He had been taken to the hospital for evaluation following the unruly demonstration, and Mark sank inside. He hoped the pastor would be all right.

They needed to hurry. Working quickly through the aisles, he picked up flour, cornmeal, rice, beans, powdered milk, condensed milk, sugar, salt, coffee, tea, tang and juice boxes and powdered drinks. He loaded case lots of vegetables in cans and twenty pound bags of potatoes and onions. Dried fruit, eggs, and butter rounded out his purchases. They needed some meat, and he got a second cart. He purchased a cooler and some ice and some fresh milk, half-and-half, and butter. They had about two hours of driving to go, and the perishables should stay safe in the cooler.

He passed on the beer aisle. He needed to keep a clear head. He was trying to think of what else they would need when the girls caught up with him. They had their cart full of socks, underwear, jeans, boots, and undershirts. He saw a coat for Sofia and a jacket for Maria as well, and Mark approved. He looked at Sofia.

"I think we have a problem," he said. "We have three carts, and we need another driver. Do you think you could do that?"

Sofia smiled and walked over to the least stuffed grocery cart. She was tall enough now with her straightened back and legs to see over the handle, and Mark led the way to checkout with Sofia behind him. Maria trailed the two of them, and he looked back to catch her look away from him.

Mark picked up a bag of chocolate candies in the checkout aisle, which made him think to ask Maria about toothpaste, but she beat him to the answer, saying they had already put some toothbrushes, floss, and paste in the cart. Shortly, it was their turn to check out. The cashier glanced at Sofia repeatedly but didn't seem to recognize her. They exited to the parking lot and loaded up the SUV. Their haul filled the cargo area.

Nesting supplies around the cooler, Maria asked, "Is this really the best plan?"

Mark didn't have an answer, but he tried to reassure her.

"Honestly, I don't know," he said. "I'm not the smartest guy, and I've made plenty of mistakes, but right now this doesn't feel wrong."

He saw her eyes widen and examine his face closely before she turned and followed Sofia into the Jeep, securing her safety belt. Maria settled on the seat with her arm around her charge, who nestled against her and was soon asleep. After all, that was Sofia's first time pushing a loaded grocery cart, and it was heavy.

Mark pulled back out on the highway and drove toward their destination. While he drove on in silence, he wondered over the events that brought the two of them under his care. He missed his wife and daughter fiercely, but he realized with surprise that he hadn't thought of his lost family all afternoon. He felt guilty again but couldn't stop thinking of the way Maria had looked at him in the parking lot.

President Maureen Thomlinson brushed back a lock of auburn hair. Even in primary school, she had learned early how to manipulate those around her. She had always been adept at reading other's emotions and anticipating what they needed or wanted to hear. Eventually, she really didn't have to think about what to say or how to say it. Her subconscious mind processed responses, and she glibly added whatever she needed to pursue her goals.

That she was attractive didn't hurt. She knew looks were important no matter what anyone said, and she worked hard to maintain her own. Eschewing any habit or action which could degrade her appearance or performance, she could never understand how others could allow otherwise.

Setting her sights on the most powerful office in the world, she had worked diligently toward that goal. Finally, her party had come to her and begged her to run for the presidency. She won, and the old guard rejoiced. They thought they had control of her, but they didn't know her at all. She was a skilled chameleon at policy, changing to whatever showed her to best advantage and kept her in power. She was also a woman who never forgot either a favor or a slight, and many had learned to their regret that getting on her bad list was a path to ruin.

The party hated her, but they needed her, and better to be needed, she thought. Who cares if they liked her. She sure didn't like any of them. Pretenders, imposters, and sycophants all, her political colleagues merely confirmed her opinion of almost all humans around her.

She wouldn't let anyone or anything interfere with her agenda to shape an America that fit into the rest of the world. She had plans, and she had been maneuvering the various pieces on the board. Soon, very soon, she would have the votes for her comprehensive package, and she would drag this country kicking and screaming into the current century.

But at the moment, this preposterous group of small-minded men sitting across from her had told her something she couldn't quite believe.

"Please tell me that again."

She wielded her voice like an ice pick and knew how intimidating it would be to the academics and political hacks in front of her.

Professor Barry Michaels, her science advisor, was the exception. Maureen had never been able to push him into any kind of corner. He was the most unflappable, apolitical man she had come across. Strangely, she found herself attracted to him, and she dismissed that thought just as quickly. She already had a stage prop husband, and he performed his tasks well. Functions that did not include late-night sessions with the president. Separate bedrooms had worked well for them from the onset, and she made sure his dalliances were exceedingly discrete.

Barry leaned forward and placed his hands on the table, a rare display from him.

"Madam President, the West Coast suffered a massive series of earthquakes this morning. Preliminary results suggest the magnitude at approximately 9.6 on the Richter Scale. The damage from the earthquakes and accompanying tsunamis is unimaginable."

Maureen absorbed the news about the earthquake. California had earthquakes all the time, however she could see from Barry's face that this might be different.

"How much of the coast?" she asked.

"Our best estimate so far extends from British Columbia though most of California and inward from the coast approximately twenty miles and more in some places. The Cascadian fault let go, followed by the San Andreas. Massive tidal waves from Vancouver to San Diego followed the devastating earthquakes. Hawaii will feel the effects any moment, and we are alerting other countries around the Pacific Rim."

Maureen didn't feel guilty that her first thought went to the loss of voters from California. That state helped push her over the Electoral College bar, and she would have to put extraordinary energy into the assistance efforts, probably a road trip for public relations photographs, but this couldn't have come at a worse time. She tried to keep her face impassive despite her inner turmoil. She had the presence of mind to ask about Foals Canyon.

"As you know, Madam President, Foals Canyon Power Plant was already well into shut down mode and permanent retirement, but there was still some nuclear fuel present on site. We have not been able to reach them since this morning," said Bryce Thornton, energy secretary.

He had arrived after short notice and was wearing an open collar, a no-no at a cabinet level meeting with the president.

Maureen nodded her head. So we don't know, she thought. Barry still looked ready to expound. She nodded her head at him to continue, and he sighed. Oh, this will be bad, she thought.

"There is something else, Madam President," said her science advisor. "There are reports of simultaneous earthquakes around the globe and unusually high tides on our southern and eastern coastlines as well as similar monster tides elsewhere around the world."

Maureen had no patience for tortuous explanations. She had just been handed a major delay to her agenda. She stood to punctuate her impatience

"Spit it out, Barry," said the president.

He didn't bat an eyelash at her bark, and she sighed inwardly. Why couldn't she have found him twenty years ago?

"Usually, Madame President, our moon, or rather the attraction between the Earth and the Moon, is largely responsible for the tides on our planet."

"Yes, I believe that is common knowledge," she replied.

"Yes, Ma'am," he said. "But we checked and found something odd."

Maureen cocked her head at Barry. Cute or not, she would castrate him if he took one more moment to get to the point.

"The Moon has moved," he said.

President Thomlinson reached down and grabbed her chair. She pulled it out to sit down and slowly adjusted her seated position, acknowledging to herself that she would need to invest some time in his explanation to understand it.

"Go on," she said.

Barry leafed through some notes in front of him.

"Please understand Madam President, the Moon moves approximately three centimeters away from Earth each year," he said. "However, we found orbital movement on the order of five meters with laser ranging just a short time ago."

The entire room sat in stunned silence for a moment until Maureen surprised them all by asking her science advisor a question.

"But shouldn't that make the tides smaller?"

Barry smiled in appreciation.

"Yes, Madam President, the tides should be smaller as the distance between the Earth and our moon increases," said her science advisor. "However, that was not the case this morning, so we investigated further. Somehow, the mass of the Moon tripled overnight."

President Thomlinson wanted to respond, but didn't quite know what to say. She sensed there was more and knew she didn't want to hear it.

"Go ahead," said the president.

Barry shrugged his shoulders in resignation and continued.

"Something massive passed behind our moon and disturbed its orbital position. The additional mass added to its gravitational attraction and caused the high tides and probably caused the severe earthquakes along the West Coast and elsewhere this morning."

Professor Barry Michaels described the object as twice the mass of the Moon based on limited observation. It might be a truly massive Kuiper Belt planetoid which had fallen in from the outer solar system or a rogue planet not bound to any system. Radar reflected poorly from the dark planetoid mass, and its approach from behind the Moon allowed the rogue planet to pass without warning.

"Pass us to where, Professor Michaels?"

Bryce had uttered the obvious question.

"We have only had a few brief observations to calculate orbital geometry, but it appears the object is falling toward the Sun."

"And what will happen when it strikes our sun?"

This question came from the head of FEMA, who had been strangely quiet until now.

Maureen could already see the panicked headlines. She would be in reaction mode for the rest of her presidency.

"Yes, Barry, what will happen when it hits the Sun?" she asked.

Maureen waited to hear the worst. She thought she was ready. She was wrong.

"We wish it was going to hit the Sun," said Barry. "It still might. As the object gets closer to our star, the gravitational attraction will be immense, and our sun may capture it despite its velocity. That might trigger a solar flare or other perturbation. Frankly, no one knows. We have never seen this before."

Maureen was scared now. She couldn't let anyone else see it. She was the president, and looking scared was a luxury she wasn't allowed. Barry's face scared her. He always looked calm and in control, but at the moment his face cast a sallow, sad countenance like he was standing over his grandfather's casket. She had not seen him like this in the three years she had known him and couldn't imagine it from him.

"You said that you wish it would hit the Sun," said Maureen. "You don't think it will?"

She hadn't wanted to ask, but no one else at the table would take the lead into what she suspected was a rabbit hole lined with teeth, large rending and slashing teeth.

"We think it will swing around the Sun," said Barry. "And if its orbital path remains unchanged it will emerge on a linear trajectory to intercept our orbit on or around May twenty-first of this year."

Barry let his shoulders sag even more at the end of his statement, which to Maureen carried all the punctuation she needed.

"My God. That's only five days."

That involuntary comment came from the energy secretary, Bryce, and he immediately looked sheepish. He knew how the president felt about religion.

President Thomlinson placed her hands on the table, and the group quieted. She leaned closer to her science advisor and said, "If that happens what can we expect?"

Barry had to have expected this question, had to know it would come, but his voice still faltered.

"If it passes us anywhere inside our moon's orbit, there will be effects similar to this morning," he said. "The closer it passes, the greater the damage. If it's close enough, it doesn't need impact to destroy us."

Maureen pressed him. She had been an excellent attorney and knew how to get information even when someone was reluctant.

"And you think it will be close, don't you?" she said.

Professor Barry Michaels shook his head slowly, sadly.

"No," he said, and he looked down at the table.

The others in the room exhaled loudly in relief.

Maureen remained locked on Barry. She knew him at a glance.

"Tell me," she said, and her voice cracked a little.

Barry raised his head and looked at her.

"I think it will hit us," he said.

CHAPTER SIX

Sofia woke up to the crunch of tires on gravel. The Jeep rolled to a stop, and Mark exited and opened a gate. He returned to the driver's seat and pulled up the driveway to park in front of a house which looked at them with sadness, like a pet ignored too long. There was a wrap-around front porch, a gray metal roof, and white painted wood which peeled slightly here and there. An old barn with gray weathered boards and a similar gray metal roof waited around the corner in back of the house.

"We're here," said Mark.

He got out of the front seat and walked up two stairs to the porch. He pulled a key out of his pocket, unlocked the front door, and walked inside.

Maria turned to Sofia and said, "I know it's a different place, but it will be okay. I think he means well. We can stay here a day or two until we get things figured out."

Sofia nodded and wanted to answer. Other than Sister Magdalena at the children's home, Sofia had known no one like Maria, and Sofia also felt sure that Mark wanted to help them. She could hear and move her tongue now, but the stranger had warned her not to speak or use her gifts until it was needed. "You will know," he said.

Mark walked out the front door to the porch.

"It's good," he said. "A little dusty, but nothing is disturbed. Let's get unloaded."

He walked down the steps to the back of the Commander, opened the liftgate, and began carrying supplies into the house. Maria made sure Sofia was out of the Jeep, then she went to help.

Sofia walked around the front yard. She could see the trees by the road and had never been anywhere with so much space. It felt good to stretch her legs and stand without her walker. She jumped up and down, reveling in her newfound ability, and paused to look up at the evening sky with wonder. She held her arms up and gave thanks.

She felt a presence and looked over to see a white dog with upright pointed ears and a long face emerge from the bushes at the edge of the house and examine her face-to-face. She smiled at the animal, which cocked its head to the side and took several steps forward. She extended her arm, and the dog licked her fingers and put his head under her hand. She knew what he wanted and scratched behind his ears until his feathery tail wagged back and forth.

"Sofia? ¿Quién esta el perro blanco?"

Maria moved toward Sofia, and the white dog pushed between Sofia and Maria, clearly protective of the little girl. Sofia said nothing but looked at the dog and then at Maria, and in a moment, the dog wagged its tail again, laid its ears down, and quivered its entire body in delight.

Mark walked back out on the porch to see his helpers surrounded by a wiggling white tornado. He watched the dog jump up and lick Maria on the nose. Sofia smiled and clapped her hands together, and Mark pushed back a wave of bittersweet memories.

"Who's your new friend?" he asked.

"We thought he was yours," said Maria.

"Nope. Never seen him before," said Mark. "Seems friendly enough. Maybe Walter knows him."

Maria had her arm around Sofia, who was running her hand over the dog's white fur from head to tail much to her new friend's approval.

"Who is Walter?" asked Maria.

"He lives in the house through the trees over that way," said Mark. He waved toward the barn. "He's a neighbor and a friend, and he watches over the house for me. Don't remember a white dog, though? We'll probably see Walter tomorrow. He'll notice that we're here."

Mark walked down from the porch, and the canine immediately positioned between him and the girls. Standing on all fours with ears erect, the furry visitor studied him. Mark paused after Sofia walked two steps closer and the dog maneuvered to stay between her and him. She looked at the dog and put her hand on its neck, and the dog sat beside her. The shepherd continued to regard Mark as if to say, "Well, okay, for now, but he better not try anything funny."

Mark grabbed the cooler from the rear of the Jeep, and Maria grabbed the bags of onions and potatoes. Sofia followed them into the house along with the white dog, who turned around twice in a circle and settled down on the hearthrug with his head down and eyes open, watching them.

Here I am, thought Sofia, with Mark, Maria, and a new friend. She had always wanted a dog and wondered where he had come from. She could tell Uriel was a boy dog. She wasn't a baby. She knew lots of things and felt like she knew more every minute. She didn't know how she knew that the dog responded to Uriel. She just knew. She also knew he was hungry. She was hungry too, and she followed Mark and Maria into the kitchen.

Mark took a lantern down from the shelf and lit it, and the yellow glow brightened the dim kitchen in the waning afternoon light. Maria shooed him out of the kitchen, saying he should get some heat going as the house felt cooler each minute as evening gathered.

Mark went into the living room, and in the corner was a collection of split wood. Sofia watched him step over the dog and apologize which was only polite. He arranged some wood in the fireplace, placed a pine cone and a piece of fat wood under the kindling, and lit it with a lighter. The flames caught and soon the fireplace was throwing out heat and light. The dog delighted in his position in front of the hearth and rolled over onto his back and dozed with his front paw stretched up in the air.

Mark fired up the wood burning furnace in the basement, and the house warmed. Maria called from the kitchen, and Sofia went in to find pancakes and bacon and milk. She was followed by Mark, who was stretching his arms and yawning after securing the Jeep and walking the perimeter outside the house. They sat at the table, and Maria said grace. Mark waited politely until Sofia reached out and grasped his hand and bowed her head, and he copied her. When he raised his head, she looked at him and smiled.

The dog padded into the kitchen, and Maria filled a bowel with a portion for him, which the animal wolfed down. Soon they finished eating, and Mark helped Maria do the dishes. The two of them were careful to keep their distance from one another. Sofia looked at the shepherd who gave her a doggie grin as if to say, "What did you expect?"

Mark said, "I'm in the bedroom at the end of the hall. I wasn't sure how you two wanted to bed down. For now, maybe you can share the room on the right. I put lanterns in both rooms. Just blow out the light when you're ready to sleep."

Sofia thought sleep sounded good. She was really tired, but she also knew her new friend needed to go outside before bedtime. She went over to the door and pointed to the dog, and the animal came right over and stood by her.

Mark opened the door, and the canine shot out, found a spot quickly, and came right back. Mark started to say something about the dog being indoors with them, but a look from Maria caused him to pause. He shrugged his shoulders and turned for the hall, but Sofia looked at him with an upturned face and raised both arms.

Mark choked up at the familiar gesture and hesitated for a moment, but then he crouched down, and Sofia jumped into his arms and hugged him. He patted her on the back before he disengaged and walked down the hall and entered the bedroom that had belonged to Maddie's parents. He closed the door.

❖

Samuel Branchwater sat at his favorite stargazing spot a mile from home. Growing up on the reservation had never been easy, but being a teenager is difficult anywhere. He would graduate soon and had plans to pursue a degree in astrophysics at the state university in the fall. He'd already been accepted, and with the scholarship money and some part-time work on campus, he calculated he could just swing it financially. He had worked a part-time job at a local automobile garage throughout high school and saved for college. He would end up with some student loan debt, but it would be reasonable.

Always quiet and reserved, Samuel cherished time with his passion, and the sky had promised to be exceptionally clear tonight with the low humidity typical for Wyoming. Nights were cool to cold most of the time on the reservation, and he pulled his jacket close. His home-made Newtonian reflector telescope sported an eight inch primary mirror he had ground and coated himself from a glass blank he had ordered through the mail. Built from plywood, the telescope consisted of a rectangular tube that rested on a wooden swivel base. The first time he set it up in his backyard, the tribal police came because someone reported that he had some kind of cannon. That was embarrassing.

He oriented himself as the stars popped into view. Finding the constellation Andromeda, he tracked carefully up from the star Mirach until he saw the smudge and centered it. Changing his eyepiece, he brought the Andromeda Galaxy, Messier Object Thirty-One, into view. Two million light-years away and the closest spiral galaxy to our own Milky Way Galaxy, it never ceased to amaze him. He had been hooked since an elementary school field trip to the planetarium in Casper.

Samuel had checked out every book in the library on astronomy and space science and learned he would need to excel in math and physics to do serious work in the field. Engineering concepts and chemistry were important too, and he worked hard in English because communication and writing skills were important in all aspects of science, but sitting in the dark, bundled up, and searching for that next great surprise in the eyepiece was still his favorite.

He could see Jupiter hanging in the eastern sky along the ecliptic and aimed his primary at the planetary gas giant. He deftly brought it to center focus and worked for the clearest view.

"Samuel?"

He had heard no one approach and jerked away from the eyepiece. He liked this spot precisely because he was unlikely to be bothered by some of the other teens on the reservation who seemed to have anything on their mind but a plan for the future. Softly, the voice spoke again.

"Samuel, I didn't mean to startle you," said a shadow walking up to him. "I saw you out here, and I wanted to come and say hello. Would it be okay if I stay awhile?"

It was Beth Songbird, and Samuel knew her from school. They had talked a few times, but always about homework or projects or inane stuff. He didn't know her plans after high school and wondered if she was considering going to UW.

"Sure," he said. "I have an extra folding chair in the truck."

Samuel got up and walked over to his old Ford Ranger. He bought the little truck from someone who had tried to wrap it around a tree. He had straightened and reinforced the frame, rebuilt the engine, upgraded the interior, and sanded and repainted the exterior. He pulled out another folding chair from the bed of the truck and set it down beside his own chair. Beth sat and pulled her jacket around her.

"What are you looking at?" she asked.

Samuel could never be nervous when talking about his favorite subject, and his passion shone forth as he talked to her about Jupiter. Finally, he realized he was rattling on and apologized for monopolizing the conversation.

She smiled and said, "It's nice to see you excited about something. You are always so quiet at school."

He didn't know how to respond, so he busied himself centering Jupiter again. He let Beth look, and she let out a soft "wow" while peering through the eyepiece.

"Wait a moment," he said.

Changing eyepieces for more magnification, he checked quickly that the field of view still held the gas giant planet and motioned for her to look again.

Beth took her time.

She said, "It moved."

They changed positions at the eyepiece, and Samuel centered the image and adjusted focus again. She moved in to take another look and brushed his hand as she reached for the focus adjusting knob. Samuel felt an electric sensation up his arm to his heart. That was new.

This time, Beth looked for a good long time and described what she was seeing. When she mentioned two enormous eyes at the bottom of the planet, Samuel said there should only be one giant red spot.

"Well, there's two tonight," she said. "Maybe it got lonely."

She giggled.

Samuel looked at Beth, and her teeth gleamed white in the night starlight. Maybe so, he thought, as he looked through the eyepiece and froze. He had looked at Jupiter a hundred times. It shouldn't look like this. There was The Great Red Spot, constituting a three-hundred-year-old superstorm, but next to it was a black spot, almost as large and angry looking. He knew what that was. He had seen photographs of the same sort of spots on Jupiter during the Shoemaker-Levy Comet strike in 1994.

"Beth, you're right," he said. "Something gave Jupiter a black eye, and you found it."

He smiled at her, and she smiled back. Samuel breathed in the cool night air full of promise, but before anything else, he needed to call the astronomy event hotline at the university and tell them to point at Jupiter. Something big had happened.

After getting off his cell phone, he pulled out his notebook and began sketching everything he could see and remember regarding the image. Beth looked over his shoulder and watched patiently in the red light from his headlamp. She leaned in close until they were almost cheek to cheek, until the pencil felt unsteady in his hand, and thoughts of two instead of one kept time in the rhythm of his heart. She put her hands on his shoulders to steady herself as she leaned against him, and laying his sketchbook aside, he maneuvered until she was sitting in his lap. Unlike how he had ever felt around any other girl, it seemed like he had always known her.

She snuggled into him and smiled like they shared the world's biggest secret, and Samuel understood then that Beth had planned this. She had bewitched him in million-year-old magic, and he realized something profound. He didn't feel lonely anymore.

CHAPTER SEVEN

Mark dreamed of Maddie telling him a story of another trip from her childhood with her parents. She was talking to keep him awake on the drive back from the lake while Faith slept in the back seat. Faith had screwed up her courage and swung out over the water on a rope swing for the first time, and after the first attempt, she repeated it no less than twenty times, laughing all the time. He loved his little girl when she laughed.

Maddie fell asleep in the front seat, and his eyes traced the curve of her neck to her shoulder and her slender fingers and the way her cotton shirt lay across her chest. He chuckled at her story describing her parents before he looked to his left at light and shadow and felt the noise of rolling off the road.

That part of his dream always ran in slow motion and led to waking in the hospital to unceasing worry below cold fluorescent lights until Father Romero entered the room and answered his unspoken question. All the air fluttered out of him at that moment like a moth and left him a husk of memories, never quite able to complete that interrupted breath.

Mark coughed and woke up to a wet tongue licking his face. He opened his eyes, and the dog sat expectantly beside the bed with a goofy canine grin. He remembered he was in Maddie's parents' bedroom. He never thought of it as his even though Maddie had told him that was what her parents wanted for them.

Mark swung himself up to sit on the side of the bed, and the shepherd wagged his tail and put his cold nose in Mark's crotch to encourage him. He didn't hear any other noise at the moment. There had been chickens and even a rooster on Maddie's farm in the past, but living far away in the city, there had been no way to care for them. That might need to change. Well, maybe not the rooster, he thought.

He put on jeans, boots, a work shirt, and a jacket. The dog paced back and forth in the bedroom but didn't bark, and Mark thought that was considerate of the exhausted girls, who were likely still sleeping. He needed to get moving. If they were going to stay here, they needed more supplies, and he had some storage in the basement he needed to check.

Walking quietly down the hall, he opened the front door, and the dog shot out quickly to do his business. Mark retrieved some wood from the porch woodpile. The house interior had cooled down overnight. There were embers in the fireplace and probably the same in the house furnace. The shepherd explored the woods bordering the fence line searching for any living thing brave enough to trespass. Well, somebody needed to, and the mutt might as well earn his keep, he thought. The dog stopped his inspection and turned to look back at him, and Mark imagined he saw the animal nod.

Going back in the house, he soon had the fireplace blazing again and saw to the house furnace. While in the basement, he checked the storage area. Since they weren't at the farm all the time, he felt they should have some supplies stored but hidden just in case someone broke in. Walter looked after the property, but he couldn't be here every hour of the day. Mark approached some wooden shelving along the basement wall and reached up to trip a small concealed catch, and the shelving swung out easily. He had lubricated the hinges heavily in the past, and there was little noise.

Walking into the ten-by-ten-foot room lined with dry goods and long-term storage food brought a smile to his face. This was mostly Walter's idea. Their eccentric and older Marine veteran neighbor was cantankerous and didn't hesitate to let you know if he thought you were being foolish, but he had a kind soul. Walter had taken to Mark right away, maybe because he had been in uniform and shared some of the same stories. Mark hoped he would see the old man today.

The storage room looked dry, and there was no evidence of rodents or other pests. Mark opened the gun safe. That had not been fun to dolly down the basement steps, but he was glad of its contents. He stored several rifles and pistols along with ammunition and some currency and silver dimes. Walter's idea again, but it sure felt good at the moment. Mark exited the storage area and closed the shelving and thought about breakfast and coffee.

Checking the front door, he found the dog sitting expectantly, and Mark let him in. The shepherd circled and lay in front of the burning logs and looked at him. Mark sensed a pattern. He got coffee started on the propane stove and quickly scrambled some eggs with added ham. Potatoes and onions would be a nice side item, he thought. He heard a slight noise and turned to see Maria standing in the kitchen doorway, covering a yawn with her hand.

"I'm sorry," she said. "I haven't slept this late in years."

She held her hands together, fingers entwined, and her dark hair had been brushed and tied back in a ponytail. She wore a light blue sweater purchased the night before.

Mark tried not to stare.

"I'm sure you were exhausted," he said. "I would have slept later if I hadn't had an alarm clock visit my room."

He nodded at the dog, who had placed his nose against Maria's thigh.

"Breakfast will be ready shortly," he said. "I'm thinking we have a few chores today to make ourselves ready to spend some time here."

Maria's forehead furrowed when he mentioned staying, and she nodded absently, clearly in thought. They both heard small footsteps coming down the hall. The dog disappeared from the doorway and escorted Sofia into the kitchen, circling around but never bumping into her, and the young girl ran her hands over his fur, entranced with the animal's greeting. She shyly stood smiling inside the doorway, her face shining and hair tousled, and Maria hugged her.

Mark plated out breakfast: eggs, ham, potatoes and onions, and toast with milk and orange juice and coffee. The dog looked at him with striking blue eyes. Okay, okay, Mark thought. The mooch did patrol this morning but getting some kibble for him had to be at the top of the list today. He portioned some breakfast for the animal, and soon the shepherd was licking his lips over an empty bowl.

They were finishing breakfast when there was a knock at the door. The door opened, and the shepherd was up with a low growl.

"Hello in the house. It's your neighbor, Walter. Is that huge ass dog going to eat me, or can I come in?"

Mark called out, "Dog."

He got up and walked into the living room and put a hand on the shepherd, who immediately stopped growling and sat while watching the visitor intently.

The lean and weathered man in overalls and worn boots smiled and looked around.

"Mark? Thought it might be you, but I wanted to check and make sure," said Walter. "I see you're not alone?"

They shook hands, and Mark invited him in for a cup of coffee. Walter begged off breakfast, but Mark soon had a small plate in front of him, and his old neighbor ate as Mark knew he would.

Walter sat and sipped his coffee after introductions and made a face, which was his routine.

"Still haven't learned to make decent java, I see," he said.

Mark played his role and said, "That doesn't stop you from drinking it every time you're over here, old man."

"Just being polite," said Walter, his eyebrows elevated in a comical way.

It was Walter's standard answer, and he could say it in half a dozen ways with different inflection and facial expressions both praising and condemning as needed.

"Mr. Lawson told us you were his neighbor," said Maria. "I had the impression that you two were friends?"

She looked confused.

Sofia and Dog smiled, and Mark put his face in his hands. He knew what was coming next.

Walter sat back in his chair, coffee cup in hand, and proceeded to give a brief history of Mark's first appearance at the farm when Madelyn had him in tow and announced that he was the one. Of course, Maddie's father had other ideas about their only daughter marrying some young police officer from the city, but Maddie had been set.

"She always was jest that stubborn," he said.

He grinned over at Mark, who shook his head from side to side.

"I thought you were a teacher," said Maria to Mark.

Mark hesitated and wasn't sure how to answer. It had been Maddie who had talked him into working on his master's degree. She'd had ideas for when he retired from police work.

"Now, I wonder if anyone else here could be that stubborn?" asked Walter.

He grinned, looking at Maria and Sofia, and Maria started to protest.

Mark changed the subject and mentioned his thoughts about getting a few more supplies today. Walter nodded his head thoughtfully.

"Ought to be able to get most of that at Landry's Store," said Walter as he rubbed his chin briefly. "Might be a good time to think about some seed."

Mark was hardly a farmer, but Maddie's father had tried to teach him everything he could each time they visited until Mark realized it was her father's way of telling him that he had accepted Mark and wanted him to take care of Maddie just as he would, so Mark had tried to learn. Walter was right, as usual, just like Maddie's father. The lessons never stopped if Mark would listen.

"The tractor?" he asked.

Mark referred to the old Ford 8N tractor in the shed beside the barn.

"I been checking it each month," said Walter. "Fired right up last time I tried. Might stand an oil change though."

Mark considered Walter's advice, and his necessaries list was growing. He would probably spend a good part of the day gathering supplies and would need every bit of room in his Jeep.

Walter seemed to anticipate Mark's thoughts, and said, "Well, Mark, it's good to see you back. Thanks for the coffee. I guess I better get to my chores as well. Got a cow that needs milking, you know. Might need some help one of these days."

He looked directly at Sofia when he said that, and the little girl practically jumped up out of her chair while Maria looked worried.

Walter walked out to the porch, and Mark followed while Dog led Sofia and Maria down to the yard

Walter watched them and said, "Might have a good one there, Mark."

His neighbor paused, and Mark knew he had something else on his mind.

"Besides that terrible mess on the West Coast," said Walter, "news is buzzing this morning about a missing little girl who is supposed to be kind of special."

Walter glanced at Sofia running across the yard and back at Mark.

"You know, I'm thinking it might be a good idea if those two were to lie low for awhile."

Mark played along.

"I believe I'll need all the room in the Jeep for errands this morning. You think you might keep an eye out if I ask the girls to hang around here?"

"I believe I could find something for them to do, if'n they was willing?"

Walter had a sly look to his face, and Mark couldn't keep from laughing.

"I'll just sit here a moment if that's all right," said Walter as he perched in the porch swing. "I don't want to miss the show."

Mark was confused.

"I'm waiting for you to go and tell the womenfolk that they can't go into town to the store."

Walter winked, and Mark realized his cagey neighbor was right again. Still, it had to be done.

Mark grimaced and turned to walk down the steps to the yard while Walter grinned.

Tomás returned overnight and broke into the church and rectory before dawn. He found the communicating hallways and realized immediately the direction taken by the little girl. There had been a woman with the child according to several witnesses from the church, and some said that the woman was a nun or training to be a nun. Tomás had catalogued every detail having learned never to take anything for granted.

He found nothing else at first until he searched Father Romero's quarters in the rectory and found a telephone number by the bedside. He called and listened to the woman on the other end of the line respond before he hung up the phone. It was a religious order.

So, the priest or perhaps the woman with the child had called a convent, and maybe the woman was a nun. Donovan Giulanti had told him that he arranged for the girl's arrival into the country, but Tomás needed more information and would need to report to his patron later today with an updated plan. Giulanti expected results, and so did he. It defined being a professional.

Tomás thought for a moment. If they left via the church office door and exited the yard to the alley, they would have headed to the far side of the block and not back toward the church. He headed up the alley and emerged onto a street along with the morning sunshine only to see an older lady sitting on her front porch. She looked like she missed little that happened on her street, and he forced a smile as he walked up the sidewalk.

Tomás bowed slightly.

"Good morning, Ma'am," he said. "It's a nice day so far."

She smiled back and said, "Yes, it is. Are you out for a walk?"

She leaned forward in her chair.

Careful, he thought.

"Just stretching my legs," said Tomás. "I needed to get out and walk around. I'm feeling restless after what happened yesterday. It's a shame about the church, isn't it?"

He saw her animate and knew he had her.

"Oh yes," she agreed. "People can be so senseless."

The Sun was warm, and Tomás wiped his forehead with his arm. She noticed his gesture and asked if he would like some water.

"Yes, ma'am," he replied. "That would be nice. Thank you."

He walked up the stairs to her porch, and she disappeared into the house but shortly reemerged with a glass of water and a small plate of fresh cookies. He took the glass from her with another thank you and sipped some cool water.

"I guess people got a little excited yesterday," he said.

"Oh my, yes," she said, introducing herself. "I saw a little of that on television. I'm a parishioner at Our Blessed Mother, but I attend Mass on Saturday. I wasn't there to see His glory."

Tomás introduced himself with an alias and asked a question.

"So you believe it was a miracle?"

"Oh yes," she replied with an emphatic nod of her head. "I know it was."

She seemed very certain.

Interesting, he thought. He needed to choose his words well.

"I guess, Ma'am," he said, shrugging his shoulders. "I think I would have to see it with my own eyes."

She sat back in her chair and seemed to struggle within, but her need to share won out.

"I saw her," she said. "walking on two good legs up this street yesterday with my own eyes."

Yes, he thought.

"Really?" asked Tomás. "What did you see, Cora Mae?"

He didn't have to feign excitement.

"Why, I saw Sofia walking," she said. "That girl was a cripple. I know, because I have seen her before at the church. She was with the young lady working with Father Romero. Maria, I think, is her name. There was a man with them. He looked familiar, but I can't place him. I think he used to go to our church. They got into a car and drove away."

"That's amazing," said Tomás. "Everyone is looking for her, and you're the first person I've heard that knows anything. Have you told anyone else?"

"No," she said. "I was going to talk with Father Romero, but now, I don't know."

She looked down at the porch with her lips moving silently, no doubt saying a prayer for her pastor's recovery.

Tomás agreed with her sentiment. He had wished no injury to the priest, but he reminded himself that his first obligation was insuring the successful completion of his mission. That path brought honor.

"Where do you think she was going?" asked Tomás.

He pushed the conversation along.

"I don't know, but they seemed to be in a hurry, too much of a hurry to talk anyway," said the elderly lady.

Tomás knew she was complimenting him for being social, and he accepted with a slight nod. His grandmother had taught him to always treat people with respect.

"You know this might be very important," he said. "I mean, there are so many people looking for her. What kind of car were they driving?"

She set her water glass down.

"I'm afraid I'm not very good with cars," she said. "I think it was some kind of Jeep. I remember seeing that name, and the license plate was blue and white with the letters HD at the end."

Tomás considered very carefully. Right now, at this moment, he was the only one who knew this information. This woman living alone in the last years of her life was obviously lonely, and he couldn't have her telling anyone else. Donovan Giulanti had told him whatever it takes, and he knew of only one way to ensure that. He would be kind. She had helped him and deserved that much.

"Would it be all right if I had more water?" he asked.

She smiled and said, "Of course. I'll be just a moment."

She stepped through her door and walked inside.

Tomás waited a moment while he put gloves on, and he followed her inside. He eased softly back toward the kitchen where he found her at the sink, and she didn't hear him approach until he was behind her.

Cora Mae turned to see him, startled and disbelieving. The glass she had partially filled dropped to the floor and rolled to a stop in front of a long cabinet.

Tomás could see her certain knowledge that there would be no bargaining, but then her eyes squeezed shut, and she raised her hands and clutched her chest in pain. Before he could advance, she slumped to the floor, and after a long wheeze, she stopped breathing. He looked at her in silence and reminded himself that he hadn't directly laid hands on her. He felt strangely grateful for that.

He walked outside a few minutes later and closed the front door firmly behind him after wiping down his glass and any other surfaces he might have touched. It was unlikely she would have visitors today, but he didn't want her home invaded without her permission.

Tomás now knew two things. First, Cora Mae believed in the miracle, and he would share that with Donovan Giulanti. Second, she made very good oatmeal raisin cookies. He took another bite.

CHAPTER EIGHT

Paul Peterson emerged from the courthouse downtown. He had contacted Martin, and his cameraman knew to be ready to capture video footage of Paul's statement after victoriously emerging from wrongful imprisonment. The police had detained him overnight and charged him with inciting a riot, but he had simply explained himself to the judge.

"I spoke the truth for all to hear," he said. "That is all."

In the end, the district attorney didn't have enough to make charges stick, and the judge dismissed the case. Paul stood on the courthouse steps and gave his version of the events at the church.

" . . . furthermore, no one seems to know who this miracle child is or the man purported to have performed the miracle," said Paul. "We don't even know her location. The pastor of the church has been injured in this madness and cannot tell us. I understand the authorities are looking at this carefully and may pursue charges pending further investigation."

Martin zoomed in on Paul's face as he continued speaking.

"Meanwhile, I remind all of my faithful listeners that a child is involved in this unfortunate situation, and we desperately need to find her. We will post all relevant information today on our website. I urge any of you who might have information regarding her whereabouts to call the authorities. We at *The Probative Truth* will help in any way we can. And believe us, dear listeners, we will call out any subterfuge to all."

Martin cut off the recording and said, "Nice one, Paul."

Paul nodded to acknowledge the compliment.

"Where are you parked?" he asked.

Martin led the way to his worn compact car, and they headed back to the studio. Paul's skin crawled like the opening to an ant colony, and he shifted in the front passenger seat. Why were people so gullible? They always looked for some supernatural answer instead of scientifically looking at the physical world. Even unlikely outcomes happened eventually. Just look at lottery winners. He unclenched his hands and rubbed his palms on his trousers.

He had a passion for his point of view, but yesterday got out of hand. He remembered stepping up on the light post base like he was someone else. The crowd had hinged on his every word and stormed the church, and the news was still talking about it. He looked out the front passenger window at a crowded stone square in another town long ago and once again pushed the memory away as a remembered nightmare like he had done for so many years. Anything else would be insanity.

Something inexplicable was happening, and he could feel that now was his time. Finding this missing child would surely bring more people to his point of view.

Father Romero had evaded disclosing her whereabouts, and Paul tried to focus on that and not think of what he had seen looming over the prostrate priest in the church, something that brought back terrible sleepless memories. He shivered involuntarily as nerve endings propagated muscle twinges up and down his spine.

The police had been skeptical when he said he had nothing to do with the priest's injuries, and Paul didn't speak about what he had seen hovering over Father Romero. The little girl held the answer. Her story and disappearance polarized people, and he had to find her. If he could somehow show the event as a misunderstanding or better yet, a cleverly orchestrated hoax, he would finally gain enough listeners to garner some genuine support.

Arriving at the office, he entered to find Felicity on the phone. She looked up at his arrival but put her head back down and wrote another note before handing over the stack of messages waiting for him. Paul glanced through them, noting the general trend of support for his message of logic and patience.

Paul walked over to his desk and wrote a quick statement for an impromptu broadcast later today. While he was writing, he looked over at Felicity. She had been with him since university. Her Ivy League family didn't care for him, and he couldn't help that. She had stuck by him, though. They had limped along for several years, barely staying afloat, but in the last couple of years, his online message had been better received with growing patronage and donations. This was their opportunity, and that little girl was the key. He kept seeing the smart phone video of Sofia standing in the church. The shock and awe of that moment had gone viral, and people were flocking back to church in waves.

That's what the news stations reported this morning, and he could see on his computer that many were looking for the reported miracle man. So far, there was no trace, but Paul sensed something coming. That momentous certainty occupied his thoughts constantly now.

He saw a news update that Father Romero remained unresponsive in the hospital, and in the stack of messages and mail, he found an overnight injunction forbidding him from trespassing on the property of Our Blessed Mother Church. Apparently, the archbishop's influence carried some weight with the local judiciary. Well, it wouldn't be the first time he had broken the law in pursuit of the truth.

Paul chuckled to himself while keying up his notes for the webcast today. He needed to pay Father Romero's parish church a visit. Just a little snooping, and hopefully, he would track down this little girl and expose the truth of her miracle for what it really was, another charade. It was time for the world to understand.

Paul summarized his thoughts aloud.

"We need to find out as much as we can about the arrangement at the parish concerning that child," he said. "Have we come up with any other contacts?"

"Not yet," said Felicity, looking on with anxious eyes as Martin wheeled his chair over to compare notes with Paul.

❖

Mark drove his Jeep Commander away from the farm. It was the first time he had seen Maria that displeased, and he hoped it wouldn't happen again soon. He had explained his concerns about either she or Sofia being seen off the farm for now, and Maria understood but pointed out that the authorities were already looking for them.

"Perhaps," she said. "it would make more sense to let the authorities offer us their help. Any other approach might be seen as keeping the child inappropriately or even kidnapping."

She had asked him if he wanted to face such accusations, and he had to admit while meandering along the road that she made some valid points. Standing there in front of him, all five feet and seven inches, she had rapidly listed all the ways their current course of action could go wrong while searching his face for any clue that she was getting through. Yes, she had heard him make a promise to Father Romero, but what if nobody believed her? And what were they supposed to do while he was out driving around?

Maria was probably right, and logic suggested her course of action made sense, except he knew in every sinew of his being that it was wrong. He didn't know how to explain this growing certainty. He was feeling his steps, which he seldom did. He had survived as a police officer and detective by anticipating the risks of the job; expecting trouble gave him that needed half step to stay alive, but he couldn't have anticipated any of this.

After the accident and his family's death, he had closed off his emotions, but he could sense the rightness in what he was doing. He also knew he hadn't wanted a drink since this all started, and he couldn't explain that either.

He braked to a stop at the turn to the highway. Left would take him toward the county seat of Anders. Right would take him toward the local shops, the few that there were. He turned right.

Landry's Store had been in the same place by the side of the highway for nearly eighty years. The original gasoline and diesel pumps had finally been replaced with modern devices since he had last been here, and Mark pulled next to a fuel pump island and walked into the store. He knew better than to use a credit card for the fuel purchase.

The interior of the two-story building comprised dark stained wood floors and walls that absorbed the overhead fluorescent lights. Landry's was the only general mercantile for twenty square miles, and over the years, the owners had gradually added this and that product to appease their local client base. There were the usual convenience store products, such as milk, soda, and beer. There were jars of candy along a counter, and shelves held both staples and specialty items. Homemade jam and honey were marked with dates and sold on consignment for the locals who produced them, and the store also carried common hardware and auto parts, not everything, but enough to stay in business. The same family had owned Landry's from the beginning of its operation, and Mark remembered from previous visits that the grandson was running the business now.

"What can I do for you?"

The dark-haired, early middle-aged man smiling behind the counter seemed happy enough. The customer seated at a table against the wall did not.

Mark said, "I would like to fill up at the pump, and I have a list if you could help me. I also need some fuel and propane delivered."

The smiling owner perused the list Mark handed him and raised his eyebrows.

"Might take a few minutes, but I think we have most of this," he said, waving the folded paper "Why don't you start on your gasoline, and I'll work on gathering these items. We'll finish the particulars after you come back in."

The big man sitting at the side table had angled to hear their conversation. There was a television mounted on the wall behind the counter. The sound was turned down, but the news displayed a grainy photograph of Sofia and mentioned kidnapping and the FBI. Mark gave no indication that he was interested in the news and turned to walk out to the pumps. He found his path blocked by the big man, who wore a tan shirt, jeans, and a yellow name-brand outdoor jacket. He had risen from the table against the wall, and Mark sighed inwardly. The last few years, most of the unpleasant encounters he had in this area had to do with Terrence Bradley. He and his younger brother ran one of the larger cattle farms in the county, and he was a neighbor on the other side of Maddie's parent's farm.

"Lawson, I didn't think you would show back here," he said. "You staying at the Evans place?"

The elder Bradley was two inches taller than Mark and always positioned himself in such a way that he could look down at him.

"Terrence," said Mark. "Yes, I'll be tending the farm for a while. Are you doing well?"

Mark didn't honestly care, but it seemed the polite thing to say.

"Yes I am, but I could be more prosperous with that west pasture you own," said Bradley. "I'm still interested in your property. If you get the notion, call me."

He started to hand Mark a card with his number.

Mark waved the card away.

"I know where you live," he said. "I have no interest in selling now or in the future. Good day to you."

Mark felt he had been polite and congratulated himself while walking to his Jeep.

Terrence Bradley's face soured, and he marched out of the store to his lifted, red half-ton diesel truck and climbed up to reach the door. It roared loudly to life, and before he pulled onto the highway, Terrence drove in a circle, sweeping Mark with cold eyes that matched the black smoke from the exhaust stack brought up through the bed of the truck.

Maddie had once explained that Terrence and his younger brother, Robert, had been a pain as long as she could remember, and now, Terrence ran Twin Oaks Farm after his father's death. It looked like nothing had changed. Mark shook his head while filling the tank in his Jeep with premium and reminded himself to purchase fuel stabilizer when he went back into the store. He had more stops to make before heading back home.

❖

Colonel Ari ben Eitan rested his head on the back of his chair. He had been in the air defense command center more than twenty hours since yesterday evening. At least Avigail had agreed to take the children and retreat to her sister's house in the countryside.

The prime minister wanted more information, and so did Ari after relaying all that he knew. They had put up their own drone, and the enemy shot it down quickly, but the information from that drone had been frightening. Massed armored forces and supporting foot soldiers gathered about flags showing various militant factions.

It looked like there might be foreign military advisors although it was impossible to identify them from this information. Ari knew that Russia was a strategic ally of Iran and provided military equipment. The Chinese government traded hardware, intelligence, and training for oil, but he hadn't believed they would be on the ground with an invasion force. If so, he could only conclude that the Russian and Chinese leadership were past caring if any other country knew. If I were in the United States, I might take alarm from that, he thought.

"Sir, I think you need to see these."

An enlisted man handed him a report and several photographs.

"Thank you, Corporal."

Ari looked at the photographs for a moment, his eyes blurred with fatigue, and he wasn't sure what he was supposed to see. They looked like aerial photographs of the countryside in and around the rivers in Northern Iraq. Wait. What? He turned to the reports and studied the numbers and summary, and shaking his head, he stared at the photographs again. This couldn't be real?

"Lieutenant Noem, have you seen these?" he asked.

The lieutenant, who seemed to live at the command center even more than Ari, said, "Yes Colonel, I have. It must have been the earthquake. I have no other explanation."

God help us, thought Ari. The reconnaissance photos revealed only puddles where the rivers had been. If this was true, there would be no stopping them. He picked up the phone to call his superior. He had to make his leadership understand. The enemy could be here in overwhelming numbers in less than two days if they did nothing. They must be stopped while still distant from Israel's border.

"Lieutenant Noem, have we sent this to the defense minister?" asked Ari.

"Yes, Colonel, all sent by hardline connection a few moments ago."

Ari expected no less. He had grown quite comfortable with the young lieutenant in a short time. Trust had to be earned, but young Noem exceeded his responsibilities so well that he had quickly reached that threshold. Ari wondered how his boss would react when he told him what he felt they should do. He suspected any support the defense minister had for him would dry up just like the evidence in those photographs.

"Sir, Defense Minister Avraham is on the phone."

The young enlisted communications specialist relayed to the defense minister that Ari was picking up the phone.

"This is Ari. Have you seen the latest photographs? Yes, sir, I thought the same, but my staff has confirmed the intelligence, and the enemy has already mobilized. Sir, we must act. I am formally recommending a first strike with Gideon protocol."

Ari waited out the silence at the other end of the line until the defense minister asked him if he was certain.

"Yes, sir," he replied. "I think it has come to that."

Ari held the phone and tried to relax his hand. He understood that he had just severely complicated the defense minister's life. His superior asked several more questions before stating he would call back.

"Yes, sir," said Colonel Ari ben Eitan. "I will await your decision."

The defense minister now had calls to make. There was little time for deliberation, and Ari worried that his country's leadership would procrastinate. There would be an unavoidable time delay in preparation and deployment after any decision, and if he were leading this enemy attack, he would have ordered missile strikes and air attacks to precede the ground assault.

A trilling alarm came from one console, and an air defense technician looked up.

"Missile launch, sir," said the specialist. "There are two, no—multiple, eastern and northern quadrants, sir. Iron Dome is deploying, and Arrow is on line, sir. Active defense initiated."

It has begun, Ari thought. This was only the start. Their enemy would see the drying up of the Tigris and Euphrates rivers as a sign from Allah and attack fanatically. The fact that their leaders could have anticipated something not heard of in five thousand years would induce fanatical loyalty in their troops. Any foreign military partners would tag along cementing their new alliance with Iran along with new oil supplies and access to ports in the Mediterranean. Ari shook off a vision of his wife and children looking at him with sadness and asking, "Why?"

Israel would be no more, but not if he could help it.

"Lieutenant Noem?"

"Yes, Colonel."

"I am asking you to set up a strike mission pending approval from command."

Ari explained, and young Noem took it professionally. Only a hint of paleness around the lieutenant's thinly set lips gave away his tension. The world had avoided this for decades, and now, the Colonel had just asked him to play a central part in it.

"Yes, sir," replied Lieutenant Noem.

Another trilling alarm sounded with the radar detection of more missile launches, and Ari stayed out of the way, letting his well-trained staff coordinate the air defenses for his country, his birthplace and the only home his children had ever known. It would be a long night.

Ari had never been overly religious. He left that for his wife, who believed faithfully. He hoped she was right and there was a God, and he hoped that same deity would hear and help them, but would it be enough?

CHAPTER NINE

Maria wished she hadn't shared her displeasure when Mark suggested she and Sofia stay at the farm. It was a side of her she didn't want others to see. After the fact, she realized it was the last twenty-four hours catching up with her, reinforcing the reality that they were hiding and on the run. She knew the authorities would take Sofia away if they found her, but the rest of Mark's ideas . . . really? She wondered again if they had fled with a crazy man.

However, he was a man who got up and fixed coffee and breakfast and worried for them. She didn't know him yet, but he had an intentional way about him. He seemed to be a man who had seen much, and even though barely past being strangers, she instinctively trusted him. What would it take to truly know such a man? Now why had she thought that? Her hand felt cool to her cheek, and once again, she said a prayer for protection and guidance.

Maria spent much of the morning straightening up the house. If they were to stay here for now, she had a year's dust to clean up. Sofia seemed to have no qualms about spending the day around the farm. She and the shepherd ran back and forth to the surrounding trees throughout the morning, and the dog never left her side. Maria was grateful for the help.

She was sweeping the hall when she noticed the quiet. Dog had been barking a few minutes earlier. Maria walked out on the porch to see if all was well and saw a stranger walking across the front yard toward the barn. There was a large red pickup truck parked in the driveway. She remembered Mark had closed the gate to the property when he left, and she called out to the unknown visitor.

"Can I help you?"

The man wheeled and looked at her with his eyebrows raised and his mouth half-open. Then, he broke into a smile that looked forced to her, and she didn't see Sofia or Dog anywhere.

"Hello there," said the man in the yellow jacket. "I didn't expect anyone else here at the house."

He looked like he was searching for something to say, and Maria grew cautious.

"I'm Terrence Bradley, your neighbor from down the road," he said. "I saw Mark at the store, and he said I could drop by to check on something. I'll just take a look, and I can let you be."

Maria didn't know what to say. The man said he was a neighbor, and he mentioned Mark's name, but something didn't feel right. And where was Sofia? The man started to walk around the corner of the house.

"Please wait," she said. "Mark didn't tell me you were coming, and I'm afraid I don't know you. I think we had better wait for Mark to come back."

The big man crooked the left corner of his mouth and glanced about before answering.

"Nonsense," he said. "This won't take a moment."

Once again he started to stride forward, and a low growl sounded, no less threatening than a rattlesnake twitching its tail. The man paused in mid-stride and looked around. A snout pushed through the ornamental bushes at the side of the house, and the shepherd slowly emerged with raised hackles at the top of his shoulder blades and the base of his neck. The canine padded forward like a prehistoric dire wolf, and the man shouted at Maria.

"Lady, call off your dog!"

Maria crossed her arms and said, "I'm afraid Dog has a mind of his own. I don't believe I can control him at the moment. I think another plan is in order."

Terrence looked through her in anger, and for a second, she glimpsed a shadowy emptiness about the man. Madre de Dios, she thought, and caution fled leaving genuine fear. Where was Sofia? The shepherd slowly advanced, and the warning moment waned. Maria didn't have to be a dog whisperer to predict what was about to happen.

Apparently, Terrence figured it out too, and he backed away slowly.

"This is downright unneighborly of you," he muttered, scrambling back down the driveway.

Dog stayed in the yard at the corner of the house and watched while the man climbed into his truck, which started with a grumble. The oversized pickup truck backed out of the driveway belching black exhaust and spitting gravel until it roared off leaving the gate open.

Maria took a breath.

Dog flagged his tail like a military unit's pennant and bounded up the stairs to the porch. She looked at the shepherd, who looked back at her with shining eyes and a grin. She could have sworn he was telling her he had it all under control. She thought of Sofia again.

"Dog, where is Sofia?" she asked.

She felt silly, but it felt right asking such an animal.

Dog ran down the stairs and around the side of the house, and shortly, the little girl came walking out, herded by the shepherd. Sofia stared up at Maria with wide, tear-filled eyes. She looked like she wanted to say something, but all she could get out was a grunt. Dog seemed to understand though because he pressed up against her. Maria ran down the stairs to the yard and hugged the child tightly while whispering soothing words like a blanket around the both of them.

"Está bien mi pequeña."

Maria knelt and held Sofia and wondered if this was how mother bears felt when their cub was threatened. She had never seen herself as a violent person until that moment, and she learned a new truth about herself. Dog nestled up against both of them, and Maria reached to rub between his ears.

Sofia stayed by Maria's side the rest of the afternoon until she fell asleep on the couch. Later, when Mark drove up the driveway in the

Jeep and pulled around to the back of the house, Maria stepped out of the back door to greet him as he got out of the SUV. He looked at her with a smile.

"I could have sworn I closed the gate when I left," he said before walking back to the vehicle's liftgate.

Maria came down from the back porch to help him unload. She hesitated as she approached, and Mark paused and focused on her while he held the seed bag he had picked up.

"Sofia's all right," she said. "There's something we need to talk about."

Tomás let himself into the modest home through the rear sliding glass door. He preferred to be methodical in his work and would have taken longer to scrutinize the location, but he needed answers. He had found his way here after hacking into the Department of Motor Vehicles and searching the partial license plate number learned from the delightful Cora Mae. It made sense to him that the SUV belonged to the man seen driving away, and a search of vehicle titles had yielded several local prospects.

He needed to eliminate each possibility, and this was the first candidate. His current target worked evenings and was likely asleep at the moment. Like many, he lived online in social programs, and Tomás already knew where this man worked and his divorced dating status. Tomás pushed impatience aside. Anything approaching human emotion only impeded his work.

After adjusting his mask, Tomás worked his way through the house, quickly clearing rooms until he arrived at a bedroom where the man lay sleeping beside a woman. There was no sign of the little girl. So far, this subject seemed unlikely, and Tomás thought ahead to the next target on his list.

Unexpectedly, the man sprang out of bed and grabbed a chrome-plated pistol from his bedside drawer. Tomás knew what he should do. He should dispatch the man without hesitation. Keep the mission clean and simple. No loose ends.

Instead, he leaped forward and grasped the man with one hand around his wrist and placed his other hand around the man's throat. He squeezed with his right hand, and the man struggled briefly before he passed out. Turning his body, Tomás bore the man to the floor almost without a sound. Kneeing the man across his neck, he slid the man's dropped pistol out of reach and injected his target with a prepared dose of midazolam and ketamine. The man would not remember how he came to be on the floor when he woke up.

The minimal noise from the brief struggle had disturbed the woman. She opened her eyes to see Tomás beside her, and she looked at him in disbelief that turned to terror as she saw her lover's limp form. The woman grabbed at the sheets to cover herself, and Tomás dismissed her action with a wave of his pistol. He had a job to do.

"Never mind that," said Tomás. "I will ask you only one question. Answer, and I will leave. Understand?"

A cloying smell filled the air, and the sheets grew wet as the woman's bladder emptied.

"I don't know who you are or wha—what you want," she said. Dense letters formed flat words in the struggle to breathe through her panic. "Wh . . . why are you doing this?"

"Where is the little girl, Sofia?"

The woman looked at him with a blank face. Tomás had his answer, but he needed to be sure, so he ground the muzzle of his pistol against the outside of her thigh. The woman screamed, and Tomás aimed his pistol at her face. The screaming stopped.

"One last time," he said. "Where is the girl, Sofia?"

Clutching at her thigh with trembling hands and gasping for air between sobs, she said, "I don't know. I don't know who that is. I swear I really don't."

Tomás had his answer, and there could be no witnesses.

"Thank you," he said, and he didn't move.

He knew what he needed to do but surprised himself when he said, "If you speak of me to anyone, I will find you. Do you believe me?"

The woman stared at him like he was the original serpent and nodded. In her terror, she had no air left to speak and hid her mouth behind blanched lips.

"If you want to live, close your eyes."

She blinked twice before complying. Tomás struck the woman across her temple with a knife-edge open hand and left her lying limply on the bed as he had promised, insensible but alive. He paused at the foot of the bed, thinking over the scene, and almost reconsidered, but he ignored the unconscious bodies and walked on.

He lived by a code and never broke his rules. Mission first, always, except for today, apparently. If his patron found out, he would not understand, and Tomás didn't know if he could explain, but he didn't turn around. Shaking his head, he cleared his mind and moved on to the next possible target.

Four hours later, Tomás approached the house of the last prospect with caution. He had excluded the other four candidates, and this was his last hope. He saw no vehicle in the driveway, and the garage door was closed. The grass in the small front yard had not seen a lawn mower recently. He observed for thirty minutes and saw no movement other than the occasional neighbor walking down the sidewalk. School children arrived at the corner by bus and walked down the street to other homes but not this house.

Tomás left his vehicle and entered the backyard along the side of the house. There was a wooden fence tall enough to shield him from view, and he examined the home while donning his mask and gloves. He suspected a home security system and searched for exterior cameras. Depending on the type, he had various methods to defeat it. He hated feeling rushed, but he had to enter. Otherwise, he would have nothing to tell Donovan Giulanti, and that was not a good way to stay alive.

Entering the house through the back door, he saw a blinking red light on the security pad. He keyed in a master code used by technicians servicing this particular brand of system, and the red light turned green. Success. He had time now since the alarm had tripped for only a few moments.

He walked through the empty house until he arrived at the living room. It looked like someone had been sleeping on the couch. There was an empty vodka bottle on the floor, and there were dishes in the sink. The walls looked bare, and Tomás found framed photographs stacked face down in one bedroom. A family photograph displayed a man, woman, and child. They were standing on a front porch, but not the front porch of this house. The man in the photograph looked familiar.

One hour later, Tomás sat in his vehicle in a parking lot three miles away, weighing what he should and shouldn't say when he called Donovan Giulanti. He had searched through county deeds on his laptop, but so far he had no exact address for the unfamiliar porch in the photograph. He suspected the county from an advertisement found at the bottom of a bathroom wastebasket, and he had checked under Mark Lawson's name without success.

He folded the scrap of notepaper he had found—the one with the name of the church and Sofia printed in block letters—with his weak-side hand in precise folds until the shape of a crane emerged. It was good for hand strength and dexterity. Everything related to training.

He called in his progress report.

"There is nothing on the homeless man involved at the church. He might as well be a ghost, but I've got a lead on the girl, and I'm running that down now. "

"Forget the so-called miracle man," said Donovan. "The girl is everything. I need you to find her and bring her to me alive. It is vital that she is unharmed. Do you understand?"

"The girl is not to be harmed, and I'm to bring her to you before the police find her," said Tomás repeating back Donovan's instructions over his phone. "A man and a woman are helping the girl. I don't know who the woman is, but the guy is your old friend, Lawson."

There was silence on the phone for a moment.

"Are you certain?" asked Donovan.

"It seems very likely," said Tomás.

He waited on the phone.

"I see," said his patron. "And the priest? Was that necessary?"

There was no censure in Donovan's voice, just resignation.

"He was resistant," said Tomás. "He still lives."

Tomás was not excusing himself, just pointing out a fact. If the priest was conscious, he would have visited him in his hospital room to have further discussion.

"It is time for Mr. Lawson to come to a timely end," said Donovan. "But again, the girl is everything. Anything else is secondary."

"I understand," said Tomás. "I will find the girl before the police."

Tomás held the burner cell, waiting for any further instructions. There was silence for a moment.

"The girl is the priority," said his patron. "You will keep me informed?"

Donovan could ask a question and make it clear it was a command.

"Yes. I will be in contact later this evening," said Tomás.

The phone call ended, and Tomás continued to work on his laptop. He would need to rest soon, at least for an hour or two. He knew he could find her. She would likely be with Lawson, so if he found him, he would find the girl. Now, where did they go?

CHAPTER TEN

Captain Dwayne Everett sat in the bridge of the aircraft carrier, USS Integrity, flagship for Carrier Strike Group Five. Carrying over ninety aircraft, the carrier's mission served to project force abroad while implementing United States policy.

Captain Everett joined the carrier group just before this deployment, and their current mission involved keeping station in the Arabian Sea. Their presence deterred aggression in the region and protected international shipping, especially American shipping. Captain Everett had dispatched two vessels to the Persian Gulf, the destroyer, USS Bainbridge and the minesweeper, USS Honorable.

The crew of the minesweeper had been kept busy clearing mines from the Straight of Hormuz, which naval forces of the Islamic Republic of Iran replaced nightly. Just the day before last, Iranian missile boats had attempted to overtake and board a British tanker ship, and the Bainbridge had fired warning shots at the boats, persuading them to change their intentions.

Dwayne looked at the bow of his flagship dip and rise as the nearly eleven-hundred-foot-long vessel bobbed in the five-foot swells, lost in the immense power of the ocean. Technically a fleet admiral, he had come up in rank the hard way, starting as a baby-faced recruit. Now approaching sixty years of age with forty years of experience in the Navy across multiple ships, he finally had a flag command, and his people sat right in the middle of a pressure cooker about to blow.

His executive officer, Commander Dillon Boyd, approached him.

"Too quiet," said Commander Boyd.

He didn't say more, but he was right. Usually, the Iranian government complained long and loud to all who could be fooled internationally, stating their case in support of actions that could only be construed as barely more than piracy. This time they had been stymied, and there was nothing from the Iranian leadership. There was nothing from Fleet Forces Command either, which was distinctly odd. Usually they were clamoring for information or back seat quarterbacking responses in the aftermath of impossible situations. There had only been a reiteration of their rules of engagement with a caution regarding escalation. Not exactly ringing support for what Dwayne saw as completely within their mission envelope. Where was their intelligence? He suddenly realized something else about the quiet. Turning to Commander Boyd, Dwayne asked a question loud enough for all on the bridge to hear.

"Is there any chatter on Iranian civilian air traffic frequencies? Anything at all?"

"You think they have grounded their civilian aircraft?" asked Commander Boyd.

Radar Intercept Officer (RIO) Spurlock called out suddenly, "Contact!—intermittent and faint; estimate one hundred nautical miles on track zero one five."

Commander Boyd responded, "Type?"

Difficult to say, Commander," said Spurlock. "Contact is subsonic and suggests either aircraft at low altitude or small surface vessels."

"Lieutenant Williamson, identify and warn them off," said Boyd.

Lieutenant Devon Williamson ran the carrier's combat information center (CIC) and had already executed the order.

Commander Boyd glanced at Captain Everett and they both understood each other without having to say anything. It had been too quiet.

"Commander Boyd," said the captain. "Sound general quarters and launch the reserve combat air patrol fighters."

The executive officer gave the orders, and sailors dogged watertight doors and jumped to their assigned stations all over the ship while all interior lighting went to infrared. Ready at the catapults, two F-18 Super Hornets launched and climbed to circle overhead and join with others on combat air patrol over the fleet.

Lieutenant Williamson sent coded commands to the ships in the fleet, authorizing defense against attack. Specialists multitasked as communications and combat information systems blurred with intense activity.

"USS Leyte Gulf reports multiple intermittent contacts flying at low altitude just above the surface," said Lieutenant Williamson. "E2C Hawkeye confirming, Captain. Looks to shape up as an attack formation." Williamson looked tense. "No answer to identification queries, and there's been civilian chatter about ongoing missile attacks against Israel all night, Cap'n."

The Hawkeye, a turboprop driven airborne radar asset, circled high above the fleet.

Boyd looked at Everett and said, "Captain?"

Dwayne had worked for command, and now he had it whether he liked it or not.

"Radio all ships that the codeword is Flash One."

He had just committed his forces to active defense. Whoever was headed toward them was about to get a very warm welcome.

He looked at Commander Boyd and said, "Light them up."

Additional sirens sounded around the carrier, which zigged slightly, staying into the wind. Other ships in the force tightened their concentrated defensive circle around the carrier.

"Hawkeye reports multiple missile launches, sir," said Spurlock. He didn't take his face away from his scope but relayed information received through the headphones he wore. "Same track as earlier contacts."

Spurlock's face said it all. They were operating a half step behind in this gunfight. Dwayne felt the ship shake slightly as additional F-18 Super Hornet fighters catapulted off the deck to fight from the air. Missile launches blossomed from the guided missile cruiser, USS Leyte Gulf, and the destroyer, USS Niyol, as the escort ships launched standard SM-2 missiles to intercept the incoming enemy attack, which Spurlock declared as hypersonic.

The five-inch guns on the cruisers and destroyers went to continuous rapid fire, throwing a curtain of explosive ordinance between the fleet and the incoming missiles. Ninety miles passed quickly in the face of missiles traveling at three times the speed of sound. They could see several explosions in the distance. However, one missile made it close enough for the radar-guided Phalanx CIWS twenty millimeter cannons to open up like angry burping bees. A sound that every sailor both loved and hated because it meant the fleet had failed in its defensive screening.

The hail of cannon fire caught the attacking hypersonic missile one hundred meters from the side of USS Integrity, and even though the missile broke up, the momentum carried it amidships into the starboard side of the carrier. The warhead had lost guidance but detonated with the impact, and the resulting explosion tore through the starboard mid-deck elevator housing, rendering that elevator mechanism inoperable. Fourteen crewmen vaporized in the explosion.

Thrown against a bulkhead on the bridge, Captain Everett righted himself and called for a damage report. Meanwhile, the CIC and RIO called out the ongoing pursuit of the attacking aircraft from the fleet defenses. Suddenly, CIC Operations Officer Williamson called out.

"Sonar contacts—tracks 344 and 030. Torpedoes in the water! Torpedoes in the water! "

Everett knew the Islamic Republic of Iran had at least two diesel submarines. They had waited in the confusion of battle and attacked in layers. He called out orders, but CIC Officer Williamson was fighting the ship and had already launched countermeasures. The USS Integrity turned along with the screening vessels.

The USS Leyte Gulf and USS Niyol targeted ASROC missile launched torpedoes at the presumed submarines attacking the fleet, but the four enemy torpedoes were still inbound.

"Sonar confirms flying fish, Commander," said the operations officer.

Boyd answered Williamson without thinking.

"Probably Hoots," said the commander. "The rumors were true."

There wouldn't be much time. The Iranian Hoot was a supercavitating torpedo which used a solid rocket engine for propulsion and released bubbles around the skin of the torpedo to decrease drag, giving it a reported velocity underwater of over one hundred and seventy knots. Supposedly, the range was limited in the Iranian version to six miles, but the submarine contacts were fifteen miles out.

Commander Boyd looked at Captain Everett.

Everett shrugged his shoulders and said, "They've improved them."

Countermeasure Anti-Torpedoes launched from both the cruiser and destroyer screen along the incoming track of the enemy supercavitating torpedoes. Two of the attacking torpedoes fell prey to the intercepting torpedoes from the fleet screening vessels. One was lured off course by towed AN/SLQ-25 Nixie decoys, taking it astern of the turning vessels. The final supercavitating torpedo lanced through the ocean and headed straight for the USS Integrity.

Captain Everett thought of his wife at home. One more deployment, he had told her. She knew his sea mistress would have him one more time, and like always, his wife supported him. He had told her he would be back, and he desperately wished for a chance to say he was sorry and tell her he loved her one more time.

The supercavitating torpedo detonated beneath the ship, blowing out the bottom keel. The resulting explosion lifted the USS Niyol above the surface and dropped her into a well of displaced ocean water where there was nothing to support the escort vessel. The ship broke in two as the steel was subjected to instantaneous loads it was not designed to support. The Niyol's captain had managed to slide his destroyer in front of the aircraft carrier just in time, sacrificing his ship, which broke apart and sank in less than thirty seconds.

From the bridge of the USS Integrity, Captain Everett saw a handful of sailors in the flickering oil slicked waves marking the site where the USS Niyol had been moments before. Like everyone else on the bridge, Dwayne was stunned to silence at the sacrifice made by the destroyer's captain and her crew.

Lieutenant Williamson broke the silence.

"Leyte Gulf reports sonar detection of ASROC impacts and confirmation via HELO sonar," he said. "We got 'em, Cap'n."

Commander Boyd ordered search and rescue (SAR) operations for the sailors in the water.

Captain Everett thought of the ships alone on escort duty on the other side of the Straight of Hormuz.

"Have we heard from Bainbridge and Honorable?" he asked.

Radar Intercept Officer Spurlock tried to contact them without success.

Commander Boyd called the flight officer for a situation report. There was ongoing fire and smoke from the midship starboard elevator, but two of the ship's catapults still functioned. Shortly, a pair of F18 Super Hornets were on their way to check on the ships tasked away from the fleet. Their rules of engagement were simple, fire on any hostile target.

Everett took a breath. This was a commitment of force from Iran tantamount to war. What was happening? He thought of the USS Niyol again. In his mind he saw her captain steer her into harm's way and knew he would see that image over and over for the rest of his life.

Smoke billowed from the angry wound in the ship just ahead and below the command bridge while the ships damage control detachment continued to pump hose sprays of water and firefighting foam into the wreckage.

Radar Intercept Officer Spurlock listened on his headset and said, "Sir, Stray Cats Five and Six report no sign of Honorable. Bainbridge is smoking, but still underway. They're reporting that they repelled a missile attack, but their long range comms are out."

Everett replied, "Signal them to move to the widest point of the gulf and keep station. They are to defend against any attack. We will provide combat air patrol for them. Further orders pending."

Captain Everett turned to his XO, who was already calling the CAG officer to task the additional combat air patrol mission along with an unmanned tanker drone. His executive officer had anticipated Everett as usual.

"Send Benson?" asked Boyd.

He referred to Captain Ward Benson, who commanded USS Joss, an Arleigh Burke class destroyer with the fleet group.

Everett nodded, and Boyd relayed the orders. Captain Benson was an excellent choice. A cool head to shadow the damaged Bainbridge in the gulf.

"We need orders from Fleet Command before we respond to this," said the captain.

Boyd said, "Cap, we can't let this stand."

"I feel the same, but before we commit to war, let's call for back-up," said the captain.

Captain Everett gave a thin smile. He had no intention of letting this stand. He felt his anger grow by the minute, a cold, swirling whirlpool of emotion which threatened to engulf any thought of peace or forgiveness.

"In the meantime," he said, "We need to plan for the fight that's coming."

The armored column lumbered across the drying riverbed. Where once the Tigris River had flowed, damp ground remained, riddled with shallow puddles of standing water. Reports were similar from the advance scouts at the Euphrates, and the troops were shouting that this was the moment of prophecy. Other officers and noncoms rejoiced that the hated Israelis would soon be no more and proclaimed that a reborn nation state of Persia would once again rule from the Arabian Sea to the Mediterranean. It had to be the will of Allah. Blessed be his name.

Captain Farhad Esfahani led his tank squadron and had an excellent view from the turret of the T-72 tank that he commanded. He saw smiling faces all around. Many of the foot soldiers were laughing and joking that the enemy would be driven into the sea, and the women would be taken and used or sold as slaves. The victory would be glorious.

Farhad didn't know any of that for certain. His commanding officers said to attack, and he marched out. That was how he had been trained. Still, it was difficult to account for the sight before his eyes.

He glanced up nervously. The overlying cloud cover had parted earlier than predicted. Farhad had requested to spread out his advancing forces, but Major Ghorbani had been most specific. They must cross both riverbeds before the day was out.

"We must not squander this miracle of Allah," he said.

Farhad had worried about Israeli air power, and the major had assured him that the Israelis were busy defending against the rain of missiles currently targeting them from all corners of their little country. He even mentioned missiles from the sea. Farhad didn't know how that could be, but looking at what was once the mighty Tigris, he was ready to believe anything.

He looked out with pride at his fellow soldiers manning great war machines grinding toward a new future for his country. This could be a rebirth of his culture, and history would record this day. He daydreamed that perhaps, just perhaps, he now played a role in the beginning of another Persian Empire. Maybe he might be worthy enough to see the Mahdi himself.

Farhad doubted that would happen. Faith had never driven him like some of his countrymen. Of course, he was careful not to reveal his doubts. However, he remembered a fragment of prayer asking to find the right path under grace, and he hoped that he might lead his fellow soldiers well. One could not look on this day without feeling that somehow grace had come. How could anyone oppose this?

Farhad raised his medium height frame behind the turret hatch of his T-72B3M tank. He had special plans for his one hundred and twenty-five millimeter gun once in Tel Aviv and imagined what he might accomplish. He thought of his hidden calendar at home. The one he leafed through when he felt sure of no interruption. The calendar featured women of the Israeli military, and he hoped to meet such women. Oh yes, he had big plans.

Turning his attention to their progress, he called ahead to the advance units to slow momentarily and maintain their spacing. They had already crossed and were racing to join the scouting units one hundred kilometers ahead. They would report direct visual confirmation of the Euphrates crossing in the next hour if all went well.

He and the other troops had seen missile contrails all morning east to west, confirming the major's words. They cheered at first and randomly even now, but slogging through the riverbed was taxing, and the cheering had eased. Still, it was heartening to see the ongoing air cover overhead keeping Israel's defending aircraft away from them like a sheltering umbrella.

Farhad had reached the rank of captain in the Iranian ground forces and commanded the spearhead tank division. He was no fool. They were exposed on these river plains, and any concentrated air attack by the enemy could decimate them. He would have preferred spreading out their forces, but he had been told to hasten as their window of opportunity could close unexpectedly. So, the attack pushed on, and he saddled the very tip of the spear.

Overhead, the black specks continued to maneuver high in the sky, as they circled and darted abruptly. The Iranian air force held some very skilled pilots, and Farhad felt proud. He saw a bright flash, and an aircraft spiraled to the plains below. One less Israeli defender, he thought. Now, he could see others looking to the sky. The explosion caught their attention, and the death dance above kept all of them on edge.

One by one the attackers fell, but so did the more numerous Iranian aircraft. Until finally there remained one lone aircraft which appeared damaged but flew more or less steadily toward the center of their forces. Almost directly in front of Farhad, the single aircraft climbed and detached a black dot like a slow-pitch softball player from several thousand feet up. The dot arced up toward them, reached its apex, and began to fall. The crippled aircraft turned away in an attempt to flee but exploded as one tank down the line made an exceptional shot taking off its wing. The jet, which Farhad could now identify as an Israeli F-16 fighter, spun in flames toward the ground.

Some cheered, but Farhad did not join them. His eyes riveted on the object falling toward them, and he saw the dot enlarge to a white oblong with fins. Farhad knew what it was, what it had to be.

The attacking Israeli fighter pilots had sacrificed themselves against overwhelming odds to get this lone aircraft through and deploy one munition against a concentrated attacking force. Surely the bomb falling toward them would turn into an eagle and fly into the Sun as foretold. He waited for the miracle to happen.

The B61-mod11 thermonuclear device fell on its gravity descent as designed. One stream of twenty-three millimeter cannon shells from a hastily deployed ZU-23-2 towed anti-aircraft gun barely missed the bomb, tracing just behind its path in the sky. The Iranian ground forces gunner hastily adjusted the aim of the automatic cannon at the urging of his sergeant.

Captain Farhad Esfahani had a moment of hope as a fresh stream of tracers tracked toward the enemy weapon. He thought the fluttering he saw trailing back from the munition was venting from a hit by the anti-aircraft cannon fire, but then he made out the drogue parachute stabilizing the bomb's descent.

His lifetime of military training and discipline almost suppressed the lizard-like panic at the hindmost part of his brain as he watched the bomb fall with the miniature parachute trailing behind. It impacted approximately fifty meters directly in front of his tank and left a crater in the riverbed, but it didn't detonate. The miracle had occurred. Allah be praised!

The bomb held true to its design. Its reinforced casing survived the ground impact with the help of the retarding Kevlar parachute, and the weapon burrowed approximately three feet into the riverbed bottom. The barometric pressure triggered altitude fuse had failed, but the failsafe internal timer continued to count down.

At thirty-one seconds post release, the firing circuits sent a charge of electricity from capacitors through the sequenced wiring designed to simultaneously detonate the shaped charges surrounding the primary sphere of uranium isotope compressing it to criticality.

The fission reaction in the primary sphere raised its internal temperature to one hundred million kelvins. The primary first released its energy in glowing thermal x-ray photons which channeled within the radiation case, bathing the secondary stage. The pusher-tamper imploded the secondary plutonium to fission criticality and internal temperatures of three hundred million kelvins brought the surrounding secondary lithium deuterium to fusion reaction. The resultant unimaginable heat and neutron energy caused the more stable uranium casing to fission, releasing a third stage of ruinous energy.

All of this occurred in a blink of Farhad's eyes, and his relief arrested in a flash of agony as the blast wave disintegrated the attacking formations up and down the river bed. The mushroom cloud rising from the mixed remnants of the attacking army scattered Farhad's atoms into the memory of history.

CHAPTER ELEVEN

Maureen Thomlinson, president of the United States of America, needed more sleep. Yea right, like that was going to happen. Every hour had been worse. Millions of her taxpaying voters on the West Coast had disappeared, presumed dead, and a trillion dollars in infrastructure had been scoured away.

She had gone on television last night in a presidential address to calm the country, and the political pundits had described her as wooden and unemotional on the screen. She thought she should have earned an Excellence in Acting Award, sitting there telling the country they would recover and how each person should look to help their fellow citizen.

It was all complete and utter crap. The whole time she was thinking of some massive rogue planet crashing into them. Barry had said even a close pass would destroy civilization. Something about continents sliding around and massive pole shifts. She had tried to comprehend what he was describing until her brain shut down, silently screaming.

Please, no more!

They had contained the information for now although she couldn't fathom how. There had been problems like the young high school age amateur astronomer in Wyoming who had reported an impact on Jupiter and a change in the Moon's orbit. Threatening people with death was less effective when they realized they were going to die soon anyway; however, she had told her inner circle the gloves were off, and threats to family and significant others helped maintain secrecy. The country was barely hanging on at the moment, and America's enemies gathered, testing for weakness.

That's what this emergency session was about in the wee hours of the night. She had directed United States military units to return home. With the impending catastrophe on a global scale, they would be needed, Posse Comitatus be damned. However, it appeared the world had other plans. She entered the briefing room and settled herself at the head of the conference table.

"Okay, Let's have it."

Admiral Johnson Boatwright, Navy, Chairman of the Joint Chiefs, glanced at a sheet of notes in front of him, and said, "Madam President, a little over four hours ago Israel employed a preemptive nuclear strike against massed forces of the Iranian Military crossing Iraq in a clear invasion attempt. Israel had been defending against massed missile attacks overnight which were launched from sites in Syria, Iraq, Iran, Palestine, and the Mediterranean Sea."

The president interrupted.

"Those lunatics used a nuclear weapon?" she asked.

The admiral's face remained impassive. If he was annoyed at being interrupted, it wasn't apparent.

"Yes, Madam President," he said. "Initial reports suggest it was a thermonuclear weapon of our manufacture delivered by fighter aircraft, also of our design."

The admiral gave the president a chance to respond, but she could tell he had more to say.

"Please continue, Admiral."

"Additionally, Madam President, nearly simultaneous attacks occurred against our carrier battle groups in the Arabian Sea and the Mediterranean. The attacks were repelled, but there have been serious losses."

Admiral Boatwright paused again, and his voice faltered. He might have been thinking of the lives lost in that simple statement.

Maureen digested the admiral's summary. Israel was under attack along with their own forces. She had never considered the alliance with Israel to be healthy for the United States, and now they were being dragged into a conflict again just when she was attempting to disengage American forces internationally.

"I need written specifics, Admiral."

She turned to look at her Secretary of Defense, Donald Davis.

"Don, give me your take on this," she said.

"They hit us hard, Madam President," said the SecDef. "Iranian missile platforms disguised as freighters, jet fighters, and diesel submarines overwhelmed the group defenses."

He gave her a brief rundown, including the loss of the USS Honorable, the USS Niyol, and the damage to the USS Integrity.

"Madam President, we think some of the updated weapons may have been recently acquired, and there is some evidence that there were foreign military advisors embedded in the Iranian army."

Maureen could see it now. While they were sitting here, discussing what had happened, the Russian and Chinese governments were doing the same, likely considering their next moves and what she was going to have to recommend, but would the Russians and the Chinese wait this out?

"Admiral, I wish us to go to DEFCON ONE," said the president. "I also require options for a response toward Iran at this point."

The admiral nodded and leaned back to confer with his adjutant. Orders would go out immediately.

National Security Advisor, Valerie Merchant, sitting beside the Admiral said, "We need to consider the possibility that domestic Iranian sleeper cells will activate as well."

"I would agree with that, Madam President," said Homeland Security Advisor Yates.

Heads nodded up and down the table.

Maureen glanced to the end of the table where her Secretary of State, Daniel Cooper, slumped in his chair, looking defeated. His people had been working with the governments of Israel and Iran, and this outcome put an exclamation point on their lack of progress. She knew the enmity between the two countries stretched back decades, and for just a moment, she despaired. Did it really matter whether they blew themselves up or some massive body from space obliterated them? The effect would still be the same. Most at this table didn't know, and that would need to change.

There was always the chance that Barry's calculations were off. He admitted the math had been based on difficult and brief observations that might have been faulty. He had told her they would know in another day or so once the rogue planet appeared from its trip around the Sun, but would any of them still be here then? That was in doubt now.

"I think we all know we have to respond," she said. "Regardless of my personal beliefs, we are a signatory ally to Israel. In addition, the Iranian government attacked our own forces. We must respond overwhelmingly. I would like to avoid it becoming nuclear, but we must prepare for what may come."

President Thomlinson hoped she sounded presidential, but she felt hollow inside. Somewhere along the way, she suspected her essence had disappeared, consumed in the fires of her ambition, and that left no anchor against the winds of destruction reaching out for them. She would eventually address Congress as a formality, but today they would plan options for striking back against Iran's leadership and military.

The entire world would want to censure Israel. Yes, it looked like the attack toward them had been overwhelming, and they likely felt they had no other option, but unfortunately, their choice threatened to drag the rest of the world into the same fire.

❖

Maria woke early on Tuesday morning and let Dog out. The shepherd quietly did his business and started his morning patrol. She walked into the kitchen, put water on for coffee, and arranged bacon slices in a pan. She had learned to love the quiet start to a day at the convent and missed the orderly routine and discipline more than she thought she would. Life changes no matter what plans we make, she thought.

She had been happy to see Mark last night when he returned and felt safe with him at the farm. That was new and startling. She had been alone since her family died, and entering a life of service had seemed a perfect fit. Devoting herself to the one who promised to always be with her still felt right. She offered a prayer of thanksgiving as she mixed batter for pancakes and started on her Rosary for the day. Reciting the prayers always calmed her heart and filled her with purpose.

She needed reassurance today. Less than four weeks ago, she had been a struggling novice in the convent, and now, she was fixing breakfast for her family. Wait, did she just think that? What was she doing here?

Sofia was a living miracle, even before the hand of God touched her, and Maria knew that was exactly what happened, no matter what anyone else said. From their first meeting, Sofia had looked at her with questions only Maria's soul could answer. Whatever the little girl saw must have reassured her for Sofia had accepted Maria and continually filled her heart with those shy smiles.

Maria didn't want the little girl hurt, and she knew when the authorities found Sofia, they would rip her away and place her where they would. Maria was familiar with that pain, and no child should have to endure that.

As for Mark, she tried not to think again of how happy and relieved she felt when he returned home last night. Home? Since when did she think of Mark Lawson's farm as home? She had tossed and turned last night, trying not to wake Sofia, and trying not to think of how he slept only a few feet down the hall. No, she didn't need to think about that.

God had called her, and she was willing but felt confused. The years after the death of her parents left her adrift in loneliness and grief. At first, she had gone to live with her maternal grandmother, and she knew and loved her abuelita, but then that awful morning came when she found her grandmother still and cold. There was no one after that.

She finished high school but felt little in common with the other teens at school. She had always been quiet, and knowing that she was not attractive helped her build walls between herself and others. Her foster parents were not unkind, but they had several other foster children that kept them busy. They were grateful that Maria caused them no concerns, and they let her be. She was thankful for a place to sleep with minimal drama.

She worked her way through college and earned a teaching degree, and one of her instructors recommended her to a first job in a catholic high school for girls in Louisville where she taught English and Spanish and found a family in her pupils. She had told herself she was happy, but a quiet voice inside longed for more.

When Maria first arrived at the convent with the Sisters of Devotion, she found herself surrounded by other women in training for service to God. She prayed daily for guidance but lost weight anyway and visited with Mother Mary Margaret several times in her office. The elderly nun would counsel her, and they would pray together. Afterwards, Mother Mary Margaret would slide two candy bars across her desk and tell Maria to eat them in the bathroom.

Her days cascaded in shades of gray, but her dreams spun spiderwebs of interconnected purpose at night, and at the center was her relationship with God. She continued in her discernment, and after twelve months she had adapted to the sparse life and discipline of daily prayer. On the morning of her last day at the convent, Maria opened her eyes to stare at the white ceiling with a burning question.

"What do you require of me?" she asked out loud.

She had been thinking of seeing Mother Mary Margaret again when she was summoned to find the archbishop waiting in the office to plead that a young girl needed her, but she hadn't known how much her life would change. She had always felt like a shadow in a black-and-white cartoon until Sofia clung to her side and pulled her like a phoenix into a world bursting with color.

Maria flipped bacon gently in the pan and thought of Mark. Dare she think of him by his first name? Although he tried to hide it from them, he seemed as sad and lonely as she remembered feeling before the still voice that directed her toward the convent. She had learned indirectly from Walter that Mark had been a police detective before becoming a teacher, and Father Romero had mentioned that Mark taught history and religion and had lost his wife and daughter in a terrible accident. She had only just met him, but she had seen Mark act decisively for Sofia and for her, and he listened to her concerns and explained his reasoning without rancor or impatience.

Maria sensed that Dog was ready to come back in, and she walked to the door where their guardian and protector awaited his usual praise. He wagged into the house, reassuring her that all was right out in the yard, and quickly found a place underfoot in the kitchen, no doubt hoping bacon would magically fall between his paws. Dog seemed to be okay with Mark, and that spoke well. Maria already knew if Dog didn't like someone, she could never trust them.

"Good morning."

Simple and familiar words, but they startled her. Mark stood in the kitchen doorway.

"Smells good," he said.

"Thank you," she replied. "Breakfast is almost done, and Dog has been out already."

Mark looked at the canine who looked back at him as if to say, "Glad you're awake, but I have dibs on the bacon."

They both heard the padding of feet in the hall and Sofia popped her head into the kitchen and wove a sleepy path to the table. She sat there smiling between the two of them.

Mark stretched while standing.

"I'm sore from hauling those supplies," he said.

Maria blushed, and Sofia grinned at both of them.

Mark did not look bad at all in the morning, and for just a moment, Maria thought of what it might be like to rest with his arms around her. She flushed with the thought, and it scared her. Something was happening here beyond her understanding, and for the first time, she understood that Sofia might not be the only one at risk of getting hurt.

CHAPTER TWELVE

"We are going ahead with the podcast this afternoon, right?" asked Martin. "We should press on with our message while the news is hot."

"Yes, we should," said Paul.

He looked away from Martin and tried to get his head clear. Being near the church had stirred up long-suppressed memories of the day he turned eleven. The day his father's friend and partner came to stay with them, and later, the afternoon when he saw his mother and the friend.

He had prayed for God to make it go away, but the image wouldn't fade. He had wanted to say something to his father, but what about his mother? He wet his bed that night and didn't get up in his shame of contemplating a confession to adults who wouldn't want to hear. His guilt weighed him down day after day until his only thought was finding a way out.

One night, relentless voices answered his plea, and as he searched for the source, he almost lost himself until he climbed back into bed with his remaining strength and pulled the comforter about his head from what beckoned in the dark. He survived, but the torment of that offer had scarred him. Somehow his father found out anyway, and their lives were never the same.

He knew now that his memory of that night was only a persistent nightmare. His fight back to reality had become a life mission to show his faithful listeners and all his detractors what he had learned. There was no God and no Heaven or hell other than what we made for ourselves. What we did in our lives was the only truth. It had to be. Otherwise, he really would lose his mind.

The phone rang. Martin answered and handed the phone to Paul, who identified himself and listened before replying.

"That will be satisfactory," he said. "I will be there at seven tomorrow morning."

Paul hung up the phone, and Martin looked at him with an unspoken question.

"That was the local affiliate," said Paul. "They want an interview for the morning news show."

Felicity looked up from her work and waited for him to continue.

Paul said, "This is a chance to tell people what they might not want to hear. I need a way to discredit this miracle. C'mon guys, give me something."

Martin inclined his head and stroked his chin in thought.

"The girl," said Felicity. "Where did she come from? Why was she staying at the church? Who was looking after her? How do we know her baseline medical status? Did a physician see her, and if so, who? There is no way to understand what happened without knowing the answers to those questions."

Paul knew in an instant that she was correct. He would concentrate on what was potentially wrong with the situation and acknowledge nothing supernatural. Felicity was quiet, but he had learned to listen when she spoke. Sure, her hair was mousy, and her eyes hid behind thick glasses, but she was loyal and warm, and he thought about how they had missed their Sunday afternoon together this week.

Martin talked to himself as if he were the one doing the interview and began writing out the questions. Picking up the phone, he made a call to the archdiocese. He had the number memorized and ran through his list of questions to the person on the other end who answered with a noncommittal response that the situation was being scrutinized.

Paul had heard the same responses long ago, and his muscles quivered with the urge to pile up all the papers on his desk and set them afire. He tried to resist but felt pulled against his will until he stood on sweat-drenched paving stone and clay surrounded by a screaming crowd.

"Crucify him!"

The words echoed just like that night under his bed. Paul's friends had goaded him when he tried to talk about it, and he could still hear their laughter. He couldn't understand, so how could anyone else? But now he had encountered the same nightmare again in Our Blessed Mother Church, surrounded by smoke and flame and madness, and he didn't know how to account for that.

"Paul, are you all right?" asked Felicity, stretching her hand out to him.

Martin sat across the room concentrating on his computer screen, unaware of the interaction between the two of them.

The sensations passed, and Paul swallowed his fear, but didn't trust himself to speak for a few moments. Afterwards, like always, he felt amazed to be alive, and he gazed at Felicity with a surging passion he could not contain.

"I missed you," he said in a low voice.

Felicity blushed, and Paul knew she was shocked at his open declaration. He felt like he was seeing her for the first time again and walked to her desk. She was the only good he could remember happening in his life, and he wanted to caress her face in an irresistible urge to kiss her.

"Paul, have you seen this?"

Martin had turned on the television and wasn't looking at Paul or Felicity. The network anchor confirmed in breaking news that a nuclear detonation had occurred in Northern Iraq, and the picture cut away to a video feed of the Israeli Prime Minister stating that Israel had a right to defend itself. Martin shook his head in disbelief.

"I knew this would happen eventually," he said. "Now what?"

The whirlwind of death and destruction had been unleashed in the Middle East, just as the shadow in the darkness had told him, and with that thought, Paul felt the remembered nightmare reach for him again with the mocking revelation that man would find out where genuine power resided as a wave of unrestrained destruction reached around Earth sifting billions of souls like chaff for eternity. The image made Paul reach down and grip the desk to keep from falling, and Martin scrunched his eyebrows and stared at him.

Something within his scarred past wanted to laugh and shout, but it was too soon for open celebration, and Paul fought for control. He wanted to tell Martin and Felicity to run away from him, but that thought was tamped down ruthlessly, and in that moment, Paul realized he had lost control again and froze in place somewhere between his desk and Felicity. These moments when he wasn't himself had become rare, but whenever they occurred, he always felt like a small, confused boy who could trust no one.

Felicity came to him in his confused state, and she took him by the hand and led him back to his desk. She hugged him while he huddled within himself, lost among the imaginary voices crying for release until he found his way back to the present.

❖

Cardinal Ronaldo Ricci left the Apostolic Palace after reporting the latest conclusions from the Academy of Sciences and walked hurriedly along the Via del Belvedere, deep in thought. Ronaldo had hated sharing Professor Bernard's answer with Pope Anastasi in his weakened condition, but the aged pontiff took it in stride and asked Ronaldo to pray with him. Afterwards, they sat and talked, and Anastasi related stories from his childhood until he tired.

Professor Bernard had assured Ronaldo of the entirely natural means of their coming destruction. The normally dispassionate scientist summarized his findings, and the professor's hands had shaken only a little as he gave his pronouncement while sipping tea.

"Unlucky, yes," the professor said. "God's anger, no."

But Ronaldo could feel the conflict between God and the fallen, who loved to manipulate from the shadows. Ronaldo had no more courage than any other man, and his soul could be corrupted as easily as the next, which is why he studiously prayed and invoked sacramental protections daily. He actively avoided any interactions which might allow transgression to slip through his door. The Church taught that it was dangerous to talk with the evil one, and he knew it from experience.

Oh, to live in such a time. He had no fear for his own life, but for the many misguided souls who preferred the secular to the truth. Ronaldo knew the world would end at some point, but he was only a man, and by himself he could affect nothing.

Ronaldo passed the intersection of the Via del Pellegrino and the barracks for the Swiss Guards to his right. The soldiers offered protection against human interlopers, but today, Ronaldo sought a different protection. Saint Anne's Gate faced him, but he didn't intend to exit Vatican City.

Finding the Church of Saint Anne to his left, he walked up the stairs to the front door, nodding to a uniformed Swiss Guard, who came to attention at his presence. Ronaldo entered the beautiful pontifical parish church of Vatican City and made his way to an alcove on the left. He produced a key and opened a locked door, leading to stairs winding down beneath the church.

The underside of Chiese d'Santa Anna reflected its true age. Built since the sixteenth century, the alcoves in the foundation were little known. It was an excellent location for a prayer war room, and he entered to find a dozen priests and nuns gathered. The rest of the world scoffed at the prophecy of destruction revealed in Revelation, but the Church had never discounted John's visions. Jesus said the hour was not known even to him, and religious warriors manned this room around-the-clock and prayed for the fate of the world.

Ronaldo took a position at the hewn wooden table, polished dark with use over the centuries, and knelt on a green prayer cushion. He meditated, hoping for any answer other than what he feared, and prayed for guidance. He had word from an archbishop in America regarding his friend, Father Romero, and the information that his friend lay injured tore at his heart.

Whenever he thought of Francisco, he saw him as he first knew him as a parish priest in Venezuela at the Colombian border. Father Francisco Romero had been a vigorous and sturdy middle-aged man, comfortable with who he was and what he was about. He had bid Ronaldo welcome and put him to work immediately.

Together, they provided comfort to the people in and around the area, even as the rebel unrest in Colombia threatened to engulf their parish village. One night, a knock at their door revealed not rebels, but two villagers requesting help. Ronaldo had watched in confusion as Father Romero gathered a few necessaries and motioned for him to come along.

They followed the men out of the village into the surrounding forest and arrived at a clearing around a great stone strand jutting up from the ground like some land-locked iceberg surrounded by twin walls of layered rock forming a natural enclosure. Several villagers were gathered about a young teenager secured to a makeshift bed at the mouth of the rock formation. The teen girl rambled and cursed and alternated between pleading tears and sneering laughter. Father Romero seemed unaffected, but it horrified Ronaldo. He had read of such things, but to see and experience it, well, it had shaken him to immobility.

Father Romero seemed well versed in the prayers for exorcism and proceeded at once. The two of them worked together, praying to force the demon out of the little girl. At one point, the girl looked directly at Ronaldo.

"He won't spare you."

She sounded like a lost little girl at first before her voice changed to a coarse, almost animalistic, bass as if more than one presence fought to speak.

"He approaches even now, and his followers grow daily. You will see the master arrive at the destruction of this world to rule over its survivors."

Those words had shaken a younger Ronaldo, and a vine of doubt choked his faith. Writhing, the girl broke free of her bindings and lashed out with one foot, striking Ronaldo a powerful blow to the side of the head. Dazed, he fell backwards to the ground.

"You will not win," she growled like dogs fighting over raw meat. "We are many, and long have we hungered. Our moment is soon, and the favored one will not stop us."

Father Romero held steady, Bible and crucifix in hand, and intoned ancient prayers while his faith echoed off the overhead rock like one of the original twelve. The girl flailed and cursed and suffered a generalized convulsion as a shadow drifted from the bed between flickering torchlight into a shaded corner of the overhanging ledge and disappeared.

The girl lay still afterwards, exhausted and unconscious but breathing. After some time, she awoke and recognized her distraught family but had no memory of the last few days. The mother sobbed and held her daughter and stroked her child's hair. Lost but found, she had been joined with her parents again, and Ronaldo knew it was due to his friend, Father Romero, a humble priest who never wanted more.

Later that morning after returning home, Ronaldo had prayed for understanding before collapsing on his bed from exhaustion. He had tossed and turned while dreaming of a great shadow covering a world of smoke and fire. Over and over, he saw the same events reach the end of everything, and each time he sought a way back only to start anew. He woke up drenched in sweat to see blood on his pillow and wiped at his eyes, but the scene was the same, except, now, he was sitting upright in his bed and everywhere he looked, people ran in desperation, screaming and fleeing what couldn't be escaped. Somehow, he fell asleep again and when he finally awoke exhausted, he stumbled upright and washed his face, but the images continued, seared into his brain scene-by-scene.

Sitting at a small table with a bowl of soup and a piece of bread in front of him, he saw Father Romero stumble into the kitchen. Tired and subdued, Ronaldo wondered what he should say. Father Romero's eyes were red and his face looked drawn, unlike his usual calm and cheerful appearance. He fixed a bowl of soup and picked up a chunk of bread and sat across from Ronaldo and said a quiet blessing.

"Did you sleep?" asked Father Romero, dipping his bread in the soup.

Ronaldo nodded hesitantly, then said, "Yes, some, but I found my sleep troubled by a dream."

Father Romero shrugged his shoulders as if he expected it. He didn't ask about the nature of the dream, and Ronaldo hesitated to continue.

"Francisco," said Ronaldo, addressing Father Romero by his first name. "What I saw . . . "

Father Romero nodded and said, "Few have beheld what you saw last night." He took a spoon of his soup.

"Yes," said Ronaldo. "I mean no, not that. I do want to talk about the girl and what she told us. I didn't believe it was real. I mean that's important, but I wanted to talk about my dream. There's something I can't get out of my head and feel I have to tell you."

Father Romero set his spoon down and waited.

Ronaldo composed himself and began to recite from memory.

"The reckoning arrives when a broken one is made whole—"

Interrupting, Father Romero said, "under a covered sky."

Ronaldo struggled to breathe around the thumping of his heart. How could Father Romero know what he was going to say? Unless . . .

Each began to talk in surprise at having the same dream until Ronaldo found his appetite and ate his soup. They continued with coffee and prayer and more discussion and planning, and Ronaldo agreed to share their mutual vision with the Vicar of Christ on Earth when he returned to Italy.

After his return to Rome, it amazed Ronaldo when the new pontiff agreed to see him. Humbly, he had shared his experience and vision with Pope Luke Anastasi. His Holiness sat quietly for a few moments, and Ronaldo had been sure in that moment that he would be doubted. Anastasi had called for some water and after Ronaldo sipped, the pope spoke.

"You must help us prepare," said Anastasi.

And Ronaldo had stayed, wondering what difference he might make as a humble priest. Later, he had been appointed a bishop by the pontiff, and still later, a cardinal, at the behest of His Holiness. Ronaldo, unknown to anyone else, was tasked with searching for any sign of the prophecy, and the Holy Father bade him and Father

Romero to confidence. Over the years, the pontiff had called for Ronaldo often in closed discussion regarding Church policy and other topics ranging from sports to family matters.

Ronaldo had diverted resources to his cause with the quiet support of the pontiff. Finding the money for the purchases had not been easy and had generated some jealously and hard feelings among his colleagues. The other clergy called him "formica impegnata" and targeted him for his efforts to fund disaster planning on behalf of the Church, but Ronaldo endured in silence as he had been directed by the pontiff.

He knew he could affect nothing by himself, but he had a staunch ally in his God, the I Am, and in His embrace, all things were possible. Perhaps, through the blessed blood of His Son and the entreaties of the faithful, humanity might still be spared.

Ronaldo prayed to understand what he should do.

He couldn't find a definite answer, but he kept imagining Father Romero alone and in pain. The one thing he knew was that he couldn't abandon his friend. He would need the pontiff's blessing if he was going to travel to America.

CHAPTER THIRTEEN

"Paul Peterson is our guest this morning," said the television host. "He is here to discuss the recent alleged miracle and disappearance involving a young child at a local church."

Stacie Obarra paused in her introduction. An up-and-coming figure in local broadcasting, she had her sights set on the national stage. The television station had a presence at the hospital to interview Father Romero if he woke up, but so far, he remained unresponsive. The story had grown hotter by the hour, and her station manager had told her to get Peterson on the air.

"Good morning, Mr. Peterson," she said. "Thank you for coming to talk with us."

Stacie beamed for the camera.

"Not at all, Miss Obarra," he said. "I'm happy to be here."

Paul wore a simple gray suit and brown shoes and sat upright in his chair with his hands folded on his knees, his face untroubled.

"You were at Our Blessed Mother Church on Sunday?" asked Stacie.

She knew the answer already, but she wanted the interview to start smoothly.

"Yes," said Paul. "Not at the Mass, of course, but later. I was curious like so many others. I wanted to see the child standing and walking as anyone would."

"What did you see, Mr. Peterson?" asked Stacie, flashing another smile.

She needed to let him tell his story to help him relax before she got to the important questions.

"I arrived as the crowd was building," he said. "Many people showed up as you know. Claiming a miracle has happened is a sure way to bring people to your door, and I saw people with questions and anxious faces. Some looked ill and likely hoped for a similar miracle. I thought it cruel that no one from the church fully addressed their concerns, and I worried for the little girl like everyone else."

Paul prepared to continue his description, but Stacie heard the producer in her ear bud prompting her to interrupt.

"The way you describe it makes me feel like I was standing there," she said. "Did you see any person or persons around the pastor? He is still unconscious, and we are all hoping he recovers."

Paul hesitated for a moment, remembering the shadowy specter hovering over Father Romero at the altar as the priest lay still. He had said nothing to the police. What would he tell them? He couldn't explain it, and no one would believe him. It would destroy his credibility. No, the light from the windows in the church had teased his eyes, and that was all. He wouldn't say anything now for the same reasons, and he shook his head.

"I saw the pastor down at the front of the altar, but no definite assailant," he said. "Someone else called for medical help as the police came into the church."

Stacie nodded her head in agreement.

"I understand you made some remarks to the people massed outside," she said. "And the police detained you overnight. Can you tell us what that was about?"

Paul had prepared for this question and shifted in his seat to directly face the television camera.

"I believe in the right of each person to think for themselves, to question and seek evidence, and to express their opinion freely," he said. "Freedom of speech is an important human right."

"Yes, Mr. Peterson, but some have said your remarks galvanized an overly imaginative crowd into violence," said Stacie. "The church building was damaged, and the pastor was injured severely."

Her producer approved so far and told her to keep pressing.

"Miss Obarra, each of us has a right to our individual thoughts, speech, and actions," said Paul. "However, our individual decisions lead to consequences, and sometimes those results are unfortunate. The decision to make a sensationalist claim of miraculous healing has an outcome like any other action."

Paul shifted position in his chair and looked at the camera directly again.

"I believe each of us has all that we will ever need or want within us. That reality is all we can have until the moment of our death, and what we choose to do within our capabilities defines our lives."

He spread his hands as if he were weighing his words.

"Ultimately, I want each person to understand that there is only the truth of decision and action followed by consequence. The world would be a better place if each person understood and applied that throughout their life."

Paul sat back in his chair and smiled. He had just accomplished his mission statement on live television, and it couldn't be edited out.

Her producer told her to wrap it up, and Stacie knew she needed to close the interview, but something inside her couldn't let it be. She was completely ambivalent about the question of God, and if pressed, she would have said there was no direct evidence for an almighty deity and plenty of evidence to suggest the absence, just look at her last failed relationship. She knew all that but couldn't help herself.

"That is an interesting viewpoint," she said. "But what about the billions of people around the world who believe in the existence of God? What if you are wrong?"

It surprised her how much she wanted to hear his answer.

Paul rubbed his chin with one hand and nodded and considered her words.

"Yes, I have heard this question before."

He didn't add that he had heard it countless times.

"I would simply ask something in return. If there is an all-powerful

God, an omnipotent being paying attention to us in this universe, then where is he or she or it? I consider myself a rational man. I am open to any reasonable possibility, but I can't reach a conclusion without evidence, and all things being equal, the simplest answer tends to be the truth.

I trust in the proof of repeatable scientific results that reflect the physical world we live in. I hope that each person who hears me understands that each moment of every day, you and you alone are responsible for your thoughts and words and actions. The consequences of those actions determine your life and the lives of those around you. The only legacy any of us have once we have passed on is the memory of our choices."

The producer called for a wrap and station break. The blinking red lights on the cameras extinguished, and the cameramen stepped away. Stacie thanked Paul Peterson, and he unhooked his microphone and thanked her for the interview. He seemed calm and self-assured and had spoken in a logical and persuasive manner. Her producer and others at the station were pleased, and she felt she had done her job, so why did she feel uneasy? It made no sense.

Something pried at the leather surrounding the meat that used to be her heart, but she couldn't let anyone else see her pain. In her world, the wounded became a meal for any opportunistic predator.

Stacie Obarra maintained her cordial exterior and masked her inner turmoil. Yes, actions have consequences. Everyone knows that, but is that all there is? You live your life making the best possible choices and end up hurt and miserable and ready to believe any suggestion that sounds good.

She wasn't sure that was enough for her. Everything she knew around her was real to the touch of her fingers, but there had to be more, didn't there? Was it all just eons of chemical interactions and chance? Stacie watched Paul Peterson walk through a swarm of admiring staff at the station, and again the thought came to her. What if he was wrong?

❖

Tomás pulled in to a rural general store just off the two-lane highway for gasoline and directions. He had driven several roads without success, getting lost twice in the process. The area map he downloaded didn't seem current, and his in-dash GPS unit had tried to take him across a fenced field more than once.

Pulling up to the pumps, he noticed a sign to prepay inside. He walked into the general store and saw a smiling middle-aged man behind the counter.

"Hello there," said the storekeeper. "You look like you've come a ways. Can I help you with something?"

Tomás considered how locals stuck together and decided to approach indirectly.

"Yes, please. I need some gasoline, a bite to eat, and a place to sit for a moment," he said.

Careful, he thought, and he kept his expression hopeful.

The gentleman behind the counter said, "I'm Matthew Landry, and that pretty girl over there is my daughter, Patricia. She can fix you a decent sandwich if you like. Just tell her what you want, and she can have it ready by the time you finish fueling."

Tomás nodded and stepped over to Patricia, who waited for him. He asked for a turkey sandwich with lettuce and tomato and mayonnaise, salt and pepper, and hot sauce.

He smiled at her knowing it cost him nothing to be polite. He heard the bell at the front door and turned to see three young men wearing jeans and plaid shirts saunter inside. They headed directly toward him but looked beyond to the sandwich counter. Tomás guessed they were equally interested in sandwiches and Patricia. He stepped slightly to the side to give them room.

"Is that your car out there?" asked one of the young men, pointing his thumb toward the front door. The overhead light reflected from the pearl button snaps on his shirt.

The one in front of their charge to the sandwich counter had paused to speak to him, and the other two halted, following his lead.

"Yes," replied Tomás.

He had an idea what was coming, but he would not encourage these young men. He had a job to do and no time for play.

"Pretty fancy," said the young man with a smirk. "Hope you can move it right quick. We have to get back to work and need to fuel up."

Tomás merely nodded and started toward the fuel pumps.

"Hey, I was talking to you."

The stout young man grabbed Tomás by the arm and squeezed.

"Robert Bradley!" said Matthew Landry. "What have I told you about behaving in my store? You unhand that man at once. Do I need to have a talk with your brother again?"

At the mention of Terrence Bradley, young Robert released Tomás and stared daggers at the store owner.

Tomás gave no sign of the glee he felt inside. Robert's aggression toward a visitor in the country store would give Tomás a sympathy vote with the owner and his daughter and maybe a gateway to some information. He played his role of the wronged stranger and acted intimidated when he stepped outside to fill up the custom dual tanks in the Toyota. He pulled away from the pumps and stepped back inside to pick up his sandwich.

Robert Bradley and his friends tapped their boots against the varnished and worn wooden floor while Patricia took extra care in wrapping the sandwich for Tomás. She placed a pickle and chips on the plate as well, but the last straw for Robert seemed to be the very sweet smile she gave Tomás as she handed him his sandwich.

"Thank you, Patricia," said Tomás.

With his smooth voice, dark hair, and careful manner, he clearly had her attention, and Robert squinted his eyes and pressed his lips together in a frown. Tomás turned away just before he judged the young man would force his hand. He paid the owner for the gasoline and his sandwich and sat at the corner table. The sandwich tasted quite fresh. He didn't remember asking for bacon, but Patricia had placed a couple of strips on his sandwich. Delicious. Tomás ate slowly.

Finding his way here had taken some detective work, and he pushed away any impatience. The location of the property seemed to be hidden under an unfamiliar name. It had forced him to find his way to the convent at the address of the telephone call from the priest.

Tomás had talked to the sister in charge, who had been reluctant to provide any information. He had tried to charm her to no effect and had switched to intimidation with fake law enforcement credentials from the FBI without success.

It was only when he checked the phone records from the convent that he came across an area code and number from a discount super-center in Bowling Green suggesting a general direction and that he might be on the right path. His efforts had eaten up a day and a half, and he would need to provide some results soon. Donovan Giulanti was not a man to accept failure.

The three young men sat at a center table after getting their sandwiches, talking among themselves, and Tomás sighed inwardly. He knew what was coming. Ordinarily, he would have already dealt with it, but he needed to stay in the owner's good graces a while longer. Right now, the storekeeper was more concerned over the antics of the young trio, and Tomás needed that to continue. So, he pretended not to hear the muttered insults and comments about fancy boys from the city in foreign pretty cars.

Tomás finished his sandwich and sat at the table, but casually moved his chair back, clearing enough room to move if needed. It wouldn't be long now. They were working themselves up to something. They just didn't know yet how stupid.

Robert rose up from the table without a glance at his leavings and strode a few paces to face him. His two friends smiled and flanked Tomás to either side. The younger Bradley smirked.

"Time for you to leave, fancy-pants," he said.

Tomás watched the loud one and waited. He was ready when Robert reached out to grab his arm again. Tomás didn't stop smiling and smoothly turned his torso while seated in the chair. Robert still held his arm but was forced to extend his body or release his grip. This threw him off balance and made it difficult for him to continue to talk, but he didn't let go.

Tomás placed his right hand casually over Robert's hand and applied a wrist lock. Now it was Robert who was in trouble as he gasped in pain. Another ounce of pressure would wreck Robert's wrist and leave him with permanent physical injury. Tomás considered it for a moment, but he needed to remain focused on his mission.

Robert's friends looked on openmouthed at their leader's submission as Tomás forced Robert to one knee. Tomás remained seated and continued to smile, releasing Robert just before irrevocable damage occurred.

The younger Bradley brother slowly stood while cradling his wrist. His face showed a mixture of pain, embarrassment, and the realization that he might be playing a very dangerous game with this outsider. He slowly drew back, and his friends followed him.

"Robert Bradley, that is the last straw," said Matthew. "You leave right now and don't come back."

The younger Bradley shot Matthew a hateful look, as if he had helped Tomás complete his humiliation.

"I'm leaving," said Robert, rubbing his wrist. "We'll see what Terrence has to say about this."

The boys left the store, and both Matthew and Patricia exhaled deeply.

"He's a creep," she said. "He always has been, and his brother is worse. Dad, what's going to happen?" She looked apprehensive and embarrassed. "I'm sorry that happened to you, mister. Most people around here are not like that."

Tomás shrugged his shoulders.

"They were unimportant and a nuisance," he said, earning a smile from her. "I'm interested in what people around here are really like."

CHAPTER FOURTEEN

Mark pulled himself out from under the tractor. He had changed the oil and filter, and he considered starting it up. He had been out in the barn trying to get organized for spring planting. Well, that and thinking about breakfast time which had been pleasant except for Maria being ever more quiet. She might be uncomfortable staying here with him, but Sofia seemed happy enough for all of them. Even the dog seemed cheerful, and it brought back warm memories of visits with Maddie's folks.

He noticed a collection of something on the far side of the barn covered by a tarp. He didn't remember leaving anything there. Maybe that's what Terrence was pestering about. He started toward the mound but heard a vehicle pull up the driveway. Might as well not have a gate, he thought.

He walked out of the barn to see Sheriff Roger Murphy getting out of his duty vehicle, a Ford Explorer. Great, thought Mark, Aldona County's finest, and the day had started so well. He walked from the barn around the corner of the house.

"Roger," said Mark.

"My friends call me Roger," he said. "You don't qualify."

The sheriff stood beside his truck.

Mark sighed and said, "Sheriff Murphy, what brings you out this way?"

The sheriff nodded in satisfaction.

"Got a report of a disturbance at Landry's Store and heard you were back. Just playing a hunch is all."

The sheriff waited for Mark to answer.

Mark shrugged his shoulders. I was there picking up some supplies. I'm not sure about any disturbance. What did Matthew say?"

"He said you had words with Terrence Bradley, but if that was a crime, half the people in this county would be criminals."

Sheriff Murphy twitched the corner of his mouth almost into a smile.

"Well," said Mark. "He kinda got in my way and reminded me again that he wants to buy this farm. I noticed the great big fence he put around his place. Can't imagine how much that cost. Still, it looks like some of his cattle have been over in our grass, but I can't know that for sure, and I didn't mention it to him."

"Lots of people in this county take exception with you calling this place yours, you know," said the sheriff. "Especially after what happened."

Mark stiffened. Still the same Roger, he thought. The sheriff never cared for Mark from the first moment he met him trailing after Madelyn, and Mark later learned from Maddie that Roger had dated her a few times in high school, but nothing ever came of it. Mark remembered her explanation while she held his hand.

"He wanted a different answer," she said.

After the accident, with his family dead and only Mark left, many in the community refused to believe any explanation other than Mark being at fault for falling asleep and running off the road. Anything else was just an excuse, and it seemed the sheriff agreed with them. Well, so be it. Mark was not about to explain himself to anyone, and if they didn't want to believe in him, they could go jump in the lake.

"Mark?" said Maria in a questioning tone.

She had come out on the front porch and was looking at the sheriff and back at Mark. Roger looked surprised, and Mark could see the wheels turning in the sheriff's head. So this was how it was. Not only did Mark kill off his family in a cowardly manner, but now he shows up at the coveted Evans farm with another woman.

Maria's head tilted like she was trying to reason something out as she saw the sheriff's face twist into a hard grimace. Then, even from out in the yard, Mark saw her blush. She crossed her arms at ramming speed and squared off directly at him and started to protest, but Mark interrupted and took the opportunity to guide the narrative while Dog and Sofia were absent.

"Sheriff Murphy let me introduce you to Miss Maria Perez," said Mark. "I have been away too long, and she is helping me revive this farm. That's why I was getting supplies. I'm planning on staying for a while, and I may try my hand at planting this season."

Mark saw Maria's face color a deeper shade. His explanation didn't really explain her presence in any innocent fashion. He hoped she intuited why he danced around the real reason for her being here, but it clearly didn't keep her from being upset. She nodded to the sheriff, turned, and walked back into the house.

Roger smiled and seemed happy to cause a rift in what he saw as an inappropriate domestic situation. Mark suspected Roger would be against anything that might provide Mark a little happiness. Wait, why did he think being with Maria could bring happiness?

"How'd you find the time to get away from your day job, Lawson. I figured you'd be helping the city's finest catch whoever kidnapped that little girl on the news."

Roger's expression suggested he really wasn't interested in hearing an answer.

Mark worked at keeping his face neutral.

"So, what made you sure it was me causing a problem?" he asked.

"Matthew and Patricia said it was some slicked-back city dude with a fancy foreign-made truck," said the sheriff. "Apparently he and Terrence's brother had words, and the guy manhandled young Robert and forced him to leave. Wish I had seen that. Anyway, that's not the funny part."

Roger reached up and adjusted his brimmed cowboy hat slightly and tugged at his duty belt to adjust it on his waist. He leaned his back against the side of his vehicle like he had all the time in the world.

Mark realized he was about to find out the real reason for the sheriff's visit and felt more and more uneasy as he thought over Roger's description of the unknown visitor at Landry's Store. Robert Bradley was an arrogant young man, but Mark had seen him lift and sling two square bales of hay at a time.

Sheriff Murphy took out a cigarette and a lighter, and moments later, he exhaled iron gray smoke before continuing.

"Yeah, after he ran off Robert, the guy started talking to Matthew and Patricia kinda intense, asking questions about any other strangers in town, especially anyone with a little girl, and he mentioned your name."

Mark willed his heart rate to slow and didn't look left or right. He had been a cop once himself and he knew all the tells, but it was agonizing. They could be in somebody's crosshairs right this moment. And where was Sofia?

"Still not tracking you, Sheriff."

"Just wondering how this all connects to you, Lawson," said the sheriff. "You've been associated with just about any bad news in this county over the last couple years, and I'm just playing the odds. You can tell me now, or I'll find out later."

Mark didn't know what to say.

Sheriff Roger Murphy flicked ash on the ground and threw the cigarette into the grass.

"She deserved better from you," said Roger as he opened the driver's door and climbed into the Explorer. The sheriff made a three-point turn back down the gravel driveway and onto the county road.

Mark stared at the house and its empty porch, the half open barn door, and the fields out to the tree line trying to see past hazy ghosts dancing in front of his eyes. He didn't have the heart to be angry at Roger. In fact, Mark agreed with him.

Standing there lost in the past, a wet nose pushed against his hand. Dog pressed against him, and Sofia was holding onto the shepherd's fur. She looked at him with innocent eyes, and he wondered what she was thinking. She held out both arms for him to pick her up, and he held her. She hugged him and put her head on his chest. Dog sat and looked with knowing eyes to the house and back to the two of them and then back to the house.

Maria walked out on the porch again. She glanced at him and glowered off into the distance, her arms rigid across her chest and her chin high. She turned and walked back inside the house, and Mark sank inside. She didn't deserve any of that, but he couldn't explain the situation to the sheriff. He hoped she would understand. They had moved Sofia out of fear for her safety, and now they had confirmation. Someone was looking for them, someone who had handled Robert Bradley with little effort. She would just have to understand or not. He couldn't help it. She didn't have to like him, but she needed to trust his judgement. It was up to him to protect them.

Dog chuffed softly, and Mark understood.

"Okay, Dog, maybe not just up to me," he replied.

Captain Ryan "Kit" Carson danced his EA-18G "Growler" F18 Super Hornet in the night sky around one cloud formation and another, daring the Iranian air defenses to target him. Moonlight reflected off his wings and cast shadows on the terrain below. His rear weapons system officer (WSO), Jack "Joker" Benson, confirmed that all systems appeared functional.

Their mission to constrain and eliminate Iranian coastal air defenses fit perfectly with the capabilities of their fighter aircraft variant designed for electronic warfare. Fire suppression and damage control teams were working on the USS Integrity when their mission launched, but the ship could still fight.

A warbling tone filled their ears.

"Now we're talking," said Jack. "We've got a Bavar-373 fire unit targeting us at 075 degrees. They have a lock. Wait, there's another at 040 degrees."

"Now it's a party," said Ryan, keying his comms button. "Patriot

One has contact at expected coordinates. Dance has started. Invitations are filling. Okay to proceed when the music stops."

The follow on wave of attack aircraft from the USS Integrity trailed behind them, awaiting a path through the air defenses, and it was up to Ryan and Jack to clear this section of the coast of effective ground to air threats. Of course, that was easier said than done.

"Launch, launch. I have two, no make that three missile launches bracketing us," said Jack. "I have targets locked. Magnum one! Magnum two!"

From underwing pylons on either side of the Growler, AGM-88E AARGM "HARM" anti-radiation missiles dropped away. Their smokeless solid stage boosters ignited, and each streaked off toward the targeting radars on the ground at twice the speed of sound. The missiles would continue to guide to the point of electronic emissions, even if the targeting radars switched off.

Ryan keyed a button on his HOTAS control system and jettisoned radar reflecting chaff as he abruptly jinked left and pitched down. Two of the missiles lost lock and continued on to the end of their fuel supply. One of the Bavar-373 targeting sites dropped off the threat radar. Presumably because of a HARM missile strike.

However, one of the Sayyad-4 surface-to-air missiles turned and homed in on them with a purpose. Jack twisted around in his seat, trying to see it.

"There's a missile the size of a telephone pole headed for our rear end," he said.

Ryan dropped more chaff and jinked hard right to move inside the missile's flight envelope. He simultaneously dropped the nose and eased up on the throttle so they wouldn't black out. The g-forces already made it hard to talk.

The long range surface-to-air missile exploded behind them and the large warhead burst shrapnel in all directions seeking a reward for its hard fought climbing attack. Two fragments pierced their F-18 Super Hornet. One hit the right rudder, and Ryan felt the aircraft shudder. The other piece slivered through the gap between the titanium shielding around the cockpit and the canopy. Slowed only marginally, the fragment burrowed into Jack's right upper back and shoulder, clipping the apex of his right lung. The weapons systems officer grunted in pain.

"I'm hit," he said. "But I can still function."

Jack flipped switches activating the multiple jamming pods on the wing supports.

"Jamming enabled," he said.

The advanced counter electronics high, middle, and low band emission pods interfered with known radar detection and guidance systems. In theory, they would provide a gateway through the Iranian air defenses for the attacking fighter bombers behind them for as long as their aircraft stayed on station.

"You're wounded, Jack," said Ryan. "We need to get you back to the ship."

Ryan listened for his WSO to answer.

"Those other pukes need us here, and you know it," said Jack. "Besides, I'm doing fine."

Ryan heard his weapons system officer cough through the intercom. He could only hear Jack and couldn't see how badly he was wounded because his WSO was directly behind him. Ryan tried to call back to the carrier but received a garbled, intermittent response to his communications attempt.

They were supposed to hold station for one hour, time enough for the attacking force to enter under cover of darkness and egress back to the carrier. Guided cruise missiles from the supporting ships in the fleet threaded through the coastal defenses below them on their way to strike specific targets with their one-thousand-pound warheads. To the rear and overhead, an E2C Hawkeye aircraft flew with its early warning radar dome and helped to provide overwatch. The airborne radar aircraft stayed out of range of the larger surface-to-air missiles and would have difficulty seeing through the jamming haze put out by their Growler.

Right on time, the flight of heavily armed fighter bombers roared two thousand feet above them while Tomahawk cruise missiles raced ahead inland. The attack aircraft would target designated airfields and command and control. Fleet had selected one flight to cluster bomb the Iranian admiralty and port facilities at Bandar Abbas. A group of four F-35 stealth fighters raced ahead of the attack squadrons. They had a singular mission target in Tehran.

Ryan continued flying a holding pattern and heard his WSO cough again.

"How you doing, Jack?" he asked.

"I'm right as rain," said his friend. "We'll have a good laugh about"—Jack coughed, and his voice choked up—"this later tonight."

Jack's voice sounded strained over the intercom, and Ryan checked his watch. The attacking force should return in twenty minutes, and they could turn for home. He checked fuel reserves and calculated he had enough to push afterburner to get Jack back on deck sooner.

There they are, he thought. A black shadow grew larger in the night sky below them, and tracers arced in front of their aircraft. A lone Iranian Mirage 2000 fighter jet overshot in front of them. Ryan had not detected the enemy aircraft beyond visual range because of the radar jamming. The enemy fighter pilot banked his aircraft, and Jack grunted in pain again as he called out a warning.

"He's to our left and turning behind us."

Ryan looked around. There was no sign of their attack wing. He would have to deal with this fighter himself, and to do that, he would have to disengage the jamming pods. They had two AIM-120D AMRAAM missiles mounted for defense, but they needed radar guidance to lock on. Their Growler variant sported no guns. The cannon had been removed and the space used for necessary mission specific electronic interfaces. The attacking pilot in the Mirage 2000 fighter jet had twin thirty millimeter cannons and didn't need a radar for dogfighting. His mark one eyeball would do just fine for him.

Ryan flipped off the jamming and pushed the throttles forward to afterburner to gain distance. He pulled up sharply, going vertical to gain some altitude and maneuvering space. Cutting afterburner over the top, he inverted, looking for his enemy as the force of gravity eased. The enemy pilot was below and behind, dumping fuel into his afterburner to get back within gun range. This was going to hurt.

"Hold on, Jack," he said.

Ryan pulled back hard on the stick and half rolled. He armed his

AMRAAM missiles and selected one, noting the target lock icon on his heads up display.

"Fox Three!" he called out and released the weapon.

The twelve-foot-long air-to-air missile bolted off support pylons on the fuselage and streaked hungrily toward the trailing Mirage at just under a mile every second.

Ryan had a bird's-eye view as the radar-guided missile covered the two-mile range to target in less than three seconds. The twenty-two kilogram blast fragmentation warhead shredded the enemy fighter, causing it to break apart in midair.

A warbling sound filled his headphones. A remaining coastal enemy air defense radar actively searched below them.

"Jack, are you still with me?" he asked.

Ryan got no reply from his rear. He centered his aircraft, selected his two remaining HARM missiles and launched them at the radar source. He waited for the flash of impact before he reengaged the jamming pods. There was still no response from Jack.

Out on the horizon, he saw several black dots rapidly grow in size. It was the friendly attacking force returning from inland targets. They exited the coast as a group, and Ryan turned in behind them. Engaging afterburner, he rocketed into a seamless gray and black sky toward the rendezvous point for the carrier and tried getting a response from his WSO again.

"Jack, are you with me?"

He heard a groan from the back seat.

"Ryan, do something for me, okay?"

"Sure thing buddy," said Ryan, checking his dwindling fuel gauges again. "We're headed back to the ship. You hang in there. We're gonna get you home in a couple minutes."

Ryan called in a distress call to let the carrier crew know he had a wounded man. The rudder felt sluggish again. Nothing like a loose rudder to make landing on a pitching steel deck in an ocean of night interesting, he thought.

"Tell Laurie I was thinking of her, will you?"

Jack's voice sounded far away over their mask intercom.

The rest of the flight had given way for him as he hightailed it home, and Ryan spotted the carrier. He would have just enough fuel for one good attempt.

"Sure buddy, but you'll tell her yourself later tonight," said Ryan. "Hang in there just a moment more."

Ryan made the turn to final approach, flaps out, wheels down, and hook down. He ran through his landing checklist from memory. He could see the central amber "meatball" centered between the green datum lights so he knew his glide path was okay. The landing signal officer waved him on. Steady. Steady. He felt the nose try to drift right. He over-corrected and thought he would lose it at the last moment, and then he was on the deck. His wheels touched down hard, and he jerked against his harness as his tail hook snagged the third wire. The thirty-thousand-pound fighter jet thundered to a stop in less than three hundred feet.

Ryan shut down the engines and opened the cockpit canopy as the ground crew approached. The engines spooled down as he pulled off his face mask and helmet, and the familiar smell of jet fuel underscored a tang of copper and iron. Unstrapping, he stood up and turned to see Jack slumped in his rear seat, covered in blood. His friend looked very pale, and Ryan couldn't tell if he was breathing.

"Let us get him, sir," said one of the crew chiefs.

Hands reached in on either side of the cockpit to unstrap Jack and lift him clear. The flight deck crew placed him on a stretcher and sprinted to the carrier island superstructure and disappeared from view.

Ryan's legs trembled as adrenaline bled away, but he managed to slide down the crew ladder without falling. Stumbling across the flight deck to the intake hatch, he turned to see the deck crew secure his aircraft off to the side and out of the way of the returning fighter wing. Ryan saw a basketball-sized hole in the right rudder, which explained the sluggish control. He was still not sure how he landed.

He looked to his right at the damage from the anti-ship missile which struck ahead of the island. Twisted and charred steel edges sharply merged into the night air and then slipped below the star line as the ship plowed through the sea. The bloody image of his weapons system officer sucked the air out of his lungs, and he shook away the urge to vomit. He didn't even know if his friend was still alive. What would he tell Jack's wife?

Ryan wasn't married, but there was a girl he had talked with on his last liberty. He could see her smiling face and dancing eyes, and he had her number in his gear. Suddenly, it felt very important to talk with her again. First, he had to debrief and check on Jack, and then, maybe a shower and a phone call.

CHAPTER FIFTEEN

Tomás watched as the sheriff's SUV pulled away from the farm. Lawson and the woman were definitely there, but the girl was the priority target. He had hoped for a visual confirmation before he committed, but Sofia had to be there. Whatever he did, it must be soon. Donovan Giulanti had been clear about that. He would return and enter the home with the advantage of darkness to find and retrieve the little girl.

Meanwhile, he should find a place to rest. He crept back to his vehicle and drove about a mile away from the farm looking for a likely spot. He slowed at an overgrown turnoff at a right angle to the road and found a way through the underbrush dragging at the windows. The turnoff opened up into a space by an old bridge which he deemed unsafe to cross in the vehicle, but it was off the road, and fortunately, he had overnight gear in the truck. He would go back later tonight and succeed in his mission.

He had been pushing hard for thirty-six hours, and he eased his fatigue-induced nausea by drinking water and eating some crackers and an energy bar. He turned on the small radio in his kit and scanned for information. There was little to pick up out here, but he did find an

AM news radio station on atmospheric bounce and heard a broadcast about the incident at the church. It was already fading from public consciousness with the confrontation in the Middle East and the attack from Iran and counterattack by the United States. So Israel had finally used a nuke, eh? Well, that was interesting but meant little in his world. He had his work, and that was enough for him.

Now, assuming the girl, Sofia, was there, he would pull her out early in the morning while they were still asleep. He would dispatch Lawson at the same time. Tomás resented the idea of kidnapping a child. However, Donovan Giulanti had assured him that he intended no harm to her. He had explained that his son was ill with leukemia and needed a bone marrow transplant, and the little girl could help. Tomás had heard about such a thing and knew that, while painful, the procedure shouldn't cause the girl any lasting harm, and it could save another child's life. On the whole, that equation balanced enough for him to proceed with his mission.

He discarded any hesitation. The plans his patron had for the girl were not his concern as long as she suffered no lasting harm. He would keep her safe while in his care and deliver her as promised. That left little time for rest, but he could still get a nap, and satisfied he was hidden from sight, he drifted off to sleep.

Terrence Bradley sat in a tree stand fifteen feet above the ground looking over his property fence with a view through the trees to the Evans place. He couldn't believe his terrible luck. Finally, he had found a way to get out of the hole he was in, and this happened. Lawson had stayed away for nearly a year, but now he had suddenly appeared at the worst possible moment.

A week ago, his neighbor's barn had seemed the perfect hiding place, but delivery was set for tomorrow, and Terrence was out of time.

Hopefully, that schemer next door hadn't discovered the shipment because the hard men who were his current venture partners had to get the product ready to move, and if that meant Lawson got hurt, they wouldn't hesitate. Well, better him than me, he thought.

Terrence heard his brother approach along the trail from their place. He had told him to stay back, but Robert never listened, even when they were little.

"They still there?" asked his little brother.

Robert wasn't fooling him. His younger brother just wanted his share of the money. He had had no interest in anything that didn't benefit him directly.

"Quiet," whispered Terrence. "I'm coming down."

He took his time getting down from the tree stand. He was a big man, and climbing a tree had long ago ceased to be one of his favorite activities.

"The sheriff came by and talked with Lawson," he said.

Robert said, "Do they know about the stuff?"

"No, I don't think so," said Terrence. "I didn't see them go into the barn. The sheriff left a while ago, so I think we have a chance if we don't blow it like picking fights with strangers in public."

Robert scowled and rubbed his wrist and winced.

"Yeah, well, I'd like another chance at that gent," he said. "He just surprised me is all."

"Speaking of surprise, I think we'll need to get the stuff tonight," said Terrence.

He spoke in a calm and steady cadence. He had learned long ago that even tones worked best with his younger brother.

"What about Lawson?" asked Robert. "Won't he see us?"

"He might," said Terrence. "We'll just have to make sure he doesn't want to talk about it."

Terrence waited patiently. Although his brother's impulsiveness aggravated him, he was still his brother. Robert's eyes widened some, but he nodded his understanding.

Terrence said, "C'mon. We need a few things for tonight."

He gestured at Robert, who slowly grinned, and they started back toward their house. Terrence had wanted Maddie long before he wanted her farm, and the man responsible for her death stood in his way now.

Once that troublemaker was out of the picture, there was no one else. Terrence could purchase the farm from the estate sale at auction, and no one would question why he wanted productive land next to his ranch. He would end up debt free with more land and water sources, and that sounded like a recipe for success to him.

❖

Mark walked up the steps to the front porch and sat in a rocking chair. Sofia clung to him with her arms around his neck and refused to let go; Dog followed and settled down beside them. There was an ominous quiet from inside the house, and Mark could only imagine what Maria must think of him.

Sofia lay against his chest and looked up and shook her head. What was she trying to say? She laid her head back down and hugged him fiercely, and his plan to get the tractor running and cultivate the garden seemed like a story in a book on a shelf too high to reach.

Holding Sofia brought memories stacked like wet clay tiles, one after the other, so heavy he almost couldn't breathe. He tried to clear his throat, but his nose kept closing off as tears trickled down his face. Oh God in Heaven, he missed his wife and daughter. What had ever possessed him to think he could protect anyone else?

Dog got up and laid his head on Mark's knee when he stopped rocking, and the shepherd's snout rested against Sofia and Mark at the same time. Mark reached down and rubbed the animal's head between his ears.

"It will be all right."

Mark heard his dripping words, and strangely, he didn't feel embarrassed at the tears. Both Sofia and Dog seemed to accept him, wet or dry.

"Mr. Lawson?"

Mark looked over to see Maria halfway through the open front door, and he wiped his face with the back of his hand. She walked over and sat in the other chair, and Dog shifted around and placed his head on her knee and gazed up at her. She rubbed his ears, and the shepherd licked her hand. Satisfied, Dog laid down between them and looked out to the yard.

"Miss Perez, I'm sorry about that," he said. "It had nothing to do with you. The sheriff and I have never gotten along."

Maria said nothing for a few moments and rocked on the porch, more or less keeping time with Mark. Sofia seemed to be asleep. He could feel her slow heartbeat against his chest.

"I couldn't explain about you or Sofia," he said. "The sheriff would most likely have had the federal authorities here inside of an hour."

Mark searched the trees lining the county road. The gravel driveway stretched out in a gentle curve until it disappeared in the tree line and met the cattle guard gate, which was most likely open. He would need to close that again. Might need to think about getting a lock, he thought.

Maria continued rocking.

"I know that," she said. "What did he mean about your wife?"

Mark hadn't expected her to sound so calm. He didn't want to tell her, but she had a right to know.

"The sheriff grew up with Maddie," he said. "They had some history, but she chose me. He thinks I'm responsible for her death, and he may be right."

There. He said it out loud.

Maria stopped rocking and stretched out her hand to him. Mark stilled his chair while holding Sofia. Slowly, he reached across the distance between them and tentatively held her fingers.

She said, "Tell me."

She would not let him off easy and had turned his apology into some sort of truth serum. Maddie used to do that with him. How did women learn how to do this?

He sighed.

"We were driving back after spending a wonderful day playing at the lake. We stayed longer than planned, but we were having fun."

His voice faltered. He'd agonized over this thousands of times in two years, and he still couldn't say it straight out.

"Faith was buckled in the back seat," he said. "She fell asleep right away, of course. Maddie told me she would stay up to keep me awake, but she dozed off too. We were all tired."

Mark tried gently to disengage from Maria, but she gripped his hand and willed him to go on. He practically spat out the last like poison from a snakebite.

"I must have fallen asleep," he said. "We went off the road and wrapped around a tree, and I hardly remember the accident. I woke up looking for them in the hospital."

Mark felt the tears running again. Poor Sofia's hair was going to be soaked.

Maria gripped his hand.

After a minute, she said, "It was an accident. You loved them."

Mark didn't trust himself to speak and fought to slow his breathing.

"It was my job to protect them," he said. "I ran around trying to solve everyone's problems, and I couldn't even protect my own family."

Maria didn't let go of his hand, and he felt her fingers across his palm. He tried not to move, and in the quiet, he heard a cardinal call from the trees.

"So why did Father Romero ask me to watch over her?" he asked and nodded down at Sofia.

Maria regarded him. She was the opposite of Madelyn. Petite, slender, dark-skinned, dark hair, but her eyes, the way she looked at him at that moment, made him think of Maddie.

"He said he knew you," she said. "He said you were a good man."

Maria studied him in all his imperfections, and Mark remembered she was practically a nun. She released his hand and leaned forward in the rocking chair until she stood and reached for Sofia.

She paused while holding her charge and said, "You were right to be careful in what you said. We have to protect Sofia most of all. She is special and under God's own protection, but we both need you." Maria started to head inside, but paused and turned enough to face him. "Please don't let anyone talk about us like that again."

The door closed behind her as she carried Sofia inside to finish her nap.

Dog had his head up. The shepherd had listened closely to everything Maria said and followed her every move. He regarded him now with surprisingly blue canine eyes, and Mark figured Dog was amazed that Maria let him live.

Dog chuffed at him once in agreement.

CHAPTER SIXTEEN

"Madam President, it is definitive," said Professor Barry Michaels. "We are still having difficulty radar ranging the rogue planet, but visual observation and infrared imaging provide enough data to conclude it's heading for us with tremendous velocity."

The president's science advisor sat four chairs to her right in the situation room below the White House.

President Maureen Thomlinson considered for a moment.

"What are our options?" she asked. "Can we stop it?"

She had slept little over the last three days. Each day, the earthquake disaster on the West Coast drained more and more resources and threatened to bankrupt the country. At her orders, the administration had suppressed any news of the rogue planet, but as it edged more and more in front of the Sun, there would be little chance of hiding what was coming.

A select group of government scientists with the national space agency had brainstormed day and night but offered no hope if the orbital path resulted in collision. Too bad they hadn't established a colony on Mars, she thought, at least someone would have survived.

Barry's voice held little inflection as he responded without hesitation.

"We will stop it when it cracks our planet into pieces. We have nothing to alter that process now."

He sounded tired.

"Oh, come on. There must be something we can do," said Bryce. "What about Ararat?"

Bryce Thornton referred to the classified underground shelter being hastily prepped in the Appalachian Mountains of West Virginia. The mountain substrates there were older and more stable. The hope was to shelter a portion of the population to ensure survival of the species, and Maureen thought it telling that Barry had declined to take part in the effort. Still, she needed to provide reassurance.

"Of course, we will move ahead with our plans for Ararat and for other shelters such as Mount Weather," she said. "Our military recall is proceeding, Admiral?"

Admiral Boatwright seemed ready for that question.

"Madam President, there have been minor hiccups, which are expected with such a rapid withdrawal. However, we are on schedule," he said. "The USS John F. Kennedy has reinforced the USS Integrity and we have the USS Carl Vinson in the Mediterranean. They stand ready if needed further in the Middle East."

The admiral didn't have to add that they expected no additional threat from Iran. Multiple strikes from the USS Integrity and additional forces had seen to that.

President Thomlinson nodded. She'd expected no less. However, the admiral had more to say.

"Madam President, our forces are still at DEFCON ONE. It is difficult to maintain our edge at such high readiness for an extended period. The use of a nuclear weapon and the expanding conflict in the Middle East threatens to draw us in. I do not believe Israel will withhold a further nuclear strike if attacked again, and if that happens, we will have to respond. You have seen our current assessment of the actions of those hostile to us and our goals. A firm response from us now might deter that outcome."

"You are suggesting a first strike from us?"

Maureen knew there were some in the executive ring of the Pentagon who felt similarly.

"Madam President, I suggest that you communicate clearly about the threat to our world. We may not be able to stop this rogue planet from doing what it will, but perhaps we can use the disclosure to change the mindset of our enemies. What's the point of wiping each other out if there can be no survivors?"

Boatwright and the Joint Chiefs had been apprised earlier in the day by Professor Barry Michaels and the Secretary of Defense.

Maureen considered his words, and what he advocated made sense. It might be the last chance to prevent their own self-destruction. Barry had explained to her that the shock to the planet would scour the surface to varying depths and the orbital path of Earth would likely change, maybe even spiral into the Sun. But, if there was a one-in-a-million chance for some humans to survive, shouldn't they take it?

"Our forces will have to stay on alert, Admiral," she said. "At least another three days from what Professor Michaels has told us, but your words are swaying."

President Thomlinson knew she needed to address the nation and had already scheduled the airtime tonight, but she would need to be decisive, and her speech would need updating. Better to make the announcement at midday tomorrow.

"You realize, Admiral, when I set a redline for non-aggression against Israel, we will have to be ready to respond if they try our hand."

"We are ready, Madam President."

Admiral Boatwright seemed sure of himself. Maureen liked that in a man but distrusted too much self-assurance, which tended to arrogance in many.

"Madam President, we expect some of our soldiers will leave to be with their families in this crisis."

"Yes, I understand, Admiral," she said. "That is why we will not say it will hit us, but that our best scientific calculations call for a close pass. If we tell the public that the world is ending in three days, there will be complete anarchy within three hours. Correct?"

Heads nodded in agreement with her around the table, except for Barry. He instantly understood and anticipated what she would ask him to do. One thing she had grown to love in the quiet professor was his honesty. He seemed incapable of telling anything but the truth as he knew it. That alone in Washington was beyond rare.

"Professor Michaels, how sure are you that this planetoid is going to strike us? Could it make a close pass instead?" asked the president.

"It is conceivable," he said. "My calculations are based on our observational data, and that has been difficult. For some reason, the rogue planet seems to absorb electromagnetic energy. We are seeing it weakly in infrared during its near pass around our Sun, and poorly in the visual spectrum. Still, my best estimate is that it will hit us."

"But I am asking if it is plausible that it will miss us?" she asked.

"Yes, it is possible," replied Barry. "But a close pass will still be catastrophic. There will be tectonic plate movement all over the planet."

"Then that's what we focus on," she said. "A near miss, which will probably cause earthquakes, volcanic eruptions, and tsunamis severe enough to require an all-out survival effort, but not hopeless, and if we are lucky, we suppress the fighting in the Middle East. Are we all agreed?"

Heads nodded around the table, and Maureen looked at Barry again. He was leaning forward with his hands pressed against the conference table. He looked so cute when he felt conflicted. She hadn't ever felt this way about a man. What was wrong with her? Maybe she was finally growing up. It only took the end of the world for it to happen.

❖

The quiet continued into the evening. Mark offered to set out some food, but Maria seemed to need to stay busy and had taken over dinner preparations. A very nice smell came from the kitchen. He managed a bag of kibble into the house for Dog, who studied it with his head canted to one side.

"You'll like it," said Mark. "It's good for you."

Dog laid down with his head on his paws and followed Mark with a disdainful look that implied he should eat it if it was so good.

Mark walked back out to the barn to organize their purchased supplies, and Sofia followed and tried to help. He was getting used to looking for her and listening for her footsteps. She seemed to understand everything he said but hadn't spoken a word. Maria had told him that Sofia's hearing might have improved since the event at the church. He wondered if that meant she would eventually be able to talk and thought about the miracle surrounding her. He didn't see it happen, but he knew whatever occurred had convinced Maria.

He regarded the shelved sacks of seed and fertilizer. He would get the ground for the garden worked over tomorrow if the weather cooperated. Mark turned again to the tarpaulin covered mound in the back of the barn. He would need to clear that out, whatever it was. They would need the room for storage. He pulled back the covering and found a pile of crates. Mark had no idea what they were and felt certain they didn't belong to him. Walter had said he hadn't been here in a month, but footprints in the dust suggested that the crates had been placed recently.

Dog and Sofia watched closely as Mark pulled out one crate. He found a pry bar on the wall behind the workbench to one side of the barn, and working in the fading light, he leveraged the lid off the crate. There was a layer of sawdust over several thick plastic bags filled with white powder.

He cringed inside, realizing that the pile probably consisted of drugs, likely heroin or cocaine. It represented a substantial fortune and somebody's investment. Whoever put this here would want it back and would not want anyone else knowing. Maria had told him about Terrence; did he have something to do with this?

Crap. They were all in danger.

Mark replaced the crate carefully and covered the pile. He would need to get the sheriff involved sooner rather than later. He looked over at Sofia, and she smiled at him. He didn't want to get the law back out with Maria and Sofia here, but whoever hid this would be back for it.

He could ask Walter if the girls could stay with him. That would decrease their risk, but he doubted Maria would go for it. Still, it seemed the best answer, and he thought on it as he walked out of the barn and back to the house for supper. Sofia followed with Dog as their outrider, and Mark found himself comforted that the big shepherd would let him know if anyone came around the farm.

He carried fresh wood into the house for the furnace and fireplace. The evening had turned cool, and the warmth would feel good. Dog paused at the door and stared at the trees, then padded inside after them.

Maria came to the kitchen doorway, telling both of them to wash up for supper without making eye contact with him. Mark followed Sofia, who skipped down the hall. If the little girl sensed any tension, it didn't seem to worry her as she washed her hands at the bathroom sink with him. How was he going to tell Maria about the find in the barn? Maybe he shouldn't. Did she really have to know? Wouldn't that put her more at risk? If he could get her out of here and she didn't know, then hopefully she wouldn't be in any danger from the people that stashed those drugs. Suddenly, that was very important to him.

Dinner was a pleasant surprise. Maria had fresh tortillas, seasoned chicken, and black beans and corn ready, delicious after an exhausting day. He waited while she said grace before digging in, and despite his worries, he found himself famished. Sofia ate with both hands and a big smile. Maria put a cup of kibble in Dog's bowl, but she topped it with some chicken and got a furry kiss.

Mark tried to look at Maria without being obvious, and he caught her glancing at him once or twice. He didn't see any knives in her hands, so he might be okay for the moment. Well, here goes, he thought.

"I have an idea for tomorrow. I have some chores to do around here, but I was wondering if you and Sofia might help Walter. I thought we would walk over to visit in the morning after breakfast. Would that be okay?"

Maria hesitated and looked at Sofia.

"Perhaps it might be better for us to remain here and help with your chores," she said.

Sofia grinned at both of them, and not for the first time, Mark wondered what her thoughts were? He suspected Sofia to be more intelligent than anyone realized, and Dog snorted while stretched out against the kitchen wall.

"I plan to be sitting on the tractor for hours tomorrow working the fields," he said. "I don't think there's a lot for you to do to help me with that."

It was the truth, just not quite all of it, and he felt uneasy. There was something about Maria that made him want to be completely honest, and he cringed inside. If she truly knew him, she would run away carrying Sofia over her shoulder.

Maria scrutinized him and seemed to consider his words.

"What do you think, Sofia?" she asked. "Should we spend some time with Walter tomorrow?"

Sofia reached down to pet Dog, who had moved closer, and she nodded. Maria placed both hands on the table and peered at Mark. He could tell she was suspicious. Darn women's intuition, he thought. He could never get anything over on Maddie either.

"Very well," said Maria. "If Walter doesn't mind us underfoot, we will try to help him tomorrow."

Mark tried not to look relieved. He was already calculating how to reach the sheriff. Wireless phone coverage remained poor here at the farm, and he wanted to keep his cell phone turned off as a precaution against being found.

He walked over to the door to let Dog out, and the shepherd ran out to do his business. Afterwards, the canine stopped with upright ears and surveyed the mix of hardwood and evergreen trees bordering the road for several moments. Finally, Dog turned and padded into the house. The shepherd paused inside the door and looked up. Mark couldn't read the animal's mind, but he felt their protector was trying to tell him something.

So was Sofia. She walked over to him and took him by the hand to the living room chair, and he knew what she wanted. He sat down and pulled an illustrated book about pirates and buried treasure from the bookcase. She had surprised him with her choice, but she seemed to love it. He opened it to where they last left off. The company had discovered an island and were preparing to investigate. She sat on his lap, snuggled in, and traced the words with her hand as he read, like she was memorizing them. His mind spun for a moment, and he was sitting with Faith, reading the same story. She looked up at him and smiled, and he asked her the same question every night.

"What would you do if you found treasure?"

He kissed her on the forehead.

"I would dance," she had said.

She always jumped up and twirled about the room, and he would catch her up and hold her as they swayed. She looked up at him with love in her eyes, but when he blinked, he realized it was Sofia looking at him. Suddenly, it was all too much, and he brought his hand up to his eyes and paused his reading. Sofia's smile faded, and she looked down.

Maria seemed to understand Sofia better than herself, and she walked over with her palms upturned. The little girl reached out for her, and Maria carried her to bed without a backward glance. They left Mark sitting alone except for Dog, who looked at him with a "well dude, you really blew that" look.

Mark agreed and felt on edge more and more with each moment. Anxious, he looked about, and the walls of the old farmhouse didn't seem as strong to him as a few minutes ago. His instincts had kept him alive in the past, and he had learned not to ignore them.

He got up quietly, thought over the situation, and decided he needed to be a little more prepared. He quietly found the door to the basement and the bookshelf to the concealed pantry and the door to the gun safe. He retrieved a pump shotgun and a box of buckshot. He would load and keep the shotgun in his room up on the shelf overnight. Mark had a revolver by his bedside in a quick action safe, the same one he had carried on the way out of town. He felt better with that preparation and stretched out on his bed but tossed and turned before drifting off to sleep.

CHAPTER SEVENTEEN

Donovan Giulanti stood at his son's bedside. Lorenzo needed round-the-clock nursing care and attendants to bathe and assist him. With Donovan's resources, they kept his son at home and maintained hydration through a central venous port catheter. He was fed intravenously through the surgical port for comfort. Resting his gut left more energy for breathing.

Donovan tried to visit with his son daily, but most of the time Lorenzo only gasped a few words before he paused to breathe deeply from his supplemental oxygen.

His son's physicians had suggested that Donovan should prepare himself for the worst, although the staff hoped that a suitable donor would be found in the time Lorenzo had left. Even after a generous contribution to the hospital, the donor lists were long. Donovan had considered having someone donate involuntarily, but there was the problem of tissue matching the donor. He couldn't have his people accomplish that on the street.

He had always been a man to make things happen, and he had contacts in other countries where the lines between what was right and what was legal blurred enough that a clandestine search had produced a match. A young and severely disabled girl lived in an orphanage in Venezuela. Enough money produced a man and woman willing to pose as a couple to adopt her and secure her transfer to America, and papers were forged documenting her trip for medical treatment. It all went smoothly until the woman posing as her newly adoptive mother grew a conscience and hid the girl. She claimed in her note that an angel told her to surrender the child. What a ridiculous excuse, but Donovan had not expected her to take her own life.

He had done his best to keep the true nature of his plans for the girl a compartmentalized secret, but he didn't know how much longer that would work with Tomás. The principled mercenary was insightful, just as his quiet nature suggested, but nothing could interfere with the plan. Lorenzo couldn't last much longer.

Donovan looked at his son lying in bed, and his boy's pallid complexion washed away any doubt. They must have that girl. Vivian sat across from him on the other side of the bed, and he had promised her that he would find a solution. She was smart and had probably guessed much of the plan, but Donovan was concerned about how she would take this latest delay.

Vivian stood and approached from their son's bedside and whispered to him.

"Save him," she said. "Whatever it takes."

And she walked past him out into the hall.

"Father?" asked his boy.

Lorenzo was awake.

"Yes, I'm here," said Donovan, moving to sit by his son's bed.

"It's hot."

The room was already cold. Donovan had extra air-conditioning brought in just for this reason, and the stand-alone unit plus the central air conditioning had the room chilled to a teeth-chattering temperature, but Lorenzo still complained of being hot. His physician had explained how the extra work his boy did just to breathe was driving his body temperature up.

Donovan moved the covers off Lorenzo. In a few minutes his son would ask for them again, but that was all right. Let it be, he thought. Tomás had called with a status report and had a lead on the little girl, and of all the incredible coincidences, that nuisance ex-detective

Lawson was involved. This time Donovan would not allow that snoop to cause any more trouble for his family.

"Dad?" asked his son.

Donovan startled. Lorenzo hadn't called him that in several years.

"Is Heaven real?"

Donovan tried never to lie to his family. There had been innumerable omissions regarding his work, but somehow he didn't feel right taking hope away from his son. Lorenzo had attended a private catholic school before he became ill and had gone through the Sacrament of Confirmation. Donovan had let his son soak up the education and figured the religious stuff couldn't hurt.

Donovan had grown up in the Church, but he had his own doubts about the afterlife. He was a practical man, and he believed in what he could see and what he could touch. Cause and effect were his mantra, and his creed mirrored something from a movie he had seen. Something about a man being bound by what he was capable of and what he wasn't. That is how he had made a life for himself and his family

"I don't know if I know for sure, Son," said Donovan. "What do you think?"

"I'm afraid."

Lorenzo's words wheezed out in a squeak like a defective toy.

Donovan reached across the bed to cover his son gently with his bulk and felt his own eyes wet with tears. He never cried. Could not remember the last time he had cried. Now, twice in three days.

"I'm here, Son."

He made sure not to press on Lorenzo's chest. It was already hard enough for his boy to talk. He wanted to say something else, something reassuring, but his son closed his eyes and drifted off to sleep.

Donovan adjusted the oxygen nasal cannula. It had a habit of shrinking against Lorenzo's face as he moved his head. The oxygen from the large wheeled tank coursed through the saline reservoir, and the bubbles in the clear saline rose and popped to nothing against the top of the reservoir. Just like his prayers, rising up to some unseen and unknowable God who never answered as far as he could tell. No, thank you.

He had taken matters in his own hands, and Tomás would find the girl alive, crippled or not. He would bring her to him, and his private medical team would do what was necessary.

Through her, his son would live, whatever it took.

❖

Mark felt a nose wedge into his side. Was it morning already? He felt like he'd just laid down. Still half-asleep, he felt Dog grind his teeth against his side and whine. That was new. He rolled over, and Dog grabbed the corner of the comforter in his mouth and dragged it off the bed. The house had cooled as the fire ebbed in the furnace. What in the world, he thought.

Wait, what was that? He thought he heard whispering outside his window. It was dark outside, and he couldn't see anyone. Dog looked at the window and bared his teeth with a nearly silent growl. Okay, that was good enough for Mark.

Easing out of bed, he pulled on his pants and slipped into his boots. Should he wake the girls? He tucked the revolver onto his belt in its holster. He reached for the shotgun, checked the loading gate, and quietly chambered a round. Finger off the trigger, he double checked the safety and tiptoed into the hallway with Dog ghosting ahead of him.

He gently opened the door to the girls' bedroom, and Sofia was already shaking Maria awake. He kept watch down the hall while Maria came to her senses. She didn't understand at first when she saw him in the doorway of their bedroom. Her look of confusion changed to alarm as she realized he was armed, and she sat up in bed, holding the comforter about her.

Mark held a finger to his lips and pointed to his eyes and made a walking gesture with his fingers to show that he was going to look around. He hesitated a moment, then pulled out his revolver and offered it to Maria.

"I wouldn't know what to do with that," she whispered.

She looked at Sofia again and back at him. Maria sighed and held out her hand.

"What do I do?" she asked.

Mark showed her how to hold the revolver. Then, he leaned down and whispered into her ear.

"Finger off the trigger unless you plan to shoot," he said. "Please be sure it's not me."

Maria held the revolver as if it was going to bite her and nodded grimly.

"Please don't go out there by yourself," she said.

Sofia had her hand on Maria's shoulder, her eyes bounding between them with each whispered instruction.

"I want both of you to hide," he said. "Stay quiet, and don't come out no matter what you hear. Understand?"

Maria looked like she wanted to say something else, but she glanced at Sofia and nodded and reached out her hand to him as he started to move toward the door.

"Please be careful," she said.

He looked at her face. He wanted to say something meaningful and hug both of them, but the moment passed, and he nodded and turned to his task.

Dog had been watching from just beyond the door and padded off ahead of Mark down the hallway through the living room and into the kitchen. There was no sign of an intruder. He checked, and whatever waited outside had not breached the doors to the house. He listened carefully, and it was quiet except for . . . there it was again. A clank of metal on metal echoed beyond the back of the house, and then he understood.

He had placed a chain and lock on the barn door. Somehow that seemed a good idea earlier in the evening, but right now, far less so. Really, what did he care if they recovered their product? It upset him that someone was using the farm for an illegal purpose, but better to let them get away quietly. Now it was likely that the trespassers outside were aware that he knew. What would that mean? He only wanted to keep Maria and Sofia safe.

Dog remained nearly motionless, standing in the dark kitchen looking from the door to Mark and back to the door.

Mark understood that the decision was his. If he remained quiet in the house, would whoever it was simply leave once they had their goods? He couldn't know and couldn't wait here hoping they would leave them alone. He readied the shotgun and silently opened the door.

Dog dashed through the doorway in an instant. No growl, no bark, just a swift white spirit darting across the yard and launching at a man shape beside a flatbed truck parked near the barn. Dog dragged the man who was grunting and cursing to the ground, and Mark followed down the back steps into the yard.

The shotgun had an integrated tactical flashlight, and he illuminated the scene. The shepherd remained clamped to the left forearm of the struggling intruder. Searching with the light, Mark glimpsed another man running from the barn and around the truck. Flicking off the shotgun's safety, he aimed the weapon.

"Hold it right there," he said. "I will shoot if you don't drop to the ground this instant."

The figure coming around the truck hesitated, then knelt slowly to the ground.

"Who are you?" he asked. "Why are you out here in the middle of the night?"

Neither of the trespassers responded, and Dog still held to the arm of one.

"I'll let you do your talking to the sheriff," said Mark.

He needed a way to restrain these two until he could find a way to contact Roger. Mark stepped forward but tensed as he heard a boot scrape behind him. Something slammed against his head, and he went down. He heard a distant gunshot, a grunt of surprise, and a woman's scream before everything faded to nothing.

CHAPTER EIGHTEEN

Maria huddled with Sofia. They had been bound wrist and ankle in the same dark room for several hours since the men in the backyard took them. She kept seeing Mark on the ground after she heard the first gunshot like a waking nightmare, and he didn't move, even after she screamed his name. Another muffled gunshot had seen a man in the yard stumble backwards, crumple to the ground, and crawl toward the barn. The echo of a second shot hadn't faded before the other two men sprinted up to the porch and pointed guns at her.

She had considered using the revolver, but something inside stayed her hand, and they took the gun from her while Sofia hid behind her with wide eyes. One of the intruders gazed on Sofia and spoke rapidly in Spanish. Maria understood him say they could sell the little girl for more than the usual amount. The other one said something about the boss not caring anymore, and neither of them seemed to want to move from the shelter of the house. They had loaded the bed of the truck with packing crates, and she saw another crate on the ground in front of the open barn door. One of them was named, Manuel, and the other, César.

"El jefe dijo que no debe haber testigos," said César.

The one called Manuel said, "I know, but we need them."

He pointed back to the truck and added.

"Los usamos para llegar al camion."

César shoved Mark's revolver under his belt, and he reached out and pulled Maria to stand in front of him. Manuel did the same with Sofia, and each hid behind the girls while they edged back to the truck. They crowded into the cab while staying below the dash, and no further gunfire came their way. Manuel started the truck and inched down the driveway, eyes at the level of the dashboard.

The county road curved in front of the truck's headlights again and again for what felt like an eternity before Manuel turned up a driveway. Maria knew only that she and Sofia were being taken to some other location and their fate remained in question from the conversation between their abductors. César was clearly in favor of eliminating all witnesses and wanted to go back and put a bullet or two in Mark just to be sure. Maria had seen Mark go down and knew he was past caring.

Manuel said, "Dejamos el jefe decida."

The one called César didn't look happy, but he went along, and that's how Maria and Sofia came to be tied up on a dirt-strewn concrete floor, waiting for an unknown boss.

Maria suppressed a sob. Over and over, she saw Mark crumple to the ground, and she exhaled slowly in the quiet darkness with Sofia pressed against her side. She was in over her head, and her thoughts raced with her beating heart. Did this all happen for naught? She accepted that she would die, but why save Sofia just to have her come to this end?

Maria sensed something else wrapped in layers of sorrow, hidden from her knowing and struggling to emerge. She couldn't discern the truth of it in her need to keep Sofia safe, and she prayed for wisdom and insight while keeping her ears trained for any footsteps that might portend their last moments.

Maria thought of Mark again and the way he smiled. She had seen him glance at her more than once when he thought she wasn't looking. Men paid no attention to her, and she had grown comfortable with that, but now she found herself missing his glances fiercely.

Oh God, do not despise me. I want to find favor in your eyes, but I miss finding favor in his.

As soon as she thought it, she realized it was true. She had only known the man for a few days, and now he was dead. What a fool she was. Mother Mary Margaret had known her better than herself.

Maria felt a young hand reach up and touch her face. Pale morning light had crept to the upper room walls, and Sofia's wistful eyes shimmered as she hummed a small tune which Maria recognized as a familiar hymn. This was new, and she held Sofia and hummed along.

"You can hear?" whispered Maria.

Sofia nodded with tears in her eyes.

The door to their little room opened. It was César, the one who felt they should disappear. He pulled out a knife and advanced as they shrank back against the baseboard. He crouched down and grinned around uneven brown-stained teeth before cutting the zip ties binding their ankles. He motioned for them to get up, grumbling at their hesitation, and led them out of the room. Maria's feet burned as her circulation returned, and she stumbled. César pushed her to hurry them along.

Could this be how it ended? She would shield her charge as best she could and prayed for the courage to seize any opportunity. Sofia held her arm and whimpered, and Maria tried to console her precious pequeña while wishing she could hear Mark's voice again, but that wouldn't happen in this lifetime. They wound down more than one hallway in the large outbuilding and emerged into a main room with an oversized garage door, which was open. Maria shivered in the cool air.

Over to the side, several men tossed open crates from the back of a truck into a pile. It was the same truck from earlier in Mark's backyard. Other men were packing plastic bags of something into three large suitcases.

Oh God! I left him when he needed me, but I can't think about that. I have to be strong for Sofia.

Beyond the mound of discarded crates stood a tall, stocky man and another younger man. They looked enough alike to be brothers, and she guessed the bigger man to be ten years older.

In the early morning light, she recognized the larger man as the one who had barged into the yard and wanted to get into the barn. He had said his name was Bradley, and Mark had said that Terrence

Bradley and his brother, Robert, owned the adjacent farm on the other side of his property. They couldn't be more than a couple of miles from home, and Maria stifled a sob, thinking again of Mark on the cold ground. She hadn't checked him in their captive exit, but she had seen the blood.

The younger man made a crude remark.

"Look at what we have here."

"That's enough of that, Robert," said Terrence Bradley.

A brawny man with a shaved head and tattoos on his forearms turned from surveying the pile of empty crates and faced both of them. He looked like a man who could stand all day in the glare of the Sun and never burn, and she overheard part of their conversation.

"You insisted on sending your men, and they brought those girls back to my farm," said Terrence Bradley. "That was never part of our deal."

"And I lost a man and half the shipment," said the tattooed man. "There is no more deal. We are leaving you to clean up the mess you made, and we will take the woman and the child. Their price might help compensate our loss."

The bald man looked over at the two of them briefly, and Maria shuddered. She would rather be dead.

"What if you could get the rest of your shipment?" asked Robert Bradley.

When the tattooed man said nothing, he continued.

"You could trade the women for your product," said Robert. "I know the sheriff in this county. He won't turn down a chance to save them."

The bald man with the tattoos turned and beckoned to César, who grasped both Maria and Sofia and pushed them forward.

"Si, Deylin," said César.

He manhandled Maria until she was directly in front of the powerfully built gang leader.

"You think you can convince the man at the farm to trade our merchandise for you?" asked the bald one named Deylin.

Maria suspected these men would kill all who might have seen them as soon as they had what they wanted, and she almost said no, but the two of them faced an alternative worse than death.

"Yes," she said, surprised at her steady voice. "I think he will gladly trade to get us back."

Her heart battered like a wind chime against the side of a house. Just a little more pressure and she might fall to the ground, except she couldn't because of Sofia. What man were they talking about? Everyone at the farm was dead when they left. Did this man believe she knew who shot his henchman? Maria had no idea and said nothing.

The man named Deylin spat on the gravel outside.

"All right," he said. "We try a trade, but on our terms. The sniper has to be there in front of us, and we name the time. No policia."

He turned to the Bradley brothers.

"You two will come with us," he said. "We are all in this now. Juntos atados."

❖

Tomás watched over the outbuilding at the Bradley farm. He had followed the girl here after her capture, and his binoculars gave him an exceptionally sharp view of the open garage. Sofia was there with her hands bound, and she appeared unhurt. He considered shooting the rest of them and walking up to take her, but he didn't have a clear aim at all of her captors, and he couldn't chance harm to the little girl.

He had returned to Lawson's hideout to find and retrieve the girl only to watch through his scoped rifle as the men plundered the barn. One of them shot Lawson, and still he watched. However, when they turned toward the house and threatened the girl, he had to act. His first shot saw one man go down, but the two remaining intruders scurried around the corner of the house, denying him a clear line of sight.

The raiders had proved smart in using the girl and the woman as hostages, and Tomás watched in frustration as they drove away. The woman was not his concern, but the little girl he must have for life and honor. Fortunately, he glimpsed the license plate of the truck and, over the next hour, traced it via county tax records to a nearby address. He had moved quickly and knew he was in the right place when he saw the same flatbed farm truck parked beside the outbuilding.

Tomás had barely controlled his urge to sweep the outbuilding and property no matter the odds, but he congratulated himself when he saw the meeting taking place. He had learned to read lips as a necessary part of his occupation and understood most of the conversation. If they made any move toward the girl, he would risk an intervention. However, it looked like they planned on keeping her alive for now, and that suited his purpose. He just needed to know when and where the exchange might take place. He felt it would happen back at the Evans farm. It made sense, and he could be there waiting for them, but when?

His phone vibrated against his side. It had to be Giulanti. Tomás had one bar of service for a text to come through. He didn't have to read it to guess what it said. He'd had no service for the last twelve hours and could not report. He read the text as a single word.

"Waiting."

Tomás pondered his answer and texted a reply with location coordinates.

"Located. Pending."

Tomás turned his attention back to the girl in front of him. She was being led back to wherever they were keeping her along with the woman. Would the girl continue to be safe? It was in doubt, and if anything happened to her, he knew what would happen to him. The man escorting them returned to the group in a few minutes, so she was probably safe for the moment.

Tomás let his mind wander while concealed in the underbrush. He had learned the value of patient reconnaissance as a high schooler when the neighborhood gang beat his grandmother because he would not join them. Tomás said nothing at school, but he became certain who was responsible when the gang threatened him to remain silent or their next visit would be her last. He stayed by her side in the hospital until she recovered enough to come back home using a cane, which she would need for the rest of her life.

He waited and observed, documenting who and where and when,

until he felt he had confirmed their individual and group habits. One night when ready, he tracked down and killed each of the gang members involved, including the leader. He piled their bodies across the church steps where his grandmother had been assaulted. He had disabled the church exterior camera and the camera in the shop across the street in his preparation, and after he finished, he reconnected the cameras. The church and the shop owner had done him no wrong.

He wasn't worried about being caught. He was careful and methodical by nature, and even when he had to improvise, he moved with caution, like now.

His grandmother, like everyone else, learned of the gang members' demise from repeated news broadcasts. His grandmother said nothing to him when Tomás told her before the news broke that she wouldn't have to worry about the gang any longer, and if she worried over her grandson's actions, she never showed it.

Later, on her deathbed, confused and rambling, she spoke to him.

"Never doubt that you have a special purpose in this life, and no matter how lost you feel, remember to save the one favored by God," said his grandmother. "The fallen will try to seize her for she is our hope."

He didn't know what his grandmother meant, but he had tried to live as she wanted, and he asked daily for forgiveness. In his heart, he thought it a long shot. If there was an accounting at the end of his life, he didn't expect to be judged well. He could only live with honor and hope for the best.

He had found a measure of peace in the ancient warrior codes, and he painted his life's canvas using the colors of discipline, duty, and honor. Compassion was more difficult for him, as he had always had difficulty in relating to others, but he admired those who strove for the same qualities.

Mark Lawson was a target, and Tomás was bound to kill him if the opportunity presented, but the man had shown courage and compassion in caring for the women under his protection. Tomás had seen Lawson hit hard and collapse in his yard, but he was still breathing when Tomás checked him. Killing Lawson in that state would have been dishonorable, and besides, the girl was the primary target. If

Lawson died at his hands, he would be given a swift and honorable death.

Tomás considered what he knew again. He knew Donovan Giulanti's son was gravely ill, and it was not his place to question his patron, but he couldn't help wondering what Donovan planned for the girl. His patron mentioned that he had helped her enter the country, and she was meant to help his son get well. Donovan had also told him that his son lay dying of cancer, but did the girl really possess a cure?

He knew that the little girl had been severely debilitated physically, and now she was not. The priest had said God singled her out and healed her. Was she the girl of which his grandmother spoke? Did his grandmother foretell this? He had given his word to his grandmother, and he could feel his life funnel to this moment. He wondered if that little girl held an answer for him, and if so, he sensed his soul hung in the balance.

Tomás decided he would observe and wait for an opportunity, but if they were all still there by nightfall, he was going to assault the group in stealth, eliminating any in his way. If they made a move otherwise, he would improvise. He would secure the girl, and then he would know.

CHAPTER NINETEEN

Mark awoke on damp ground to early morning light and shivered. His head throbbed, and he reached his hand up and winced as he brushed crusted blood from his tender scalp. The grass in front of his eyes dripped dew drops into the soil to water the roots of a nearby maple tree which climbed into the morning sky.

He crawled to his feet despite lightheaded vertigo that ebbed to nausea and washed out images before subsiding. The cut chain and padlock lay on the ground beside a crate in front of the open barn door. He remembered the truck, and his eyes swept left. There was nothing. He glanced to the right and glimpsed someone coming around the corner of the barn. He looked down at the ground for his shotgun and faltered to one knee.

"I thought you were dead, boy," said his neighbor.

Walter had his lever action rifle in both hands, and his eyes searched the surrounding trees.

"I have to say you've looked better," said Walter. "What happened?"

Mark maneuvered slowly to his feet, and when he tried to look down, the ground started spinning again.

"I was hoping you would tell me," he said. "I heard a noise outside last night, and came outside to investigate. I think somebody shot at me."

Walter looked at Mark's scalp, which displayed an angry, coagulated furrow.

"Uh huh," said Walter. "Looks like someone creased you good. Get a look at them?"

"No. It was dark." Mark pressed both hands to his head to ease his headache. "Saw someone messing around at the barn door, and there was a truck parked here behind the house."

He tried to look for tire tracks and immediately regretted it when his head pounded like a grating carousel. He put his hands out a bit to steady himself.

Walter said, "Yeah, I saw the tracks already. Is that your blood over there?"

Dark splotches on the ground led to the open barn door.

"I'm not sure," he said. "I had a shotgun with me when I came out, but I don't think I got a shot off, and it's not here now." He pressed his hands against his throbbing temples.

Walter walked toward the barn door, and Mark followed, trying to get his headache to lessen. The old man held his lever action carbine at the ready and entered the barn. He stepped to the left side of the door and stood there as Mark followed him in. There was a dead man lying in a pool of dried blood just inside the barn.

Walter said, "Who's that?"

Mark shrugged his shoulders. The face looked like the man in his flashlight beam last night, but he didn't know him. Mark looked over at the area where the crates had been and could see about half the pile had been removed. Why didn't they take all of it? He remembered Dog had come out with him, but he didn't see any trace of the shepherd. Walter looked at him, waiting.

Quietly, his old neighbor said, "What about the girls?"

An icy hand gripped Mark's heart, and he ignored his throbbing head. He remembered a gunshot followed by a scream and almost fell as he staggered to the house like he was wading across slick creek rocks. Disregarding Walter's warning, Mark lurched up the back steps and into the house through the partly open back door. He forgot he didn't have a weapon. He forgot everything in his need to be certain.

"Maria! Sofia!"

He called out and searched every space, including the basement. The girls were gone.

Walter came in behind him and picked up Sofia's handiwork from the kitchen table, a crayon drawing of three figures and a dog. It was easy to tell that one of them was Walter, and the old veteran's hand trembled like he was holding a hand-drawn masterpiece.

"We can't let this stand," said Walter.

Mark felt the same, but before he could say anything, he heard a vehicle's tires crunch on gravel. He peered around the front room curtains and saw Sheriff Roger Murphy's duty vehicle creep up the driveway.

Mark opened the door, and cool morning air breezed through the house. He stepped out to the front porch, and Walter followed, porting his rifle.

The sheriff parked and exited his truck.

"Good Morning, Roger," said Walter.

"Walter," said the sheriff. "Didn't expect to see you over here this morning. You hunting?"

Roger nodded toward the rifle.

"Varmints."

Walter's short response and tone conveyed much, and the sheriff nodded a fraction of an inch.

"What happened to your head, Lawson?" asked Roger.

Mark hesitated, but he had no choice.

"There's something I need to tell you," he said. "I didn't think I would ever say this, but I am glad to see you."

"It wasn't my idea," said the sheriff. "It was his."

Sheriff Murphy jerked his thumb to the right, and a white head with upright ears popped up in the passenger seat and barked once.

"He showed up at the station this morning and hopped in my truck," said Sheriff Murphy. "Wouldn't even let me get coffee. Wouldn't stop barking unless I stayed on the road to get here. He's yours, right?"

Dog sailed through the open window to bound up the porch steps and wind his way around Mark and Walter. He looked at the sheriff and barked once. Clearly the canine wanted him to join them. All three men looked at each other.

Walter muttered, "Reminds me of a television show I saw when I was a boy."

All three went into the empty house. Mark needed to sit down but felt like he should be doing something to find the girls. Walter leaned his rifle in the corner and poured some water in a bowl for the shepherd, who lapped it up. Soon, the three of them were sitting around the kitchen table with Dog at Mark's feet.

The sheriff looked at Mark closely.

"You look like hell, Lawson," said Roger. "What's happened here?"

Dog raised his head at the sheriff's tone and watched the two of them intently while Walter got up and started coffee.

"Does this have anything to do with that woman who was here with you?"

Walter grabbed an orange out of the fridge and peeled it at the table. He got up to get the coffeepot, which bubbled on the stove, and poured three cups.

"Best let him start at the beginning, Roger," he said. "It's quite a story, and Mark might just have the strength to tell it once."

Walter brought the coffee over to the table.

Mark pressed his hands against the table.

"It started for me with a visit from the dean of my university," he said.

He continued to tell the story bit-by-bit and accounted for Maria and Sofia while taking a sip of coffee. Walter passed out sections of orange to the sheriff and a slice to Mark which Dog eyed with interest.

"And I woke up in the yard to find a dead man in the barn, about half the powder that I'm assuming is drugs gone, and the girls missing. Walter found me there just before you pulled up. I didn't know if they took Dog or killed him, but apparently he went to get you."

Dog sat up and laid his head in Mark's lap for a well-earned ear scratch.

Walter just shook his head slightly.

Sheriff Roger Murphy listened to all of it and waited a moment before speaking.

"Better take me out to the barn," said the sheriff.

❖

Ari ben Eitan watched on a television at the northern Air Defense Headquarters as President Thomlinson took the podium in Washington, D.C. The President of the United States had requested other countries attend her noon broadcast, which had been touted to have global significance, and Ari hoped her words would be persuasive.

Israel and the United States had counterattacked against Iran, resulting in the loss of offensive capability for that country. The world had hovered uncertainly after Israel's defensive use of a nuclear weapon. Russia and China had gone ominously quiet after denouncing the act, and Israel had intelligence that an escalation seemed likely.

Ari could feel his own tension mirrored in the faces of the other air defense headquarters personnel, who tried desperately to tend their duties and pay attention to the broadcast hoping for some sort of solution from the United States as the president began her remarks:

"Ladies and gentlemen, members of the press, fellow citizens of the United States and countries all around the world. We are all shaken by the recent events in the Middle East and the use of defensive force by both Israel and the United States. It is unfortunate, and I know that not everyone agrees with the necessity for our actions. I hope in time, that we can all come closer to understanding. Let me say this first. The United States will stand honorably with Israel in this defensive action now and in the future."

President Thomlinson cleared her throat, wavered for a moment, and glanced down at her notes, something that Ari couldn't remember seeing her do previously, and a terrible feeling washed over him at whatever she was about to say.

"Earlier this week, the United States and other countries of the world suffered a devastating series of natural catastrophes. We now know those cataclysms had a common cause. Early Sunday morning, a large and previously unknown planetary body passed behind our moon causing a shift in its orbit. This rogue planet with a mass greater than the Moon has circled our Sun and is on a return course to pass close to Earth. We expect further devastation when this occurs, and I urge every government and every citizen to prepare for the coming catastrophe as best they can. I have ordered our overseas troops home in anticipation of our own needs. I now introduce my chief science advisor, Professor Barry Michaels, to provide further details."

President Thomlinson moved to the side as Professor Michaels stepped behind the podium. A roar of questions erupted from the journalists attending the press conference, and Barry answered as best he could, but one question stood out.

"Professor, is there any chance that this planetary body might actually hit us?" asked one reporter.

The room grew quiet, and the president's science advisor took his time in forming his answer.

"Taking observations on this rogue planet has been difficult," he said. "It is currently heading back toward us from the Sun, and the light from our system star makes direct observation difficult. Our calculations show a meaningful chance that this rogue planet will transit inside of our moon's orbit, and such a close pass may cause further fault displacements, tidal changes, and volcanic activity. Frankly, we don't know, because we've never experienced this in recorded history."

Another reporter asked, "Does it have a name, Professor Michaels?"

"We are calling it, Apollyon," he said in a flat voice.

The press room erupted again as Professor Michaels stepped away from the podium.

President Thomlinson moved to the lectern again and held her hands up for quiet.

"There will be further instructions on the hour," she said. "Like every other country around the world, we will face this as a nation. I have nationalized all broadcast facilities in the United States. I am freezing all prices as of this moment. Banks will close to foot traffic immediately, but electronic transfers, checks, and debit cards will still be honored."

The president placed her hands on the podium and looked directly into the cameras without blinking.

"National Guard units will protect homes and businesses, and any rioting or looting will be dealt with severely. Do not test me on that."

Ari listened with one ear while considering his situation. He would remain at his duty post for now. His sister-in-law kept a well-stocked home in the country. She and her husband were down-to-earth people who loved to grow food and take care of their animals. They had a basement and a prepared shelter area, and his wife and children couldn't be in a better location. He would call them as soon as he could. He suspected many in the world were thinking the same thoughts.

Fourteen hundred miles away in Vatican City, Cardinal Ronaldo Ricci had his bags packed and watched the broadcast while waiting for a taxi. He considered all that he had heard. The Vatican staff had scheduled his flight to the United States in two hours, and he felt lucky to have found a seat given the current circumstances.

President Thomlinson concluded her press conference, and a member of the State Department clarified that all non-citizen travel into the United States had been halted. A message scrolling across the bottom of the television reported that all routine commercial flights to the United States out of Rome had been grounded. What was he to do now? He still felt the urge to go to his friend, and he prayed for God's will to reveal itself.

Five thousand miles farther west, Father Francisco Romero woke up to overhead recessed lights and a television mounted on the wall of a hospital room. He remembered falling and a shadowy visage he hadn't seen for twenty years hovering over him.

Father Romero's head throbbed while he watched the President of the United States end her address, and a national news anchor recounted what had been said. He remembered Sofia and the prophecy and tried to raise his right hand, but his wrist was bound to the bed frame. He needed to get up and out of this room and pressed the call button on the remote at his right hand.

The end game was happening, and he prayed that he would be in time.

CHAPTER TWENTY

Mark waited at the kitchen table while Sheriff Murphy inspected the barn. The sheriff had been outside about thirty minutes, and Mark heard him talking with Walter but couldn't make out their words. He knew how this looked. In his previous life as a detective, you always brought in the only witness at a homicide for further questioning.

He desperately needed to look for his girls, and he covered his face with his hands. What was he thinking? He was looking after them for Father Romero and the archbishop, and it was only temporary. Mark swallowed another upwelling of nausea. No, no matter how he felt, they were his responsibility, and he had to find them.

Walter pointed to several areas in the backyard, and Mark saw the sheriff survey the ground around the barn. A few minutes later, he heard them trudge up the back steps. Walter waited outside on the back porch, and Roger entered the kitchen holding his hat.

The sheriff sat at the kitchen table and gathered himself while his mouth pursed together like he'd bitten into a green lemon. Mark knew Roger had gone to school with Madelyn. She had told him that they dated a few times, and her father had known his father. Mark knew Roger and some of the other locals never understood what Maddie saw in him, and Mark couldn't disagree with that. He waited for the sheriff to speak.

Roger asked, "When did you find the contraband in the barn?"

"Yesterday evening before dinner. I didn't tell Maria. I didn't want to worry her. I planned on bringing you here this morning. I was going to have the girls stay with Walter today."

Mark couldn't think of anything else to say.

"They took the little girl too?" asked the sheriff. "You know the feds and state police are looking for her?"

Roger's face remained neutral, neither accusing nor condemning. Mark knew most of the county folk liked Roger as sheriff, and he began to see why. He further explained about Maria and Sofia, and when he finished, Roger sat there looking at him before asking a question.

"I need you to tell me about the night your family died," he said. "I need to hear it from you."

Mark hadn't expected those words and fought for control. His last memory of them was his private cross to bear. He had shared his memory of that night only with Father Romero and told himself he didn't care what others thought, but deep down, he knew that wasn't true. That's why he was so happy to see Walter these last couple of days. Although Walter didn't say it, his actions said that he trusted Mark, and looking at Walter standing on the back porch watching the property out to the woods, Mark realized he trusted that old man too.

It felt good to trust someone again, even a little. Maybe he should try.

He sighed and said, "We were driving back from a great day at the lake."

He continued with the story's bare facts. Waking up in the hospital, learning his family was dead and his guilt, leaving the force and trying to carry out Maddie's life plan for him, his drinking and depression, and then he shared the one thing he had told no one else other than the police investigating the accident, not even Father Romero. He told Roger about the dark truck and the shadow grinning in the driver's seat just before he was forced off the road.

Roger said, "There was no mention of another vehicle in the final police report?"

Mark said, "No."

"You think they omitted it on purpose?" asked the sheriff watching him closely.

Mark clenched his hands together while stomach acid bubbled up into his throat. Maria and Sofia were out there somewhere, and bitter fear seeped from his heart to his brain until his head wound hurt.

"Yes," he said. "I think so. Have you ever heard of Donovan Giulanti?"

"Isn't he a wealthy guy in the city?" asked Roger. "Big into charities, right? I've heard the name in passing."

"I was investigating him," said Mark. "I had credible information linking criminal activity to his business organization."

Mark eased himself up and grabbed a cup of water from the sink before sitting back down.

Roger pulled out his phone and frowned and shook his head at the lack of signal.

"And you think Donovan Giulanti or someone in his association influenced the final police report?" he asked.

Mark knew how it sounded and sat there thinking of how to respond.

"I think my family died because of me," he said. "I think someone ran us off the road while trying to kill me. For a long time after the accident, I remembered little. Even now, I don't clearly remember leaving the road. I was tired that night, but I remember another vehicle slamming into the side of our car."

Roger said, "And you never said this to anyone else?"

Mark looked up and met his eyes.

"Maddie and Faith were dead," he said. "I didn't have any proof, and when the investigation discounted it, I realized anyone who actually believed me would be in danger too."

He looked back down at his hands as another wave of nausea hit him and willed himself not to throw up. He didn't expect Roger to believe him.

"I've known Walter Emmitt all of my life," said the sheriff. "I haven't seen him this upset since his wife passed. Walter believes in you, and he loved Madelyn like a daughter."

Roger drew out each syllable, and Mark suspected the lawman's brain was struggling through what he thought he knew and what he had heard and seen.

Mark pressed both hands on the kitchen table in front of him until his fingers blanched.

"I have to find them," he said.

"You don't look well enough to find your own bed," said Roger, snorting. "And I can't have you investigating as a civilian."

Mark started to protest.

"Let me finish," said Roger as he turned his hat around on the table. "I've seen an increase in drug use in my county. Down at Landry's Store, Matthew has seen a few too many unfamiliar, hard faces. I've had my suspicions but little in the way of evidence until now. I've got one deputy in a county that is four hundred square miles. I need some help, and so do you." Roger reached into his pocket and pulled out a deputy sheriff badge and tossed it on the kitchen table. "You want to find them? Do it the right way."

Mark picked up the badge and gripped it by the edges.

"What do I tell Walter?" he asked.

Walter walked in through the back door on cue. He was holding his rifle and wearing a similar badge on his shirt.

"Tell me you're not ever giving up again," said his neighbor.

Dog put his head on the table and nudged under Mark's arm and stared at him with blue eyes, waiting for an answer, his tail waving slowly back and forth. Mark held the badge and nodded. Dog barked once and put his paws up on the table, putting his head almost even with Mark.

Roger reached over to rub the shepherd between the ears and said, "Looks like we have another deputy."

Mark said, "Where do we start?"

Sheriff Roger Murphy said, "What did that truck look like again?"

❖

Felicity drove her Mercedes Sprinter passenger van toward Our Blessed Mother Church. After her parents cut her off, she had purchased the van out of her remaining savings, and it served as a business vehicle. She didn't like other people driving it and had the headlights on in the subdued afternoon light. The rogue planet, Apollyon, edged in front of the Sun more with each hour now. The president's broadcast had really shaken her up, but it didn't change their present objective.

"Does Father Romero know we're coming?" she asked.

"I tried to call with no answer, but he should be there," said Paul. "The hospital said he woke up and signed himself out an hour ago. Hopefully, if he's well enough to come home, he can answer some questions."

She nodded and turned the corner at the church and parked.

Paul, Martin, and Felicity bounded up the steps to the rectory, and the parish pastor answered the door when Paul knocked. Father Romero stood beside a small bag, and Martin recorded from the rectory porch.

"I'm afraid I don't have time for questions at the moment," said the priest.

But then he looked at their Mercedes van parked at the curb and muttered something about mysterious ways and spoke again.

"Do you want answers?" asked Father Romero.

Finally, Paul thought, trying to keep up with the elderly priest.

"Yes, we just want the truth," he said.

The priest nodded, hesitated for a moment, then spoke.

"I will tell you everything, but I need something from you," he said.

Father Romero motioned them into the living room of the rectory while he donned his jacket and the shoulder bag he had packed.

Paul couldn't resist.

"What do you need?" he asked.

"Is your van in good shape?" asked Father Romero.

He stepped past them out to the rectory porch, and they followed, trying to keep up with the elderly priest as he walked down the steps to the sidewalk without looking back.

"Yes, Father Romero, it was just serviced two weeks ago," said Felicity.

She blushed as he smiled at her.

"I will tell you anything you want to know, but the answers you seek are almost two hundred miles away," he said. "Lives are in danger, and time is running out."

Father Romero practically raced to the van, and Martin continued recording as they tried to keep up.

"What are you saying?" asked Paul.

He was thinking his thoughts about mental illness were correct and so would his viewers.

"She is the key," said the elderly priest. "Please, we need to leave now."

Father Romero examined the side of the vehicle, trying to figure out how to gain entrance. Felicity stepped in front of him and deftly opened the door to the van.

Paul grabbed the arm of the old priest before he could climb in.

"You mean Sofia?" he asked. "You know where she is? You want us to go to her?"

Father Romero forced himself to slow down.

He looked at Paul and said, "She is our hope. He's found her and won't stop until she's no longer a threat. Please, there's no time. I can explain more on the way, but we need to leave now."

Paul glanced at Martin, still taking video.

Father Romero said, "Paul, this is what he told you so long ago. This is the moment he bragged about. Remember?"

Paul's breath halted in his throat. How could Father Romero know about that? He'd told no one else, but somehow this priest knew? He couldn't explain that.

"C'mon, get in," called Felicity. "We going or what?"

She had already climbed into the driver's seat and called to them through the open door. Martin shut off the video camera and climbed into the van behind Paul and Father Romero, who sat with his bag at his feet. Felicity started the Mercedes van and showed off its turning radius as she headed up a side street to Bardstown Road.

Paul gripped the armrest on his seat and glanced at Father Romero, who looked back at him waiting for him to ask his questions. Paul didn't know how to begin and bobbed in his seat, adrift with no frame of reference. Martin had his action camera up and working again behind them, ready for a question-and-answer session.

"So, where are we going, Father?" asked Felicity from her driver's seat.

"Just outside Anders, Kentucky," said the priest. "We must hurry. He almost has her now."

Father Romero grimaced as he sounded out the syllables.

Felicity put the destination city into the navigation system built into the dash.

"Whoa, two hundred and three miles," she said. "Not bad, Father." She merged onto the Watterson Expressway and accelerated.

Paul forced himself to think through his confusion and ask the obvious question.

"Who is it that almost has her?"

He wasn't sure why he was afraid to ask.

"You know the answer already, don't you?" said Father Romero.

Paul surprised himself by thinking how understanding the crazy priest looked. He couldn't believe he was going to say it and felt like he might throw up.

"The shadow man?" said Paul, his voice creaking like a rusty screen door trying to hold back a werewolf.

Father Romero nodded.

Felicity kept her eyes on the road ahead as she passed cars to the right and the left.

"Who is that?" she asked. "What are you talking about?"

Father Romero said, "Paul, do you feel you can finally talk about it?"

CHAPTER TWENTY-ONE

Donovan cradled Lorenzo's ashen hand while his son gazed on some distant point beyond his mother, who wept silently in a corner of the room. No deity should allow anyone to suffer like this.

"Daddy, please."

Lorenzo mouthed the words and turned his damp forehead to the side.

"I know, Son," said Donovan as he pulled the sheet down.

Lorenzo's arms and chest had grown skeletal, the muscle tissue consumed in the effort to breathe while his swollen, weeping lower extremities reflected the inability of his heart to pump away his venous blood return. Donovan wondered again if his boy understood what was about to happen.

"Father, I'm lost."

Lorenzo's voice sounded far off and hollow like he was already underground, and Donovan glanced at his wife, Vivian, unblinking and welded to her chair.

"I'm here, Son," he said.

Donovan felt like a bug washed toward a drain, desperate to hang on as the precipice loomed near.

"I'm sorry," said Lorenzo, wheezing.

Donovan motioned for his wife to stand, and Vivian held out her hand. Her fingers felt like the brittle branches of a dry tree, and he held her gently, afraid she would disintegrate in his grasp.

"We're here, Son," said Donovan.

The two of them huddled by the bedside waiting for their lives to end, and Vivian trembled like a gazelle poised to flee. Lorenzo had become their sole reason for holding to each other, and trying to will their boy strength left none for anything else.

"Forgive me," said Lorenzo, murmuring at the ceiling. He closed his lucent eyelids and drifted off to sleep. His ragged respirations slowed, but didn't cease.

"Oh, Son, there is nothing to forgive," whispered Donovan. "You are the best boy a father could ever have."

Why was his son asking forgiveness after only living thirteen years? His boy was blameless. Donovan pondered this and heard his wife protest. The surgeon he had placed on private retainer had come to the opposite side of his son's bed and shook his head in answer to her silent appeal. Fresh tears spilled down Vivian's face, and Donovan watched Lorenzo take a gasping breath in sleep. His son was a much better person than he would ever be.

Vivian's hand slipped from his, and Donovan wondered if he would ever feel it again. Did it even matter? You work and strive to build a life that can be embraced only to realize it's all temporary. Vivian trembled with her back to him and mewled hushed sobs. Donovan thought to comfort her, but she didn't want to feel his touch. He had failed to save their son, and she would never forgive him.

He stood there in near graveyard silence thinking of how it might have been different if the girl had been brought to him as planned, but she had disappeared along with the hope for his son's recovery. Sorrow and frustration gave way to icy anger. The couriers were dead, which would have happened anyway, but it wasn't enough. Donovan hated excuses from himself and couldn't abide it in others; but had he really failed?

Tomás had reported cryptic updates that Lawson had escaped with the girl along with a location. Donovan's mind bounded from known to unknown. Tomás said he knew where she was but hadn't called back.

His son was dying. Lawson. His son was dying. The girl. His son was dying. Lawson.

Donovan had built this life, and all those around him did his bidding. He promised himself that Mark Lawson and anyone who had thwarted him would die by his hand if possible, but on the life of his son, they would die. First, he had to retrieve the girl before his son ran out of breath, and if he couldn't bring the girl to his son in time, maybe there was another way.

Donovan stepped away from Lorenzo's bedside and summoned one of his more trusted lieutenants. After whispered instructions, the man assured him that he would mobilize the medical team and make immediate arrangements. Most of them were on payroll, but a couple, including the surgeon, had been persuaded through other means.

Who else could know where the girl and Lawson might be? Donovan's source at the hospital had informed him that Father Romero had recovered, and Donovan tasked another subordinate.

"Be discreet, but find the priest and bring him to me," he said.

Donovan seethed and made himself a promise. He would find her, no matter what, and then they would all pay.

Felicity joined up with the interstate heading south from Louisville and kept her eyes ahead for any change in traffic. She had the radio on low volume for any further news, but Paul could tell she was listening to them. Martin kept his action camera rolling.

"I'd rather hear your story, Father Romero," said Paul. "You did promise to answer our questions."

The priest arranged himself in his seat.

"Very well," said Father Romero. "Twenty years ago, I worked as a village priest in the border country between Venezuela and Colombia, and one night I was asked to see a young girl thought to be possessed."

"What, like with a demon, Father?" asked Felicity from her spot behind the wheel.

She tilted her head to the side to hear his answer without taking her eyes off the road.

Martin asked, "Aren't pretty much all of those cases explained away through non-supernatural causes after investigation?"

Father Romero looked at Paul closely.

"Yes," said the priest. "That is true most of the time."

Father Romero hesitated, and Felicity urged him to continue.

"That night the villagers led a fellow priest and myself to a suffering young girl," said Father Romero. "I can only say that after much effort, we observed the demon leave her body though the grace of our Lord and Savior."

Father Romero paused after his words, and the elderly priest's eyes searched to and fro, perhaps for memories from years ago, confirming the details again in his mind.

The sound of tires rolling on asphalt filled the van.

A mile passed by the windows, and Paul remained uncharacteristically quiet while Martin continued recording. Felicity broke the silence without taking her eyes off the road.

"But how did you see the demon?" she asked. "I mean, you could actually see it?"

Father Romero looked at Paul and waited.

"Paul, maybe you'd like to answer that," said the priest with a kind smile.

"What does he mean?" asked Felicity.

Paul didn't want to talk and didn't understand how Father Romero could know his secret. He licked his lips, but his tongue was too dry to moisten them. If it had been anyone other than Felicity asking, he wouldn't answer.

"I saw something I shouldn't have when I was younger," said Paul. "And one night, after my parents had a terrible argument, I didn't want to live and cried myself to sleep. I woke up terrified, and I glimpsed something move along the floor. I couldn't stop myself and leaned over the edge of my bed."

Paul took a breath and hesitated.

Martin squirmed and asked, "What did you see?"

"Nothing at first, but I had to know," said Paul. "I looked under my bed into an empty darkness that swallowed the glow from the night-light. I don't know how to explain it to this day, but I reached out and there was no floor, and somehow, I fell, or maybe I was pulled. I don't know, but everything became gray around me, and I couldn't see my own hand. I could turn around, but there was no room to sit. I sensed people all around. I heard them moaning and whimpering and cursing, but their voices were muffled like they were on the other side of cheap apartment drywall. The grayness hemmed me in and stuck to me like dry ice. It scalded wherever it touched, and I screamed over and over until I was naked, stripped to muscle and bone, and every shameful thought or act in my life stuck to me like a hollow skin. I was branded and hopeless and so alone. That's when I met something faceless and dark."

"It was hard to see," said Father Romero.

Paul nodded. This was a memory he had repressed for the last twenty years. Now, it was loose, and his heart galloped around a truth he couldn't allow.

"Yes," said Paul. " It showed me things from the past and boasted of promises to come. Sometimes, I still hear them."

Felicity gasped from the driver's seat.

Father Romero made the sign of the cross and said, "Yes, my son, I do too. You saw it again in the church, didn't you?"

Paul choked on remembered fear and understood that this interview had turned into a confession. He swallowed a gob of sour gall before he answered.

"Yes," said Paul. "When you were hurt."

"Once you've seen him, he comes back to feed," said Father Romero. "He savors our dark moments when we doubt or fear."

"I woke up in my bed," said Paul. "I convinced myself that I dreamed it."

"The downcast glory in the shadow of lies and draw strength to convince us they don't exist," said Father Romero.

Felicity looked like she was ready to pull the van over.

Martin had mostly remained still while recording but finally couldn't help himself.

"Hey, I don't know what to say about all this, but I don't see how this proves anything," he said. "You both had similar experiences, sure, but there's no proof."

Father Romero nodded in agreement.

"Your skepticism is understandable," he said.

Paul held back. He had survived by convincing himself it was nothing more than a remembered nightmare but couldn't explain Father Romero knowing his fear.

Another thirty minutes passed, and Felicity absent-mindedly tapped the radio frequency seek symbol on the dashboard multifunction touch screen. Every news station speculated on the president's speech and the release of information by her administration regarding the approach of the rogue planet and the conflict in the Middle East. Felicity took an exit off the interstate at a prompt from the van's navigation software. She had turned on the headlights in the soft afternoon daylight but still had to slow down for safety. She was also the first to say anything.

"So how does this all relate to Sofia?" she asked.

"Father Ricci and I received the same message that day. We were told that a broken one made whole could redeem the world," said Father Romero.

Martin still had the camera up but forgot he was holding it and asked a question.

"And you think Sofia is that child?" he asked.

"Well, the world sure needs saving," said Felicity.

She gestured upwards, reminding them of the approaching rogue planet.

Martin asked, "Father, why haven't you told this story publicly?"

"We were admonished to silence until now," replied Father Romero.

Felicity called back from the driver's seat.

"So, did this shadow whatever have a name?" she asked.

"Abaddon," replied both Father Romero and Paul at the same time.

❖

Mark and Walter followed Sheriff Roger Murphy in Mark's Jeep. The sheriff had loaned Mark a portable radio which broke squelch.

"Are you sure about the design on the side of the truck?" asked the sheriff.

They had already had this discussion, but Mark realized Roger wanted to be certain before they forced themselves onto the Bradley Farm. Terrence Bradley might be an asshat and his brother worse, but he was still one of the significant landowners in the county. Sheriffs don't remain in office long by prodding prominent citizens without good evidence.

Mark remembered the side of the truck in the glow of his flashlight and answered on the radio.

"It was dark, but it looked like two spreading oak trees side by side."

Walter drove the Jeep. The old farmer had scrubbed Mark's wound and approximated it by tying the hair together in individual bundles, loosely pulling the wound edges together. At least Mark wasn't bleeding at the moment, but he still felt a little woozy.

"Okay, that sounds like Twin Oaks Farm," said Roger. "That's the Bradley brothers' place. This might get a little rough. You boys ready?"

Mark was ready for whatever he needed to do. He had put on a clean shirt and denim pants over his boots and strapped on his old duty belt with his handgun, two spare magazines, cuffs, zip ties, and flashlight.

Walter had spare ammo for his lever action rifle and wore a single action revolver in a holster rig. A fixed blade knife hung on his left side in a sheath. Appropriate, thought Mark, since they were hunting animals. Walter looked determined, and he asked a question.

"We're ready," said Mark. "Walter wants to know if we're all going in the front way? Seems like a good way to get surprised, and I'd rather be the one doing the surprising. What do you think, boss?"

A few moments went by.

"Might not be a bad idea to come at them from more than one direction," said Roger, over the radio. "Walter, do you remember their place?"

Walter kept his eyes on the road while Mark held the radio close to his friend.

"Been awhile," said Walter. "We never got on too strong, but I remember it well enough."

Roger's voice came back over the radio.

"Think you can approach the main house from the back?" asked the sheriff.

"I expect so," said Walter.

They were coming up to a split in the road, and both directions ahead ran alongside the Bradley farm. Roger slowed his duty SUV to a stop, and Walter parked the Jeep Commander behind the sheriff on the side of the road. Roger got out and walked back to the Jeep. He had his phone open and frowned again, shaking his head at the lack of cell service. He approached the driver's window, and the afternoon Sun was to his back.

Walter was the first one to speak.

"Something wrong?"

The sheriff nodded.

"I'm not sure," he said. "I got a call from Martha down at the diner earlier, but it cut off, and I haven't been able to reach her."

Now it was Walter's turn to frown.

"And she ain't called you back," he said. "That don't sound right."

Roger nodded in agreement, and his eyebrows narrowed as he looked at both of them. They still had a job to do.

"Okay, Mark, you and I will go in the front way," said Roger. "You can join me in my truck. Leave the radio with Walter. He'll drive around the back side of the property and make his way around to that side of the house. Walter, you find yourself a good spot to overwatch and wait for us. We'll give you thirty minutes. What do you think?"

"I can do that. I'll signal you when I'm set."

"Just to be clear," said Mark. "We're not leaving without them." He looked at Roger and Walter. "No matter what."

They all nodded in agreement, and Dog chuffed once, pushing his head up between the front seats.

Mark gave Walter the radio and got out, and Dog jumped out and followed him. Walter pulled out onto the road and veered left at the intersection. Mark climbed into the passenger side of Roger's Explorer, and Dog jumped into the rear seat.

"Not sure how I feel about waltzing in there," said Mark. "Wish there was some way to get a look before we drive up."

"We're on official business," said Roger. "Terrence will cooperate. If folks around here find out he's not willing to help look for a child, he'll never be able to show his face again."

Mark checked his watch. About twenty minutes to go. A dotted sun watched above the trees across the fields to the west.

"So, why did you agree to shelter those two?" asked Roger. "You know the FBI is searching for Sofia as a possible kidnapping."

Mark realized Roger knew more than he had said about what happened in the city. The sheriff reached down to the dash and turned on the radio to low volume. The top news stories rolled off quickly.

The approach of Apollyon, The current actions in the Middle East, The Recovery Efforts for the West Coast, and The Hunt for Miracle Child Sofia.

"We're not completely isolated here in the country," said the sheriff. "You have to know this might not end well for you."

Mark's thoughts raced over the last few days. His heart still ached for his lost family, but he surprised himself when he answered.

"It felt like the right thing to do," he said.

Roger nodded. It must have been a good enough answer. They both sat in the Explorer stewing in their thoughts as the radio relayed the news broadcast in the background:

. . . most overseas troops are headed home while there are protests from several countries that the United States is breaching faith in their agreements. . . . Geologists and park officials have voiced concern over the increasing ground tremors in and around the Yellowstone Caldera. . . . A report surfaced of a suspected impact on the planet Jupiter, although any association with the approaching rogue planet is uncertain according to Professor Barry Michaels, science advisor to the president.

"So what's it like living with a nun?" Roger asked.

"She's not a nun," said Mark. "Maria is in training."

"Oh," said Roger without further comment.

"It's not like that," protested Mark. "She was caring for Sofia and agreed to come with me to keep her safe."

"Uh, huh."

Another brief response from Roger.

"Look, it's not what you think," said Mark. "I'm just looking after them temporarily, and they both know that."

Mark didn't understand why he felt he had to convince the sheriff.

"It's just that I saw the way she looked at you from your porch," said Roger.

Mark let that statement go as long as he could.

"What do you mean?"

"My Nancy used to look at me that way sometimes," said Roger. "It was her way of roping me in, and I just recognized the look. That's all I'm saying."

Mark thought Roger was enjoying himself entirely too much.

"Does Nancy know you're about to brace drug runners and kidnappers?" asked Mark.

He thought turnabout was fair play.

"I don't know," said Roger. "She died a year and a half ago. Came home late and found her on the couch. Doc Higgins thought she had a hidden heart defect or something like that."

Roger managed his answer in the same flat and controlled way Mark talked about his family.

"I'm sorry," said Mark. "I didn't know. Children?"

Mark waited for an answer.

"We tried," said Roger. "Didn't happen."

The sheriff's answers were short and controlled, and Mark understood exactly. The pain was still there but compressed in a box out of the way, visited now and then, but not left open for others to inspect.

"That's why I said something about the way she looked at you," said Roger. "I remember how lucky I was to have someone care enough to look at me that way, and it doesn't come around often."

Roger sat quietly.

Dog nuzzled up between the Explorer's front seats and put his nose on Roger's shoulder, and the sheriff reached up and rubbed the shepherd's ears with his right hand.

Mark had seen the look from Maria on the porch too. It had scared him. Worrying about her made him feel things that hurt all the way through, but for the first time in a long time he felt alive. He had a purpose, and maybe, a chance at redemption. So be it. Guilty or not, he would find the girls.

Whatever it took.

CHAPTER TWENTY-TWO

Cardinal Ronaldo Ricci feared for his old friend, Father Romero. Over the years, Ronaldo hoped that he misunderstood because he was a fallible human man, but now, he knew in his heart that the prophecy had come in his lifetime as he feared it would. The story of Sofia's miracle had graced many international news outlets before the growing war in the Middle East had drawn a response from the United States.

Ronaldo walked outside and looked overhead to the evening sky. He couldn't see the outline of the rogue planet, Apollyon, as the news called it, but he could feel it pressing down on him. He had packed quickly to leave for America, but all flights had been canceled. He stood in the grass just off the walkway and prayed over what to do next. He waited quietly for an answer until he heard approaching footsteps.

The cardinal turned to see the pope's personal secretary, Monsignor Esposito, fidgeting with his cell phone and a black portfolio.

"Cardinal Ricci, I am asked to bring you to His Holiness now," said Esposito. "It is most urgent. Abbiamo fretta, per favore."

The monsignor put his phone in his pocket and grasped Ronaldo's arm.

"Per favore, Your Eminence. Fretta."

Ronaldo let himself be pulled along, and he hastened to the papal residence to see his friend, Anastasi, while Esposito kept repeating they should hurry.

"His Holiness has worsened most suddenly, Your Eminence," he said, his eyes blinking back tears.

Ronaldo walked as fast as he could without running and thought of his first meeting with Pope Anastasi. His shared experience with Father Romero had been all that gave him the courage to sit with the Holy Father. Much had changed in his life since that night outside the village years ago, but Ronaldo had never forgotten. He had dared to imagine that recollection as only a distant possibility by staying busy, but now, the memory was constantly in the background, laughing at his efforts and mocking his weak faith. He silently mouthed a prayer of contrition and admonished himself to be strong for his friend, Anastasi. He only hoped it wasn't as bad as Esposito seemed to fear. Ronaldo paced along the Apostolic Palace hallways, but in his mind, he walked the jungle at night.

The girl looked straight ahead until they approached. Her wrists and ankles had been fastened by rawhide thongs to wooden stakes driven into the ground, and several villagers gathered around her, including a woman weeping quietly, whom Ronaldo guessed as her mother.

At Father Romero's approach, an older man introduced himself as the girl's grandfather and told them she had been a happy fourteen-year-old girl until she returned from the jungle a week ago, distant and withdrawn and angry. When the girl lunged at her mother with a knife, they felt she might be possessed and sent for the priests. The family had brought her out of the village in shame to this place.

Ronaldo had listened and thought the girl functionally ill. The change was reportedly quite sudden, but teenagers often had mood swings and bouts of anger. Her family reported emotional and mental status changes but nothing supernatural in her condition. Fourteen was young for schizophrenia, though not unheard of.

The girl moved her head from side to side, saliva flinging a few feet in either direction, and her tongue flicked in and out of her mouth.

Ronaldo thought about rabies or a delirium from tetanus when she screamed and arched her back over grunted syllables.

"You have no authority here, shamans."

The village girl growled guttural sounds which clung to the surrounding rocks like dripping tar, and she heaved off her primitive bedding, inexplicably suspended above the earth and tethered only by her bonds. Ronaldo stiffened until his toes cramped. The stories were real, and he couldn't remember what he should do.

Father Romero took out a cross and a flask of holy water and began the exorcism rites while the girl raged and cursed. The surrounding jungle held its breath in the cooling night except for occasional sighs from the overhanging tree canopy sympathetic to the battle beneath.

After the ordeal was over, Father Romero and Ronaldo were reciting prayers of protection and safekeeping over the exhausted teen as she rested on her makeshift bed when a brightness surrounded her face. She remained absolutely still, except for her eyes, which moved rapidly beneath fluttering eyelashes.

She opened her mouth and said, "A broken one made whole will stand for us at the end."

Later, the village girl recalled none of it, and Ronaldo learned in talking with the family and villagers that no one else saw or heard her speak. That was when he realized the message was meant only for him and Father Romero.

Although painful to speak about, they shared a bond of prophecy and prayed to understand what they had experienced in the context of world events while keeping in touch, at first in letters, but later by email and video chats, thanks to advancing technology. Now, they were at the fulcrum, and the next few hours would determine their collective fate. Ronaldo had never felt so certain in all his life.

❖

Sheriff Roger Murphy drove up the asphalt driveway to Twin Oaks Farm with his duty vehicle's roof light bar pulsing blue reflections off the main house and outbuildings. There could be no mistaking their arrival as other than official business. Somewhere out in the tree line, Walter watched and waited, having keyed his portable radio twice to confirm being in position.

Mark exited the Explorer with Dog beside him and waited impatiently while Roger knocked on the oak and glass front door of the Bradley estate house, a rambling colonial style two-story home with six round white columns supporting a grand half-moon style front porch. No one answered the door.

"Now what?" asked Mark.

He wanted to search, warrants be damned.

"This doesn't feel right," said Roger. "Terrence has a half-dozen men working this farm. Where is everybody? Look around the back while I call our location in on the radio."

Mark walked around a corner of the expansive home, and Dog ranged a few meters ahead. They walked past two central air-conditioning units at the rear of the house where a pool with surrounding deck and bar beckoned with the scent of chlorine. Mark took a moment to knock on both the back door and a sliding glass door that opened to the pool area without response.

Dog pricked his ears up and stood still. The shepherd curled one front paw and stared at a large outbuilding which looked to be a garage and workshop.

"Seems like a good place to check, huh," said Mark.

He carefully approached the metal sided outbuilding. Other than some gravel crunching underfoot, all was quiet. Dog paced back and forth and put his nose to the ground. The shepherd looked back at Mark as if to say, "Quit wasting time; let's go!" All the exterior doors were closed, and Mark tried a locked doorknob.

"I couldn't get through on the radio," said Roger. "What do you have?"

He had walked around the other side of the house and joined up with them.

"Not sure, maybe something," said Mark. "Dog seems worried about this outbuilding."

"I see that," said the sheriff.

Roger stepped up to the door and broke the glass using his jacketed elbow. He reached in and turned the doorknob to open the door, and Dog squeezed past him. Roger followed with Mark.

They entered an office-like setting with another door opening to an expansive garage space which housed a large gray tractor and some attachments up against the wall. The rest of the floor was bare except for some empty packing crates which looked the same as those Mark remembered from his barn. He nodded at Roger.

Dog stopped and crouched with his ears up and his fur bunched between his shoulder blades like an enraged grizzly bear. The shepherd darted in a run as a man leaned into a far doorway and aimed a Kalashnikov-type rifle at them. He hadn't counted on Dog, who leaped up and clamped his mouth around the man's arm, drawing blood and forcing him to the ground with his weight. The man's rifle clattered to the cement floor as he tried to fight off the shepherd.

Mark called out, "Dog, enough."

Instantly, the shepherd released the man and trotted back to sit beside Mark. Roger kicked the man's rifle aside and kept his service pistol pointed at him.

"Where are the girls?" demanded Roger.

The man cradled his mangled arm with his right hand and stared at them.

Mark stepped around the sheriff and picked up the dropped rifle.

"Dog and I will check the back," said Mark, moving around and through the doorway to find another hallway.

He tried several doors leading to other work rooms. The last door on the right was locked, and Dog immediately jumped up and began scratching at the hollow-core door. Pulling the shepherd to the side, Mark gathered himself and kicked in the locked door. Inside, huddled against the far wall, he found Maria weeping with her torso partly covered by her torn shirt. Sofia hugged her knees beside Maria and rocked back and forth with tears in her eyes.

Mark positioned the captured rifle carefully against the wall of the room and knelt beside them. He tentatively reached for Maria, who jerked away from his touch at first, but then her eyes widened as she recognized him, and she reached out one trembling hand, her other still holding on to the remnants of her shirt. Mark scooped her up and held her tight against his chest. Sofia jumped into his embrace and the three of them knelt together in a group hug. Dog nosed in with them.

"I've got you," he said. "It's going to be all right. Don't worry."

Mark exhaled a half-sob and felt their faces against his while wet tears merged into a common family pool on their skin and clothes and floor. Maria and Sofia gulped air in great heaves which gradually lessened to washed-out exhaustion. Dog licked the tears off Sofia's face and laid his snout on her neck and shoulder, and she buried her face in his fur.

"Mark, you back here?"

The sheriff appeared in the open doorway and took in the sight of Dog nosing in between the three of them huddled together.

"We've got to hurry," he said.

Mark helped Maria stand and Sofia pressed against his leg.

"What?" asked Mark.

"I persuaded the guy out front to talk," said Roger with a grim smile. "The rest of the gang is due back any time."

"Bradley brothers?" asked Mark, reaching for the captured rifle with his right hand.

"And then some," said Roger. "We need to get out of here while we can. We can come back with reinforcements, but we need to move."

"There are other girls, Sheriff. Please help them," said Maria, no longer leaning against Mark.

She held to her tattered shirt while Mark picked up an old blanket on the floor and draped it across her shoulders.

"They left to bring them here," she said. "Those animals were planning to sell all of us."

"César said there were other girls," said Roger. "I thought he was trying to confuse me."

Maria shivered at the mention of her captor's name.

"By the way, look what I found on him," said Roger.

The sheriff handed over a revolver with a four-inch barrel which Mark recognized as his and placed in his jacket pocket.

The group made their way toward the door to the garage area where César sat handcuffed to a support pole, looking the worse for wear. Maria walked past him without a glance, wearing her horse blanket like a queen's regal stole, completely beyond him. Sofia walked beside Maria, hand in hand, and Dog padded over to César, who cringed at sight of the animal. The shepherd hiked a leg and sprayed César with a reminder of their encounter.

They were at the door to the yard when Roger received a radio call from Walter.

"Sheriff, trouble coming. Get out of there."

Looking out the doorway, they saw a dust trail coming up the driveway. Mark could see the Bradley's flatbed farm truck with the twin oak trees decal on the door. There were nearly a dozen armed men in the back of the flatbed truck, and an older short school bus trailed close behind on the long driveway.

Mark looked at Roger. They were trapped.

CHAPTER TWENTY-THREE

The vehicles roared up to the front of the house and parked behind Roger's parked Explorer. Several men jumped off the back of the flatbed truck and pointed rifles in the general direction of the sheriff's vehicle while two men carrying rifles exited the doors of the school bus and motioned for someone to follow.

Four women stepped down from the short bus. Their clothes looked soiled and torn, and two of them cried while the youngest swayed with halting, zombie-like steps and stumbled. The teenager was caught by the oldest of the women, who looked to be around thirty years of age, and the high-school-aged girl clung to her arm. The two armed men pushed them toward the outbuilding, and Mark watched through the slightly open door as the captives shuffled toward them.

"Those are the girls they were talking about," said Mark. "The deal must be tonight."

"That's Martha holding the youngest," said Roger, his face set in a hard mask.

A decisive, balding man exchanged words with Terrence Bradley while the rest of the men in the flatbed truck climbed down and spread out, awaiting instructions.

"I'll brace them," said Roger "and you run out the back way." He started to reach for the door of the outbuilding.

"Are you crazy," said Mark, grabbing his arm. "Don't be a hero. I've got an idea."

Mark motioned for Maria to hide with Sofia and Dog behind the desk against the wall, and he and Roger ducked to either side of the opening door just before the captured girls were pushed inside, followed by their captors.

Mark and Roger pounced on the two kidnappers herding the women inside the building, and both dropped after being hit from behind. The women shrank back and swayed in place, unsure what to do. Maria and Sofia stood up and held their fingers to their lips, motioning them to be quiet. Martha recognized Roger and reassured the other girls while Mark grabbed a spare work-shirt for Maria from a hook on the wall by the entry door. He held the blanket up for cover, and she managed to quickly change.

There was no time for introductions as they moved past César, who stank of urine and tried to shout through the duct tape covering his mouth. Making their way along the hallway to the back of the building, they opened a door, and the fields behind the house beckoned in front of them. Gray daylight outlined freshly furrowed ground and a fair amount of open space to cover with frightened women who looked dehydrated and worse, but what choice did they have?

Roger said, "Ladies, stay low, and move as quietly as possible, and no matter what, don't stop. Let's go."

Mark guessed they had another minute if they were lucky, and Roger took the lead. The sheriff picked his way across the field while trying to keep the outbuilding between the escaping group and their captors. Mark brought up the rear and kept looking back. He held the newly captured rifle at the ready, and the group had about one hundred meters to get to the safety of the tree line. Stumbling his way across the broken soil, Mark began to hope they might make it.

A shout went up from the corner of the outbuilding. Someone had spotted them.

Roger shouted, "Run!"

The sheriff started pulling and urging the exhausted women to the trees as the hornet buzz of a bullet overhead followed by the crack of a gunshot helped hurry everyone.

Mark stopped and took aim with the compact rifle. He held upper center mass of the man shooting and estimated the range at just over a hundred meters. He squeezed the trigger, and the carbine bucked against his shoulder. Three rounds fired before he released the trigger. When he looked again, he saw the man had disappeared. More shooting came from the front of the outbuilding, and the gang no longer appeared to be paying attention to them. Mark hurried to catch up to Sofia and Maria, who raced ahead into the trees.

A cacophony of gunshots echoed behind them. Somebody was covering their escape, and Mark wondered if Walter might be the source, but that was an awful lot of rifle fire. Who were the other shooters?

He didn't have time to consider further and hustled after the group, which had disappeared among the trees. He found them hiding behind some brush and ducked down beside them.

"We got some help," he said. "Walter and maybe someone else. What's our next step?"

"We need to keep moving, but"—Roger nodded toward the girls who looked like they wanted to drop—"right now, I imagine they are sending some men to cut us off."

Dog whined to get their attention, took a few paces, turned around, and chuffed at them. Clearly, the shepherd thought they should keep going in the same direction. At least somebody had an idea what they should do.

Coaxing the freed captives, they stumbled on. Weaving around a pair of red maple trees, they made their way past basswood and white pines to a ten-foot fence topped by three strings of barbed wire. It was the Bradley farm perimeter fence, and it might as well have been thirty feet high to the exhausted women, but there had to be a way.

Mark saw a hollowed out hackberry tree sagging toward the fence with its roots pulled partly out of the ground. He walked over and pushed against the tree and felt it move, but it didn't fall. Roger joined him, then Maria, and then the other women, who all tried to push with the last of their strength. Dog ran up and leaped over their heads against the tree, and it crashed to the ground, dragging the fence and barbed wire down beneath it. Mark looked up and saw the shepherd on the other side with his tail wagging, urging them on.

"Where did you get that dog?" asked Roger, shaking his head.

The sheriff picked up the freed teen captive, slung her over his shoulder, and walked in short quick steps on the fallen tree across the downed section of fence. Mark helped each of the other female captives get onto the tree, and they shuffled carefully over the makeshift bridge. Martha stumbled at the end just as Roger reached up and lifted her off the tree and onto the ground. She held her arms around his neck and stood with the sheriff for a long few seconds.

Just as Mark attempted to help Sofia and Maria get up on the tree trunk, the ground bucked them off their feet. Violent shaking lasted more than a minute making it impossible to stand. Dust riddled with bits of earth billowed between the trees until Mark could barely see Maria and Sofia beside him on the ground.

The ground finally stopped moving, and Mark helped Maria and Sofia stand upright. They were shaken but unhurt.

The tree bridge, fence, and the intervening ground had disappeared into a ragged crevasse twenty feet across. Fortunately, the sheriff and the rescued women were intact, but there was no way to cross the chasm in front of them. Dog paced back and forth on the far side.

"Roger, get them out of here," called Mark, pointing to the four women captives. "We'll find another way."

Mark could tell the sheriff wasn't happy, and Dog frantically ran along the edge of the cleft trying to find a way back across to them. But there wasn't another answer, and any moment pursuit could come across the fields. Roger waived that he understood, and Mark saw the sheriff attempt to make contact on the radio as he led the group of freed captives into the trees on the other side of the miniature canyon in front of them.

"What do we do now?" asked Maria.

She held one arm about Sofia and tried not to cough in the dusty air.

"We hide in the trees and head toward my place until we can find a way across."

Mark picked up Sofia with his left arm, and she wrapped her hands about his neck. The three of them paced around brush and between partially uprooted trees. He couldn't see the Bradley farm for the dust and the smoke in the air.

"I'm sorry, Maria," said Mark.

He stepped carefully across the uneven ground while Sofia clung to him.

"I'm sorry for not protecting you," he said. "This happens to everyone who depends on me."

Maria walked beside him, choosing her steps carefully. She said nothing at first, and Mark didn't press her.

"I thought they had killed you," she said. "Sofia trusted that you would come. She was so sure."

Mark cringed inside. He understood. She was telling him indirectly that he was right.

"But then you saved us just before that animal . . . "

Maria was crying again, sobbing as she walked. Mark set Sofia on the ground and brought her between them as he hugged Maria. They clung together tightly, swaying heart to heart and drawing strength from each other.

The shooting at the farm had stopped, and Mark hoped Walter was all right. The repetitive thump of helicopter rotor blades broke the silence, and a sleek turboshaft helicopter screamed overhead and descended to Twin Oaks Farm.

Sofia pulled back from both of them with wide eyes and opened her mouth like she wanted to speak, and Mark sensed a presence behind them.

"No!" shouted Maria.

Mark turned to look, but his muscles spasmed in clicking agony. He fell hard and felt a pinprick while he lay immobile on the ground. A pair of hands reached for his girls, and he tried to get up, but his vision narrowed to a haze filled sky swirling about the treetops, and beyond that, the angry, red Sun trying to push away a growing black dot eating the light like some video game.

The helicopter approached the fissured driveway leading to the main house of the Bradley estate, and the pilot gingerly touched the landing gear down, testing the asphalt surface to ensure it was stable. Glimpses through the dust and smoke revealed that the main house had collapsed at one end, and flames licked at the exterior through an exposed and twisted window frame.

Donovan Giulanti stepped off the helicopter, along with two of his trusted lieutenants, and marched with purpose until he stood in front of the burning estate home. His men had attacked from the trees with machinelike precision and corralled the surviving members of the gang. The outbuilding where some had holed up still burned. The sparks from massed gun fire through the metal exterior had ignited something flammable inside which devoured the building and its contents in a conflagration. The muffled screams from inside had died out, and several bodies littered the ground outside where they had fallen. Donovan only hired the best, and his men were all expert marksmen.

In front of him stood three captive men. Donovan judged one to be the leader of the gang, and one of his lieutenants leaned in and confirmed their identities.

"Where is the girl?" asked Donovan.

The gang leader called Deylin sneered.

"You don't know who you are messing with, cabrón," said the muscled, shaven-headed thug.

Donovan had known there was a source of competition in this part of the state. He just hadn't expected to find it himself.

"Today I don't care," said Donovan, his eyes flat and hard.

At least the man was smart enough to know his fate, thought Donovan, as he raised his handgun and shot Deylin in the face. What was left of the gang leader dropped to the ground like a marionette who has had his strings cut. Donovan already knew some of the associates for which the man worked and would deal with them later.

"Who are you, and what do you want?" asked the shorter of the remaining two men. He looked like a younger version of the big man standing beside him, and Donovan knew from one of his men that these two were the brothers who owned this farm.

"Where is the little girl?" asked Donovan.

The younger one spoke quickly before the older brother could reply.

"The gang had her prisoner in the back of the garage that's burning down," said the younger Bradley brother as he glanced at the ruined outbuilding and twisted his mouth in a crooked grin.

In an instant, Donovan's rage dwarfed the heat from the fire. To be in that storage building would be unsurvivable. He leveled his pistol and shot the younger brother between the eyes. The young man's next remark died on his lips, and he dropped limply to the ground like a wet sponge, blood pooling around his distorted cranium.

Terrence looked at Robert's still form and said nothing as his shoulders sagged. A resigned look appeared on his face, and he exhaled a long sigh before he spoke.

"Who are you?" he asked.

"Do you want to live?" asked Donovan.

He waited for an answer and raised his pistol.

"Yes," said Terrence, looking away from what remained of Robert. "I want to live."

"Where is the girl?" said Donovan. Each word cracked like ice about to give way beneath the feet of the last living Bradley brother.

"My brother and I didn't take those women," said Terrence.

He was trying to excuse himself. Donovan hated men who tried to justify their actions. It resembled apologizing which equaled weakness. That was one thing the military had right. No excuses. Do or don't do and be done with it. His patience waned.

"The little girl," said Donovan. "The one called Sofia. Where is she?"

"She was here," said Terrence. "They brought her here along with another woman. I didn't know they were going to do that. They took her from the Evans farm down the road, and I had nothing to do with that. I only allowed them to run some stuff through here—you know—warehouse it and take a small cut as a storage fee."

Terrence stopped talking.

"And," prompted Donovan.

"We went to pick up the other women."

"That you had nothing to do with?" asked Donovan.

He hated liars.

"Look, we were trying to save this place," said Terrence, his voice breaking as he looked once more at what was left of his younger brother. He was almost crying now. "That's all. We didn't mean to hurt anyone."

Donovan Giulanti knew without a doubt that Terrence Bradley would die by his hand, but he needed an answer first.

"Was she in there?" he asked, pointing to the smoldering pyre of an outbuilding.

"Lawson and the sheriff took her," said Terrence. "Had to be the sheriff. That's his truck." Terrence pointed to the Explorer. "He and the sheriff came out here and took those girls. We were chasing them when your men attacked."

"And where did Lawson take her?" asked Donovan.

"Either to the sheriff's station in town or back to the Evans farm, I guess."

Terrence spoke eagerly now.

One of his men brought Donovan a piece of paper folded into the shape of a crane.

"Found this about two hundred meters out, Boss," he said. "There's no sign of anyone now."

Donovan held the folded shape. Tomás was here? Was he involved in the rescue of the girls? Had he turned against him? Very well. He would deal with him. Right now, he didn't care if he had to kill everyone in this county. He would set it right. His son hovered at death's door, and they were all guilty.

"Gather the men after they sweep the property. We are moving out with the usual clean-up instructions. We are going to pay a visit to a neighboring farm first and then the sheriff's office." Donovan had another thought. "How far to the local hospital?"

Terrence Bradley responded like he realized the narrow ledge his life clung to today.

"The hospital in Anders is twelve miles away, but the hospital in Paducah is about sixty miles," he said.

Donovan said, "Send some of our people to check out the local hospital in case they head there, and make sure the advance team is prepping."

One of his men nodded, and he knew it would be done.

"What about me?" asked Terrence Bradley in a ragged voice.

"Convince me that I need you," said Donovan.

He spoke while checking the load in his pistol.

Terrence looked around anxiously.

"I know this county," he pleaded. "I can help you find that girl."

"Tell me about Lawson," said Donovan.

"He keeps to himself on the Evans farm, and he's been a pain in my ass since he first came around. I've been trying to buy that property for years."

Donovan calmly reseated the magazine in his pistol.

"You know his farm and house?" he asked. "As well as your own?"

"We don't see eye to eye," said Terrence. "But, yeah, I been there when he didn't know I was around."

Terrence didn't elaborate, and Donovan didn't care.

"Take him with us," said Donovan, looking at one of his men. "If he tries to run, kill him."

Three armed men grabbed Terrence by his arms and bound his wrists with a flex-cuff. Donovan holstered his pistol. This would be a day to pay debts. His son would live or have a pile of corpses to memorialize his death, and on the top of that mound of bodies, he would stake out Lawson and Tomás and the little girl and anyone else that came to mind. Donovan tried to take comfort in that, but he felt nothing, neither good nor bad, only a hunger for vengeance that needed feeding.

"Sir, look at that."

One of his men pointed at three figures walking out of the trees at the edge of the fields. Donovan borrowed binoculars and saw Tomás escorting the girl and her caretaker.

There was still a chance! Donovan felt giddy. Lorenzo was even now being flown to them with his private medical team. The surgeon had said they could do the procedure in the nearby county hospital with the proper support, and Donovan already had some of his men there.

They would lock down the hospital and the town. The locals would cooperate or lose their lives and the lives of their families. If they thought this disaster was bad, he would give them a new frame of reference.

CHAPTER TWENTY-FOUR

Tomás escorted the holy woman and the girl across the field. The broken ground shifted with each halting stride, kicking up tiny mushroom clouds of doubt which clung to his boots and threatened his resolve. He thought over the holy woman's words again. Remarkable. But he was bound to fulfill his contract, and he pushed his uncertainty away.

Sofia hid her face in Maria's side, and they made their way step-by-step until Tomás faced his patron. Donovan's men fell in behind them, taking Maria and Sofia under their control.

"You brought the girl as I asked," said Donovan, looking from the captives back to Tomás. "You did well. What about Lawson?"

Tomás waited as a competent young man in a flight uniform approached from the helicopter.

"Mr. Giulanti, we are ready," said the pilot, and he leaned forward to say a few words in private before heading back to the rotary aircraft.

Donovan waved his hand, and two of his men escorted the girl and the woman under guard to the waiting helicopter. The nearest hospital was damaged, but it would do. He relayed further instructions to one of his retainers.

"Tell the medical team to use the county hospital," said Donovan. "I have already spoken with the administrator."

The confusion in the aftermath of the earthquake should work to his advantage and allow him to commandeer what was needed. Specialized surgical equipment and a military-grade industrial generator were making their way to the local hospital. The staff would see Donovan as a benefactor in a time of crisis, and he congratulated himself. His wife might even talk to him after today. Tomás remained silent in front of him. The man was inscrutable. The fact that he didn't needlessly talk was one of his best qualities, but Donovan still required an answer.

"Well?" he asked. "And Lawson?"

"He lives," said Tomás. "It was necessary to persuade the caretaker to help with the little one, and the girl was more important."

Donovan did not want to debate with Tomás and nodded. He had learned to accept what this vassal said at face value, which was a rare thing for a man of his station, but drawing information out of the assassin made Donovan wonder again how soon Tomás would have to die. The hired killer knew too much by association, but for now he still had usefulness.

"Will you be able to complete the requirements of the contract?" he asked.

Tomás watched as Donovan's men forced the struggling woman and little girl into the helicopter, and he faced Donovan again.

"Yes," said the stone-faced samurai. "I will do what must be done."

Donovan allowed himself a moment of relief. If Tomás promised something, it was as good as done, but the hired gunman surprised him when he asked a question.

"Is the girl to be sacrificed?" asked the assassin.

"Don't trouble yourself about my plans for her," said Donovan. "She is the price for my son's life."

The corner of Donovan's lip twitched at the thought. The girl would unknowingly serve her purpose thanks to modern anesthesia, and he wondered for a moment if dreams occurred in death. He concluded they must for at least a little while. That is what all those near-death experiences were, just the dead person's brain firing off because it hadn't figured out yet that it was dead.

"Thanks to you, my son has a chance now," he said. "Finish the job, and the rest of your fee will be in your account."

Tomás stayed before him instead of his usual exit after receiving his marching orders.

"Is there something else?" asked Donovan.

Tomás glanced over at the helicopter again and hesitated.

"No," he said. "I know what must happen."

The bronzed manslayer stepped back, and Donovan slowly exhaled. Talking with Tomás was a bit like stepping into a cage with a lion. There was always the chance that the lion would realize its place in the order of things, splinter the chair in its maw, and rend the trainer limb from limb. Donovan angered at that thought. He gave the orders and decided who lived and died. Even a lion should know that.

Donovan raised his left hand with his fingers spread wide as a signal to his men while striding to the helicopter. They would sanitize the area and follow to the hospital.

Tomás glanced back at Donovan Giulanti walking to the waiting helicopter and accepted that his patron had lied to him. He had brought the girl to Donovan to be sacrificed, and he could not get his grandmother's face and words out of his brain. At the end, she had babbled on about his grandfather waiting for her in the room with angels, and just before her last breath, she had grasped his hand and implored a promise.

"Save the one who was cast-off, and you will save us all," she gasped. "But beware the beast in shadow."

She released him and smiled with a faraway look in her eyes and breathed her last. Tomás had watched her leave him with dry eyes. He had loved her and knew she had loved him. Could the one she spoke of be this little girl? He wanted to honor his pledge to his grandmother, but what about his duty to his patron?

He tried to be logical. All he had to do was what he was exceptionally good at. Kill one more person, and there would be no one else left with direct knowledge of anything. He would collect his pay, but then what? He had promised himself that he would leave the stench of death someday and live out the rest of his days in peace, but he knew in this moment that Donovan would never let him live, and he had the resources to hunt him down. He should disappear if he had any sense, but there was something about that little girl.

Tomás prided himself on taking action after due diligence and hated indecision in others. This would be the most impulsive choice of his life and probably his last, but as he watched Donovan Giulanti fly away with the girl, he doubted his previous efforts he had thought so honorable. He had let himself be used.

He crossed the field to the tree line, pulled out his pistol, and attached a suppressor to the threaded muzzle. Ominous smoke blackened the treetops ahead, and a torrent of last words whispered to him from ghostly faces silently watching his decision. He couldn't believe what he was going to do and knew he should turn around. But if he was going to have any chance to navigate the shoals before him, he needed someone else in the boat. He picked up the pace, glad that he'd left Lawson alive.

❖

Walter picked his way through the trees. He had seen the sheriff and Mark flee across the field with the girls just before men emerged from the tree line bordering the driveway and assaulted the farm in near military fashion. By that time, he had abandoned his temporary concealment and made his way in the general direction of Mark and the girls and the sheriff. He heard the helicopter roar overhead and sensed the connection with the mercenaries behind him for that is how he thought of them. They moved like professional soldiers, but they had gone to the dark side and would look for any witnesses.

Walter knew what would happen if they found him. He needed to find Mark but was no help to him dead. He continued his creeping egress until he came to the Twin Oaks Farm perimeter fence. He again pulled compact wire cutters from his pack and snipped chain link until he was through, and he trailed to his right. The ground beyond this section of fence had torn loose and upheaved in a haphazard manner.

It was new, presumably from the earthquake, and he could see an easier way to get down the embankment about twenty meters ahead.

Walter saw the brush ahead twitch, and he moved behind paired white ash trees. The bushes parted, and he lowered his rifle. It was Dog. The big white shepherd wasn't fooled at all by Walter's concealment and trotted right up to him.

Roger emerged from the bushes behind the canine and startled at seeing Walter. The four rescued women followed behind the sheriff and looked played out. Walter was close enough to recognize the oldest of them as Martha Goodwynn. She worked at a diner in Anders, and Walter had known her father, Samuel Goodwynn, before he died. He didn't know the other three.

"Walter, good to see you alive," said Roger.

Martha moved up beside Roger to listen.

"Where's Mark?" asked Walter, dreading the answer.

Roger explained how they had been forced to separate.

"We're trying to make it back to Mark's place. We think that's where he and the girls will head," said the sheriff.

Walter didn't like the odds of Mark and the girls trailing inside that fence line.

"What?" asked Roger.

"We need to get down to the road," said Walter. "There are men combing this property trying to find us."

The sheriff nodded and gathered the women to find a way down the bluff.

Dog's ears went erect, and the shepherd looked back the way Walter had come.

Walter shouldered his rifle and leaned in so his voice didn't carry.

"Get them down to the road and stay under cover."

Roger tried to stop him, but the old farmer moved ten steps and disappeared into the trees. Dog wafted after him like a phantom warrior. The sheriff shook his head and assisted the youngest girl down the embankment while Martha helped the other two. Roger winced at the noise they made getting down to the road, but it couldn't be helped. At least none of them broke an ankle. He looked up and down the road and saw no one. The women were in poor shape for a walk, let alone running from men searching for them. Roger wanted to go back and look for the old farmer, but he couldn't leave the newly freed captives.

Back up the embankment, Walter slipped into the trees, and years faded as old hunting instincts returned from time spent in another forest where death waited around every tree or rock. Dog padded beside him, and he worried that the shepherd would give him away, but the animal waited for him to lead. A branch snapped in the stillness followed by a whisper somewhere off to the left. Someone found the hole in the fence, he thought, and he brought his attention back to the area in front of him. He waited with one hand on Dog, knowing any quick movement at the wrong time could get him dead. The shepherd tensed but didn't move.

There, just beyond the bushes in front of him, were two armed men, dressed in black and angling toward him. He slid his knife from his belt sheath. He needed to act quietly to avoid bringing anyone else. Just as the two armed mercenaries stalked beside them, he loosed the shepherd and sprang forward.

Down by the road, Roger tried to decide what to do. He thought he heard something back up the hill but wasn't sure. A few minutes later, a small bit of dirt dislodged higher up the embankment, and Dog came bounding down to join them. Walter followed carefully, holding a second rifle.

"Well?" asked Roger.

Walter looked up and down the two-lane road.

"We're clear for the moment," he said without elaborating and handed the spare rifle to the sheriff.

"Any update on Mark and the girls?" asked Roger.

Martha said, "I think I hear something."

A large passenger van topped the crest of the road to their left and slowly approached.

CHAPTER TWENTY-FIVE

Cardinal Ronaldo Ricci arrived at the papal apartments to find barely controlled chaos surrounding his friend, Anastasi, who reclined on his bed in the simple room where he insisted on sleeping. His Holiness felt the grandeur of the papal apartments to be ostentatious and not conducive to an ongoing search for wisdom, one of the many reasons Pope Anastasi was so beloved around the world.

Clutching his chest and and looking weaker by the moment, the pontiff whispered.

"Thank you for attending me."

Ronaldo knelt beside the bed and kissed the Ring of Peter Incarnate. After a moment, he stood respectfully.

Gathering himself, Anastasi said, "I am at my journey's end."

Murmured protests sounded from his secretary and the senior cardinals standing along the walls. None of them wanted to hear the pontiff say such things.

"We all walk the same path, Your Holiness," said Ronaldo. "I would pray with you."

Holding the pontiff's hand, he recited the Lord's Prayer together with Anastasi.

Cardinal Ronaldo Ricci tried to center himself in the two-thousand-year-old prayer, taught directly to the Church by Christ, but the world was literally shifting under his feet. At any moment, he felt he might spin away into space, and in his imagination, he forced out a last frozen breath in the blackness as he witnessed the end. It was all too much.

The pontiff released Ronaldo's hand and pressed himself up in bed to address all in the room.

"This is a moment in time that can suffer no loss of leadership for our Church," said Anastasi, and he paused to take a deep breath. "I am given to know that the world needs the truth now more than ever, just as the Church needs a leader."

Collapsing back on the bed, Anastasi breathed deeply from the oxygen mask provided by his medical team.

"You are that leader, Your Holiness," said Ronaldo.

Anastasi peered at him with kind eyes.

"You still haven't figured out why I sent for you, have you?" asked the pontiff.

Cardinal Ronaldo Ricci shook his head, and there was silence from the senior cardinals arrayed behind and around him.

Pope Luke Genoa Anastasi, the leader of the Roman Catholic Church, grasped Ronaldo's hand with his remaining strength.

"I am entrusting His Church to you," he said. "For the first time in more than a thousand years and in this hour of great upheaval, I appoint you as my successor. Do not fail in this, Ronaldo, for you alone know what is at stake."

Anastasi tried to hold on but sank against his pillow and drew a last shuddering breath. His hand dropped to the bed, and he was gone.

Ronaldo looked around the room at the leadership of the Church, and all eyes were on him as he tried to comprehend what had just happened.

Cardinal Benaldi, previously most favored as a successor, walked over and knelt before him.

Placing his hands on Ronaldo's forearms, he said, "His Holiness was very clear to us about this. He trusted in God's plan for His Church, and he trusted in you. You are his chosen successor, and the conclave are all in agreement. May God watch over you and His Church."

Cardinal Ronaldo Ricci blinked at the faces in the room looking to him for leadership and inspiration, and he fully understood Anastasi's efforts to remain humble. Ronaldo took a breath and tried to think of what to do next. He held his hands out to those present.

"Brothers in Christ," said Ronaldo. "We are at a moment when evil stands at the door, and we must help in every way possible to defeat the fallen. We must stand together and we are never stronger than when we kneel. I invite all of you to pray with me."

Ronaldo sank slowly to his knees, hands clasped together at the bedside of his still friend.

"Father in Heaven, receive the soul of your elect, Pope Luke Anastasi. He lived your word and taught by example that a man is often humbled by his own sureness of action, but a wise man considers all and invokes your guidance. Please grant us wisdom and guide us in the struggle we find before us, and forgive us, Father, for our errors and misdeeds. Save us from the terrible fate which hangs over us, but ever in your love for us, your will be done. Amen."

He stood slowly while the preferiti and senior leadership laid hands on him and each other in a unity harkening back to the early Church.

Outside the windows, an unnatural darkness loomed, while overhead, the dark mass of Apollyon pushed aside stars with unbearable and suffocating gravity. The leaden air swelled with abrupt endings and unreached beginnings and what could have been but never would be.

And in that room, a group of imperfect men prayed incomplete prayers for guidance and deliverance while Ronaldo added a silent prayer for his old friend in America and a child at the center of the storm.

❖

The dark gray Mercedes van slowed to a stop to avoid hitting Roger, who had walked to the center of the road and waved his arms. Walter and the women stepped onto the road, and Martha held the youngest, who looked like she would collapse at any moment. Several of them looked up as the helicopter roared overhead and flew directly toward town.

Felicity rolled down the driver's window.

"I need to get these people to care," said Roger after introducing himself with a short explanation.

Felicity motioned for them to come around to the van's passenger side. The door slid back, and one-by-one, they squeezed into the van.

Father Romero introduced himself and asked if any of them knew where Mark Lawson lived, and several people started talking at once.

"Did you say that someone abducted these women?" asked Paul.

Martin continued to video record while Walter relayed what he witnessed at the Bradley brothers' farm.

Dog wound his way to sit beside Father Romero and laid his head on the priest's knee.

"So, you believe they are still out there and trying to make it back home," said Paul.

It grew quiet in the van for a moment.

"We have to find them," said Father Romero.

Felicity gripped the wheel of the van with white knuckles and pursed her mouth in a thin line, and in the rearview mirror, she saw the woman next to the sheriff lean over to whisper in his ear.

"Yes, of course," said Roger. "Martha says we need to prioritize medical attention for these women, and she's right. We can check for Mark at his place on the way."

The sheriff tried to call over the radio to his office again without success, and Martha laid her head on Roger's shoulder and held his hand.

Dog barked once and whined, and Felicity made a three-point turn. She drove carefully, wary of sinkholes and breaks in the pavement.

Ahead of them, a line of black SUVs pulled out of the farm's gated entrance and turned toward town. Looking to their left, all inside the van could see a column of black over the trees marking what was left of Twin Oaks Farm.

After a couple of miles, Felicity followed Sheriff Murphy's instructions and slowed to make the turn for the driveway to Mark's farm.

Three hundred meters ahead, two black SUVs had parked across the road in a hurried roadblock, and several armed men milled about the vehicles.

Walter gestured and said, "Looks like they're waiting for any stragglers."

"Doesn't change our plan yet," said the sheriff. "We still need to check for Mark and the girls." Roger leaned forward and pointed ahead to the left. "Turn in here."

Walter jumped out to open the gate, and Felicity pulled up Mark's driveway and parked in front of the farmhouse. Dog shot out of the van and ran completely around the house before following Walter, who walked up the porch steps and opened the front door.

Mark could see tree tops swirling about. Where was he? He remembered running and the ground shaking, and then, he remembered the girls. What was he was doing on the ground?

He stood while bracing his hands on his legs and looked around to see brush and trees, but no Maria or Sofia. He hurt between his shoulder blades, and his weapons were gone. He bent over and dry-heaved twice. The nausea eased, and Mark slowly straightened back up to look into the dark eyes of a solemn man aiming a suppressed pistol directly at him.

Mark realized he was about to die and pictured Sofia's lopsided grin and hug. He thought of Maria's shy smile and searching eyes and ached for her. God help him, he didn't care if she was almost a nun. He hoped God and Maddie would forgive him.

The man lowered the pistol three centimeters and spoke.

"You are a man of honor," he said. "If I ask you to be still and hear me out, will you?"

Mark nodded, not sure what else he could do.

"I am Tomás," said the man. "I am sent to kill you."

Mark said nothing.

"You will have trouble remembering all that happened because I gave you some medicine, but I took the girl and the woman to my patron," said Tomás. "He lied to me that the girl would be unharmed. I know better now."

"Who is your patron?" asked Mark.

Tomás told him, and Mark stumbled back a step. Giulanti?

"He said his son is ill unto death," said the bronzed terminator.

"I don't understand," said Mark.

"Somehow, he means for the girl to save his son," said Tomás.

Mark considered the man's words. Why was Tomás telling him this, and could he possibly trust the man? If what he said was true, Sofia's time was limited.

Tomás lowered his suppressed pistol to the ready position and waited for Mark to respond. A gust of wind swirled charred scrap along the ground chasing dark tendrils of smoke stinking of burnt leather.

Mark pushed any thoughts of Giulanti aside. He could only think of the girls.

"Where are they?" he asked.

"The left in his helicopter a short time ago," said Tomás. "I am certain that he intends harm to both."

"What are you saying?" asked Mark.

Tomás holstered his pistol.

"I know where he took them," said the assassin.

❖

News spread around the world via computer, radio, and television. Nations on the brink of atomic warfare paused at the threat of imminent destruction by an unexpected force of nature. There would be time enough for long-nurtured hatreds if they survived the coming apocalypse.

The president paced in heels and tailored business apparel under the covered walkway behind the White House. She was accompanied by General Porter Harrell, a two-star sent over by Admiral Boatwright from the Pentagon to attend the president.

"Madam President, your message seems to have been effective for the moment," said the general, walking with her to the Sikorsky Sea King helicopter which would ferry her to project Ararat. "However, there is unrest in every state as people try to prepare for the worst."

"That was expected, General," said the president. "No sane person would sit by and do nothing with his family endangered. Direct our military and homeland security forces to prevent violent crime. People may obtain their supplies peaceably, but I will not tolerate violent looting. That is why I have nationalized the various state guards and tasked our military to keep order."

President Thomlinson knew the general knew this, but she needed to reinforce her wishes.

"What about the broadcast?" asked General Harrell.

The general referred to the follow-up address to the nation that her staff wanted her to make tonight to quell the rising panic. If only someone could alleviate mine, she thought.

"I will address the nation from Ararat," she said. "It will look as if I'm still at the White House." Which is why I'm leaving like this, she thought. "I need to hear from you that our governors and the military are backing us," she said. "We have to maintain order in this crisis."

General Harrell nodded and saluted, and the president turned and walked up the steps to the helicopter, which became Marine One the moment she stepped into it.

The general turned and walked back across the damp grass until he was under the covered portico in the back of the White House. They needed to keep the president safe and her movements undisclosed for the moment.

The Russian and the Chinese governments had agreed to a stand down considering the revelation of Apollyon. The media had repeated the name over and over as soon as the news came to light. There were still some sources publicly quoting a strong chance for impact, but the administration had consistently trumpeted the close fly-by story in the media along with continually scrubbing any impact conclusions from the Internet. So far, the official version of a near miss was generally accepted, probably out of hope, he thought.

If the information the scientists passed along was accurate, tomorrow morning's dawn would really scare the world with a good part of the Sun's face blocked out by the rapidly approaching planet. By late tomorrow afternoon, the eclipse would be nearly total, leaving one last day in near darkness until the end of the world.

Harrell remembered his first days in the military, incessant running, little to no sleep, and constant stress from the drill instructors followed by his baptism of fire in the Gulf War, and later, his steady advancement in the military after his decision to stay in as a career.

He had planned on remaining single during his deployments, feeling it unfair to leave a wife behind, but then he met Beverly. The first time he saw her, she stood behind the jewelry counter at the post exchange and outshone any of the shiny items in the case. Her smooth skin, bright teeth, and the curve of her neck to shoulder entranced him, and he kept turning to look for her.

In his memory, he counted approaching her at that counter more fearful than any firefight he had experienced, and she had smiled at his panic as he stood before her. Her voice made him think of candlelight and soft jazz, and somehow, she agreed to meet him the next day at a local eatery for lunch. He still remembered it as the best meal of his life, not for the food, but because she was there with him.

So much time had passed, and he still had eyes only for her. She had suffered in his absence through the years during their marriage. He did not consider himself a wonderful husband because of his work constraints, but he loved that woman. He had his responsibilities, but perhaps tonight he should take the time to tell her, and he decided that was exactly what he would do.

CHAPTER TWENTY-SIX

Walter returned to the living room with a pitcher of water and plastic cups for the newly freed captives. Three of them took the offered water, but the youngest remained focused at something unseen on the wall. She hadn't moved since sitting in a chair except for blinking now and then. Dog kept his head on her lap and looked at her with worried blue eyes.

Martin manipulated his video action camera and replaced a battery and memory card.

Father Romero paced back and forth and looked out the window again and said, "From what you have told me, they should have been here by now."

Roger nodded. He had the same thoughts.

Felicity walked over to the youngest woman, knelt down beside her, and gathered her hair back into a ponytail using a rubber band. The young woman reached out hesitantly to pet Dog, who pushed his head into her hand.

"It's okay now," said Felicity. "You're free of them. Know that it's behind you."

Paul watched Felicity, thinking of the years she had been with him.

He didn't know why he had never told her how important she was to him, and he started across the room.

Dog raised his ears and padded to the window. Roger and Walter gripped their rifles as two black SUVs pulled up the gravel driveway and stopped away from the Mercedes Sprinter van.

Six determined men emerged from the vehicles and advanced on the house, rifles in hand.

"Father Romero, please take the girls into the basement," said Walter, bringing his rifle to ready position.

Father Romero, Felicity, and Paul ushered the women out of sight, but Martin continued video recording and would not budge.

The men in the yard readied their rifles, and one of them shouted.

"Come out of the house, and you won't be harmed!"

Roger called out from inside the house.

"This is the sheriff. You men lay down those rifles."

The men shouldered their rifles and began firing. Automatic weapons fire burst through the walls of the house showering splinters about the room, and Roger and Walter dropped to the floor below window level to avoid being hit. Roger chanced a peek through the front window and saw two of the men moving to either side of the house in a flanking maneuver. A moment more, and they would be surrounded. Roger looked back toward the kitchen. That maniac, Martin, was still recording from his position on the floor.

"Walter, can you scoot to cover the rear of the house?" asked the sheriff. "They're going to come at us from the front and back."

Walter nodded and started crawling to the hallway, spry for a seventy-year-old man.

One of the men out front said, "No witnesses. Boss wants it level when we leave."

The remaining assailants switched out magazines in a disciplined manner.

Roger raised up and fired at the attackers, and one stumbled back and down, but the others resumed firing, and the sheriff fell back to the floor with searing pain in his left shoulder. He reached up with his right hand only to see it covered in blood.

The sheriff looked around for something to staunch the bleeding and felt a hand at his back. It was Martha. She had come up from the basement and crawled through tattered drywall and broken glass to find his side. She wrapped his bleeding shoulder in gauze from Mark's first aid supplies in the basement.

Martha looked into Roger's eyes.

"I've been waiting for you to make up your mind," she said. "I don't want to leave this world without telling you that I love you."

Tears glistened in her eyes in the pale light through the broken windows, and she leaned in and kissed him full on the mouth.

"Now kick their asses," she said and began crawling back to the hallway to give him room.

Roger barely had time to think about her words before he heard shots to the front and back of the house. He looked out the window and saw the attackers in front down on the ground. The shooting had stopped.

"Walter, are you all right?" he asked as loudly as he dared.

"Yeah, somebody shot the two back here just as they were getting ready to bust in," replied the old farmer. "You?"

"Same," said Roger. "Stay under cover until we understand what's happening."

Dog padded from the basement into the kitchen and canted his head and whined.

Roger saw a fit man cradling a scoped rifle emerge from the trees at the edge of the front yard. The man held up one hand to show he was not a threat. At the same time, Roger heard Walter exclaim from the kitchen.

"It's Mark!" said the farmer.

Roger slowly stood up, surprised at the effort it took, and he noted that Martin was still alive. The back door opened, and Mark stepped into the house holding a rifle at the ready.

The man at the front of the house didn't advance closer but waited with one hand up to show he wasn't planning on using his rifle.

"Mark, I'm glad to see you," said Roger, supporting his left arm. "Who's your friend?"

Roger jerked his thumb toward the man out front behind the downed attackers.

"He was sent for me," Mark replied and shrugged his shoulders. "I'll tell you on the way to the hospital."

Walter walked in behind Mark and called down to the basement for the others to come up.

Roger said, "We were planning on heading to the hospital with the women after we checked to see if you were here, but we saw those men at the roadblock. Where are Maria and Sofia?"

Mark walked to the front door, opened it, and motioned for Tomás to come closer.

"There's no more roadblock," said Mark.

He didn't elaborate, and Tomás stood in the front yard without speaking.

"They took Maria and Sofia to the hospital in town," said Mark. "I'll fill you in, but we have to move. There isn't much time."

Mark walked through the gathering group in his living room, but stopped short when he saw Father Romero.

"Father, what are you doing here?" he asked.

The priest answered, "I came to protect Sofia."

Mark nodded and couldn't argue with his pastor, at least from his standpoint. They helped the women out to the van, and Felicity took the wheel. Roger talked to each of them, and Martha assisted.

Off to the side, Tomás talked with Father Romero, just the two of them, and he bowed to the waist in front of the priest. After several seconds, Father Romero said something and placed a hand on Tomás' shoulder, and the serious dark-haired man straightened upright.

"What is that all about?" asked Walter, watching the bronzed stranger. "Do you trust him?"

Mark knew the old farmer referred to Tomás.

Mark shrugged as Roger walked over to face the two of them, his left shoulder in a makeshift sling.

"It's complicated, but I think Tomás is on our side," he said. "Donovan Giulanti took Maria and Sofia, and Tomás says Giulanti plans to use Sofia to save his son."

Roger said, "I can't let my deputies go after her alone."

"What about the rest of the county?" asked Mark. "And you're still bleeding. You need to get your shoulder evaluated, and that won't wait."

"Yeah, there is that," said Roger, wincing. "I know there has to be all hell breaking loose after that earthquake. I'm sure people are hurt, maybe dead all over the county, but I know for sure that little girl is kidnapped. If I let you go on your own, you'll get yourself killed, and Sofia won't make it. I can't live with that on my conscience. I'm sorry, by the way."

Mark said, "What do you mean?"

"You loved your family," said Roger. "I should have believed you."

Roger's voice wavered.

Mark swallowed. He knew how hard that was for the sheriff to say.

He nodded and said, "Thanks."

Roger said, "So promise me you are going to rescue Sofia and Maria and not to kill Donovan Giulanti, right?"

"Right," said Mark. "I'm not coming back without them."

❖

The helicopter settled onto the aeromedical landing pad at Aldona County Hospital without difficulty. Vehicle alarms blared in the distance while smoke arose from the county seat of Anders in multiple directions. The light from the interior of the hospital was the only visible illumination in the area thanks to the industrial generator that Donovan had supplied little more than thirty minutes ago. The hospital administrator had not questioned his good fortune.

Maria saw two automobiles stacked on top of each other and strad-dling buckled asphalt in one section of the parking lot. A once majestic elm tree had toppled, exposing its root base for all to see, and in the thickening light, she saw several serpentine cracks running between bricks in the exterior building walls leading to shattered windows.

Maria kept her arm around Sofia, who clung to her, while the two gunmen from the helicopter pulled on long, black coats to hide their slung weapons. Donovan nodded, and both of them fell in behind to escort Maria and Sofia.

"Why are you doing this?" she asked.

Donovan didn't reply and hurried toward the nearest hospital entrance, paying no mind to the traumatized visitors and patients making their way in and out of the building. Maria held Sofia's hand and desperately looked for any chance to break away.

Entering adjacent to the emergency department, they proceeded to a stairway, and Donovan led the way up two flights of stairs. Exiting the stairwell on the second floor, Maria saw more of Donovan's dark-clad men guarding the hallway.

"No one else gets up here," said Donovan.

They nodded to their boss, and Donovan whispered further instructions. All of them straightened to attention and looked about like their lives depended on it.

Donovan turned and walked toward double opaque glass doors labeled Surgery Preparation and Recovery. The doors slid open, and the guards herded them down a long hallway and forced Maria into a room while Sofia held to her. The two escorting guards stepped aside.

"What do you want from us?" asked Maria again.

She recoiled when Donovan faced her. In the artificial light from the overhead fluorescent lamps, the big man's eyes and mouth loomed like dark craters on a barren and lifeless moon.

"You are part of this now," said Donovan. "My son is ill."

"I will pray for your son, but how does that involve us?" asked Maria.

She pulled Sofia closer if that was possible.

"My son needs what she has," said Donovan, looking at Sofia. He considered Maria again and gestured with his hand slightly. "You are just in the way."

Donovan left as two attendants and a nurse filed into the preparation room. The nurse held a tray covered with a blue surgical towel, and Maria had only a moment to realize what they intended before muscular hands gripped her from either side. She tried to cling to

Sofia, but the guards held them separate no matter how hard she struggled.

"I need to stay with her!" yelled Maria.

No one in the room answered, and Maria fought and struggled to no avail while Sofia looked at her with tearful eyes and soundless cries.

The guards dragged Maria kicking and struggling from the room. She looked over her shoulder before the door closed and saw Sofia pulling away from the attendants while the nurse held a syringe up to double-check the dose.

❖

Samuel Branchwater realized he had stepped in something when men in dark suits raided his family's home in the middle of the night. Citing national security concerns, they took him into custody without a warrant. He was a dangerous high schooler who dared to report his conclusions.

Samuel didn't have a chance to warn Beth. She had patiently stayed by his side Sunday and Monday helping him collect data. Using a technique from an article in a scientific journal, he had measured the distance to the Moon with his digital camera, a tripod, and his smartphone. Making the measurements had meant spending more time with Beth and shown him that the greatest truth was sometimes right in front of you.

Using a fairly simple equation gave him an answer, which he compared to published tables. By his calculations, the Moon had moved approximately sixteen feet in one night, and that was physically impossible without a major gravimetric distortion. He discovered a couple of fragments on the Internet regarding tides and moon position displacement before they were scrubbed, which reinforced his concerns about a possible connection with the strike on Jupiter.

He had cobbled together a brief paper explaining his methods and observations and posted it to ten of the most popular amateur astronomy sites and two respected magazines. He also sent his work to several government space agencies via their published contact email addresses.

Later that night in the early morning hours brought the raid and his detainment and interrogation. How did he know the information in his paper? With whom had he shared his assumptions? What did he think it meant? He had asked for a lawyer but was taken away without any response. His own government treated him and his family like terrorists. They even knew about Beth and threatened to bring her in if he didn't cooperate. Samuel had grown up as a Native American living on a reservation, but he had never really felt like a second-class citizen until that moment.

He had answered their questions truthfully and asked them to read his paper. His conclusions were obvious and explained by his methods. His suffering at the hands of the authorities told him they were afraid, not the ones taking him into custody, but the people questioning him, and when he asked why, each of his interrogators averted his or her eyes and remained silent.

The only reasonable moment of the entire ordeal had been meeting Professor Barry Michaels, who had walked into the interrogation room and sat across from Samuel and smiled sadly.

"I'm sorry you were dragged into this," said the president's science advisor. "I read your paper," he said. "You put that together in something over twenty-four hours, correct?"

Samuel nodded, and Professor Michaels asked another question.

"I understand that you are about to finish high school?"

Samuel nodded again in reply.

Professor Michaels' smile didn't reach his eyes as he sat back in his chair, and Samuel's ribs felt like ice cubes stuck in a tray, freezing his breath to his sternum and holding back the question he didn't want to ask. Wrapping his arms around his torso, he squeezed the air from his lungs past his vocal cords until he heard his voice squeak.

"Sir," said Samuel. "How long until the rogue planet hits us?"

Professor Michaels hesitated and then placed his hands on his thighs and stood.

"Samuel, if we survive this event, would you consider coming to work on my team?"

The professor left contact information before exiting the holding room, and afterwards, the authorities let Samuel go with the condition of his continued silence.

He arrived back home just in time for the president's follow-up address and listened with disbelief. All the news channels touted a close pass of the rogue planet with almost no impact conclusions, and his gut burned behind clenched teeth. He possessed some experience with the government misinformation machine now, and the silence regarding a collision spoke volumes. The authorities had taken his computer, but he had researched the Internet heavily for his paper. He hoped he was wrong, but the response from Professor Michaels had only heightened his suspicion.

Samuel knew that an interaction with a strong gravitational body could alter Earth's orbit and displace continents. At the very least, it would cause devastating seismic and volcanic activity, and then he thought of Yellowstone. There had been reports of increased tremor activity since the West Coast earthquake. What if the underlying Yellowstone supervolcano suffered a major eruption?

His family didn't understand his passion, and didn't take him seriously. Beth's family only knew him as another resident of the reservation and someone in whom their daughter was interested. Now that he had been taken as a suspect of the federal government, they wanted nothing to do with him, and he had not been able to speak with Beth since coming back home.

A major eruption from Yellowstone would create an ash cloud across most of the United States and would be feet thick in the Wind River Area. They might not survive here with a close pass, and moving east or north would not work considering the prevailing winds. The Pacific Northwest, could be okay, but Mount Ranier might erupt, and it would likely get cold and stay cold. No, they needed to go south, but with so little elevation, Florida was at high risk from ocean changes, so maybe Texas or Arizona or New Mexico.

Samuel considered all this while knowing he needed to do something. The president's most recent address, while likely not the complete truth, quoted forty-eight hours, and that was probably correct. His own family wouldn't listen to him, but he had to put out some kind of warning. The federal agents confiscated his computer at his arrest, but Beth's family still had one, or he could stop somewhere on the road to put a warning out. He hoped Beth would listen to him. He had to convince her regardless of her family. He loved her.

CHAPTER TWENTY-SEVEN

Felicity turned on the van's radio, and through intermittent static, they listened to President Thomlinson address the country for the second time in the same day. The president stressed sheltering at home in preparation as the rogue planet called Apollyon passed near Earth on its return approach from the Sun. She urged all citizens to remain calm, and the president deferred further questions via remote link to her science advisor, Professor Barry Michaels.

Mark listened to the professor on the radio and sensed there was more than what was being said. When asked repeatedly if the rogue planet was going to hit the Earth, the president's science advisor answered the question very carefully, and Mark intuited a terrifying answer.

He thinks it's going to hit us.

Mark knew he was right. He looked around, and Father Romero looked at him like he knew what he was thinking and nodded in agreement.

Felicity slowed to pull into the Aldona County Hospital parking lot. Two outdoor light poles had fallen across a group of parked vehicles, and several automobiles had crashed on top of each other like die-cast toys.

In one corner, emergency staff attended an injury, and minute-by-minute more walking wounded from the surrounding streets filed into the hospital parking lot hoping for treatment.

"You think he brought her here?" asked Paul.

Martin echoed the question without lowering his motion action camera.

Paul swept his hand to encompass the developing chaos in the earthquake's aftermath. Even as he spoke, the van shook from a short jarring aftershock, and a vintage Ford Mustang slid off the mangled hood of a four-door sedan and crashed to the pavement.

Felicity drove around to the back side of the hospital, and a burnished helicopter squatted on the heliport.

"Yes, I think she's here," said Mark. "I'm going for them, but they are probably guarded."

At that moment, two dark-coated men emerged from the nearest entrance and scanned the parking lot before eyeing each person streaming in and out of the hospital.

"I can try to reach more help from inside, but I'm guessing their communications are no better," said Roger trying not to move his bandaged shoulder and arm in the makeshift sling that Martha had fashioned for him at the house. It was obvious he was in pain, and he looked pale. "Anyway, I need to get these ladies in for evaluation."

The sheriff was right that he needed to check in with the town leadership, and they certainly needed more help, but Mark wasn't sure how much longer Roger could stay on his feet.

"I don't think I can wait," said Mark while concealing a pistol.

Dog whined once.

"You can't come with us," he said, looking at the shepherd. "Animals aren't allowed in the hospital, and you would draw too much attention. I need you to stay in the van."

Dog looked at Mark for a moment like he would argue, but the shepherd ducked his head on his paws and snorted.

"I am coming with you," said Father Romero. "I may be able to talk some sense into Donovan."

Walter tucked his revolver under his shirt and said, "I'll help the sheriff and the women. Give me a moment."

Father Romero and Walter both looked determined. Mark didn't have time to argue as he stepped outside the van.

"If they see me, there may be an alarm," said Tomás. "I will find my own way inside." He held a cloth to his forehead and face and fell in behind a group of people heading for the hospital entrance.

Mark asked Felicity if she would wait for them.

"If we find the two of them, we may need a quick way out of here," he said.

She nodded from behind the driver's wheel.

Paul grabbed a spare camera from Martin and climbed out of the van to follow.

"What do you think you are doing?" asked Felicity.

Paul saw the concern on her face.

"This is why we are here," said Paul. "This is important, and whatever is happening in that hospital right now needs to be shared." Paul leaned over and kissed Felicity for a long few seconds, surprising her. "I'm coming back for you."

He left the van, and Felicity stayed at the wheel, her eyes tracking his every step.

The group trudged toward the emergency department entrance without Tomás, who had vanished. Mark helped support Roger while Walter faked a limp as he escorted the women. Paul hid his camera from view, and Father Romero helped support the youngest woman.

The group had nearly reached the entrance when Roger sagged and almost fell as Mark lowered him to the ground. The sheriff had passed out. Walter yelled for help, and nurses and assistants came with a wheeled stretcher.

The emergency department had filled with wounded and ill patients waiting to evacuate, and a cacophony of words, moans, cries, beeps, and ringing alarms met the group punctuated by an occasional shudder as the building wavered but decided to continue standing. Staff moved from one crisis to the next while attempting to care for the influx of patients, but there were clearly not enough hospital personnel for so many in need.

The nursing staff rushed the sheriff back for treatment immediately. Father Romero had a word with the triage nurse, and one of the nurses assisted the youngest woman back to an examination room. Martha clearly wanted to go back with Roger, but she stayed to assist the other two women until they could be evaluated.

"Well, look at that," said Walter, tapping Mark on the shoulder and pointing his thumb toward the hallway without being obvious.

A hard-looking man wearing a black coat had emerged from a stairwell door. Mark checked a directory map on the waiting room wall and hoped he was wrong.

"I want to take a look upstairs, starting with surgery," said Mark, looking at Walter. "Someone needs to watch over Martha and the girls and keep an eye on our exit."

Walter nodded and said, "Okay, go and find them."

"I will go with you," said Father Romero.

Mark and Father Romero separated from the group and made their way to the stairwell in the confusion. Paul hesitated but quickly caught up to them.

The group wound their way up two long flights of metal stairs to the second floor. The air in the stairwell felt stale and damp, and Mark tried not to think of the weight of the building over their heads as they arrived at the second floor landing. Peeking out the door, he saw two men in long black coats standing in front of sliding glass doors at one end of the hallway. Everything about them screamed security.

"I think we are in the right place," he whispered

Mark tried to think how to get past the guards and noticed that the door across the hall from the stairwell was labeled as a physician locker room. A group of anxious people hurried down the hall to the surgery annex and were held up by the dark-suited guards, who told them that no visitors were allowed because of the emergency.

"What do you mean?" asked one of the family members through clenched teeth. "You have no right to keep us from our father. Do you even know what's happening?"

While the guards dealt with the angry family, Mark led the way to the physician's locker room across the hall. He and Paul donned scrub gowns over their clothes, but Father Romero felt he should remain in his black shirt and pants. The locker room led to a main hallway, allowing them to bypass the men guarding the surgery wing entrance and the irate family.

They stayed near the wall and cautiously took a few steps in the hallway past an employee freight elevator until they arrived at the first corner. Tomás appeared in front of them while Mark was deciding which way to go.

"She is here," said Tomás. "We must hurry."

Mark didn't know what to think.

"How'd you get up here?" he asked.

"I fear his intent," said Tomás, bypassing the question. "Donovan is determined to help his ill son, and the holy woman knows too much."

Tomás eased his way to the hall corner, peeked beyond, and moved his head back, so he was not visible.

"There are two guards in the hallway ahead," he said, and he looked at Father Romero.

"I am sorry for my sins, Priest," said Tomás. "Those in my past and those I am about to incur. Please pray for me."

With that, he bounded around the corner in one smooth motion like a jungle cat and fired twice with the suppressed pistol outstretched in both hands. The group followed him, and Father Romero paused and uttered a brief prayer over the guards' bodies while Paul recorded with shaking hands.

"There will be others before this is over," whispered Tomás to Mark. "He means to use her, and he wants you dead. I know that Donovan tried to have you killed once before because you were investigating him. I say this to you now in atonement in case I do not survive."

Tomás looked at Father Romero.

"Priest, you are my witness."

Pushing down the hallway toward the pre-op staging area, Tomás led the group while Mark struggled with this additional information. What the assassin said confirmed Donovan Giulanti as the man responsible for the accident that took his family.

Mark paused as an avalanche of remorse and violent thoughts overwhelmed his focus. Father Romero gripped his arm, and Mark shook his head to clear his mind. Somewhere ahead in these rooms, a little girl and the woman he cared for depended on him.

❖

Sofia woke from her drug-induced sleep. Where was this place? Her head hurt, and she felt confused and small like a mouse considering whether to emerge from her hiding place. She remembered running through the trees with Maria and Mark to get away from the evil men. One of them had tried to hurt Maria. She remembered the helicopter ride and holding Maria in fear as the bad men brought her here and took Maria away.

Sofia squiggled on the narrow bed with its thin mattress. There were rails on either side, but she climbed over the bars and touched the cold floor. She peeked out of the room. The hallway was empty and looked familiar. She had visited hospitals before. She had to stop and press her hand to the green-tiled wall for a moment until a wave of wooziness passed, and she slowly crept up the hall, feeling tiny imperfections in the vinyl flooring beneath her feet. Someone laughed at the end of the hallway ahead of her.

Sofia peeked around the corner and saw a desk in an alcove in the wall occupied by two women, who were wearing green surgical gowns with masks hanging around their necks. Farther down the hall, there was a glass walled room with the curtains partially drawn where a boy was hooked to tubes and machines. He looked exhausted and pale, and her heart went out to him. She felt certain he was scared and didn't want to be here just like her.

Sofia crept in a low crouch past the nursing station, and the two women didn't see her. She pressed against the wall, staying low. She wanted out of this place, but she couldn't just ignore the boy. Maybe he wanted to go with her? She had to ask and crept into his room. Sofia made certain that she was not in sight of the ladies at the desk and stood slowly. She was tall enough to see the boy, who looked asleep.

Sofia tried to speak to him, but like before, she could think the words, but they wouldn't come out.

The boy's eyelashes fluttered, and he opened his eyes and looked at her.

"Hello," he said. The word wheezed past his lips.

Sofia smiled and pointed to him and the monitors and back to herself. She scrunched her face to show that she was afraid too.

The boy swallowed.

"Yes, I'm afraid," he said and gasped for breath.

Sofia wanted him to sit up and climb down from his bed, so they could sneak out of here. She pointed to herself and him and moved her fingers like they were walking.

"Yes, I think I'll be going soon."

The boy said this in a small voice like he was standing beside a train on a track about to head somewhere far away.

Sofia understood what he meant because she had seen the messengers hovering about the boy, shimmering in silence. She knew most people couldn't see them and doubted this boy could either. She knew she needed to flee, but her heart went out to him, and she tried to think of what was right. She reached out and touched his arm and prayed for him, and she saw the messengers do the same.

The boy's eyes widened as he looked about the room, his mouth open.

"Are those angels?," he asked

Sofia smiled at him, happy that he could see them too.

Mesmerized, the boy stared at one messenger, who gazed at him with a kind face.

"How do you know about my uncle and my sister?" he asked with effort.

The messenger open her hands in a welcoming gesture, and Sofia thought she glimpsed others behind the celestial guardian, but it was difficult to tell from her position. She didn't know what the messenger said, but the boy seemed to relax and sink back into his bed as a tear rolled down his face.

The boy smiled and reached over to touch Sofia's cheek with trembling fingers.

"Thank you," said the boy. "You need to run away."

Sofia wavered.

"Please go," he pleaded. He took deep breaths from his oxygen and said, "You are in danger."

Sofia nodded and stepped away from his bedside, her eyes still on him. One of the messengers ushered her toward the doorway, and she slipped out of the room. The ladies at the desk were talking with their backs to her, and Sofia made for the end of the hallway, hoping she could find her way to the outside and help. She heard steps coming toward her from the left and searched for a place to hide.

Sofia looked up and froze in place at sight of the tall, bitter-faced man from the bad farm. Terrence Bradley seized her like a mamba striking a bush baby, and she struggled in his grip.

Donovan Giulanti walked around the corner accompanied by a raven-haired, teary-eyed woman who looked at Sofia in surprise. The woman paused for a moment, then stepped around and walked down the hall and entered the boy's room.

Giulanti's bottomless eyes inspected Sofia under the ceiling lights, and her nose twitched at the odor of burnt clay.

"What is this?" he asked.

"Just taking her back to her room, Mr. Giulanti."

Terrence Bradley gripped her, and Sofia felt the tremor in his voice spread to his hands.

"You do that," said Donovan Giulanti. "Make sure she doesn't get away, and then I need you to do something else for me."

Donovan gestured at the door across the hall and leaned in to say something quietly to Terrence Bradley. He liked to give orders, but Sofia saw no messengers following him. Donovan walked into the boy's room and sat down.

Terrence escorted Sofia back up the corridor past the nurse's station where the women in the emerald surgical gowns had stopped talking and quietly looked on. He pushed Sofia ahead and back into the room from which she had escaped. He lifted her up on the bed and walked out of the room and stood by the door. He stayed outside the doorway in the hall until the nurses came into the room and changed her into a paper gown. They laid her down and strapped her hands and ankles to the stretcher. The nurses said little and didn't smile.

Sofia was afraid. Whatever they wanted with her couldn't be good, and she asked Our Mother to pray for her to heavenly Father. She had been trapped in her own body for so long, and nothing had ever been as wonderful as the last few days of freedom. She hadn't tried her best yet, but she thought she might be able to run really fast and prayed for that chance.

Please God, she thought, please make me fast. Please let Mark and Maria find me. I'm so scared.

Her heart pounded in her chest as she prayed in silence.

Please tell me what I'm supposed to do.

CHAPTER TWENTY-EIGHT

Maria paced eight steps to the wall of the small storage room, turned, and walked back to the door looking for a way out. The men who dragged her to this room had ignored her protests and thrown her inside like refuse. The shelving attached to the wall had not tipped over in the earthquake, but the windowless room offered no exit other than the locked door. She tried the door again for the hundredth time and wept in frustration. That man, Donovan Giulanti, had said his son was ill. What could he want from Sofia?

One small ray of light from the remaining unbroken light fixture on the ceiling barely lit the storage room. She needed to find a way out, but no one else knew they were here. If Mark were alive, he would come for Sofia, she thought, and wished desperately that it was so, but she had heard Donovan Giulanti order Tomás to kill Mark, and she knew that slayer of men would do just that.

She remembered the casual way Tomás had immobilized Mark and injected him with a sedative, leaving him helpless. She had offered her cooperation and even her own life in exchange for Mark and Sofia, whom God had chosen for a miracle. The assassin had promised to leave Mark alive at that moment, but she knew that was only temporary. She squared her shoulders back, exhaled, and pushed her despair aside. It was up to her to help Sofia, and she had to find a way to free herself.

There were voices on the other side of the door.

"What is this?"

She recognized Giulanti's voice.

Another man's gravelly voice sounded like Mark's neighbor, Terrence Bradley. He told Giulanti he was taking her back. Was he referring to Sofia? Maria started to call out, but she sensed the threat beyond the door as Giulanti spoke in low tones.

"No, she's not a nun," said Giulanti. "Get rid of her, and make sure no one ever sees her again."

Maria heard them move away. Sofia was still alive, but Giulanti meant something terrible for both of them. Maria looked for anything to use as a weapon, but unless she could bind Terrence in toilet tissue or paper towels, she was out of luck.

Please God, she is all I have now, and she needs me. Lord, please save Sofia. It doesn't matter what happens to me.

Maria had a momentary thought that the Holy Mother might have said similar prayers over her son, but God's plan had been larger than either one of them. Could this really be His intent?

She had planned on taking her vows and living a life of service, comforted in daily routine until her death in old age. Now she feared for a child's life more than her own and longed for one more chance.

"I'm losing my mind," she muttered, shaking her head.

She brought her hands up in supplication and whispered, "Lord, I will do as you ask. Please show me your will."

Maria looked around again for anything to help and noticed two aerosol cans of cleaning solution. She grasped at the glimmer of an idea and busied herself before breaking the remaining light fixture and crouching in silence.

Footsteps approached in the hallway, and the doorknob rattled and turned with a click. The door swung open to reveal Terrence Bradley, and his pupils bloomed in the darkness, searching for any trace of her presence as he worked the light switch.

"C'mon, sister," said Terrence. "It's time to help you leave."

The big man stepped into the room, his shoes crunching on shattered glass and his arms outstretched. Maria let him take another step before raising an aerosol can of glass cleaner and spraying directly at his face.

He cried out in pain and rubbed his eyes.

"You bitch!"

Maria kicked him in the groin as hard as she could.

He groaned and clutched both hands at his zipper, bending forward and sideways to one knee.

She slipped around him and into the hallway, trying to get her bearings. Sofia's room was on the opposite side of the preoperative holding area. One of Giulanti's men stood at the nursing station, and she needed to get to Sofia unseen. She crept to the other corner and looked beyond to see no one. She stepped out but was grabbed from behind by bear-trap hands that spun her around.

Terrence Bradley towered over her with quivering lips and blazing eyes. He gripped her with his left hand and drew his clenched fist back to strike.

❖

"Who was that?" asked Lorenzo's mother, Vivian.

Donovan looked away. What could he say? His wife knew very well who the little girl had to be. She always gave the pretense of not knowing what he did for a living, but she was a smart woman. He played the game for her and answered.

"She is a patient from down the hall," he said. "She is facing a surgery."

He always tried to tell the truth in front of his son as best he could.

Lorenzo nodded in agreement. Despite his labored breathing, he seemed calmer and more alert.

"I met her. She is nice," said his son, gulping another breath. "I want her to be safe."

Vivian patted their son on the shoulder.

"Did she say anything to you?" asked Donovan.

His son talked in a hushed voice, still trying to breathe.

"That I don't need to be afraid, and I have family waiting and praying for me."

"That's right," said Donovan. "You will be asleep, and these doctors and nurses are going to fix you right up. When you wake up, you will get better."

He wanted his son to know that his father had everything under control now.

A nurse walked in and said, "We'll be taking Lorenzo back shortly." She had a syringe in her hand. "I have some medicine to help him relax."

Donovan stepped aside from the stretcher and thought over his son's words. The little girl knew our family? That was curious.

"Lorenzo, what family?" he asked.

The nurse finished injecting a small amount of medicine through the intravenous line, and his son's eyelids fluttered toward sleep. His boy opened his lips and Donovan leaned closer to hear.

"Jack and Lucia," mumbled Lorenzo.

His son's voice trailed off, and his breathing continued, regular and shallow. The nurse noted his vital signs on the monitor.

Vivian clasped her hands over her mouth in surprise.

Donovan raised his eyebrows. His brother, Jackson, had loved Lorenzo like he was his own, but his brother had been dead for ten years. Lucia had been their firstborn, but she had died shortly after her birth. By tacit agreement, he and Vivian never spoke of her. What was this?

Another nurse joined them in the room along with the surgeon who said it was time to take him back.

"We will get started once we have him on the table and ready," said the surgeon. "I want to point out that the hospital is operating under emergency procedures and is being evacuated. We are on emergency power, and if that goes down during the procedure—"

Donovan hated excuses and interrupted, standing eye-to-eye with the surgeon.

"Then you and everyone you have ever known or loved will die," he said.

It wasn't a threat but a quiet promise. Donovan needed the staff to concentrate on his son.

The surgeon blanched but stood his ground. Donovan had forced the skilled physician to cooperate under threat to his family, and he still needed him. Donovan had decided the man would suffer some convenient accident in the months to come, but better to wait until his son was well out of the post-operative recovery period.

The staff wheeled Lorenzo back to the operating room, and Donovan watched until his boy rolled through the sliding doors. Standing in the empty hallway, he blinked back tears, and the walls faded away.

He stood on broken ground littered with untold remains. Fires raged in every direction and devoured any remnant of hope leaving everything around him colored in ash. The voices raged inside wrestling for control, and he shook his head until they were gone. It was just a stress reaction, he told himself, relieved that his son would have a chance. He slowly exhaled and focused on the floor beneath his feet and stood in the hospital hallway again.

Donovan had gone to Father Romero and asked for prayers during his son's illness. He had been raised in the Church and felt if anyone could intercede with God, it would be one of his servants, but there had been no improvement, and Lorenzo's doctors had given no hope.

If God was real but wouldn't answer him, maybe some other power would, and one night in fear of loosing his son and with little to loose, Donovan had offered all that he had and all he would be until he collapsed in the dark. He lay powerless to move through the night and witnessed all he knew end in cold nothingness over-and-over until he finally acquiesced, and then it was only him holding his boy standing on a lone hill overlooking desolation. The very next day, he received word of a medical match for Lorenzo.

Finding others who believed in practical reality as he did had not been difficult, especially when it paid well. Some aspects of his work had always skirted the law, and he expanded his influence. In this region of the country, there were smaller competitors, but they kept their distance like jackals. His plans included a political run that might land him in a seat of ultimate power. That was the legacy he wanted to leave to his son, so he had pounced on the good news of a match. A river of money passed hands, and hope began to grow.

Smuggling the little girl into the country had been expensive but not difficult, and everything had gone well until that blasted woman went soft and reneged on the deal. She had been put to rest along with her waste of a traveling companion, but the hallucinations had continued, and among the voices, one returned again and again, smoldering like wet hay spread over burning tires with a lust for power that made Donovan fear his oath would come due soon.

So be it, he thought, as long as my son lives.

Sofia lay on a stretcher, clad in a paper surgical gown with an intravenous catheter taped to her right forearm. Drowsy from the medicine she had been given, she looked around, and there was no one else in the room. She tried to scream for help, but it wasn't time yet, and she felt alone.

Where were Maria and Mark? She remembered trying to climb the fence before the ground shook, trying to escape in the woods, the silent nurses with needles, and then nothing until she woke up here. Where was Dog? She knew he would search for her. He had been meant for her. She felt certain of that.

The messenger in the church had told her she would be watched over. He told her many things before he turned bright, and her limbs stretched and twisted until her back straightened, and a thunderous clamor like all the colors of Heaven pushed aside the pain.

Sofia had always sensed I Am in the everyday dreariness of her life. She couldn't hear, and she couldn't move as other children did, but she could see the messengers come and go like daylight passing through a glass window.

In the earliest days, those around her seemed to move about their days, barely acknowledging her, but later in the children's place, she had a sense of being cared for in the gentle touch of the nun who washed and clothed and fed her. She had watched television and learned the alphabet from a children's show. The letters went together to make words, and she felt the vibrations through the speaker.

Letter by letter, she learned, and one day when Sister Magdalena read to her, Sofia pointed to the words one after the next. Sister almost dropped the book and hugged Sofia. Soon, Sister Magdalena brought in a chalkboard and worked on vocabulary daily with Sofia, and more interesting books appeared. Sofia's mind exploded with new images and information, and she always felt God's delight in her.

Then the day came when a man and a woman appeared at the orphanage. She knew the word for the place now. They asked about becoming her mother and father, and Sister Magdalena had seemed happy for her, but also sad. Sofia hadn't known how to feel. She had dreamed of being in a family, but she had found happiness with Sister Magdalena and feared change. She prayed for reassurance and felt I Am, soothing and warm, so she had smiled, and she remembered how the woman looked surprised and slowly smiled back at her.

The man remained distant while they were traveling, but the woman seemed to enjoy spending time with her. Sister Magdalena had enjoined her new parents to spend a great deal of time reading to her. For a couple with so much money to spend adopting her, they seemed to own very little in the way of books, but the woman had a children's Bible and held it for Sofia and turned the pages. Sofia could feel the woman's voice as she read, and she read along and asked questions in her mind, and I Am answered.

Then came the day when Sofia knew they had crossed into a country called Estados Unidos. The United States was the English name she knew from her reading and a place many people wanted to go, and now she was here. The following night, she had fallen asleep despite her excitement, and when she woke up, she was in a chair on a porch with a blanket wrapped around her. There was a note, which she couldn't quite reach with her good hand, pinned to the blanket. Daylight broke the horizon while her teeth chattered.

An older woman came out on the porch to pick up the newspaper and paused when she saw Sofia. The woman hurried back inside, and shortly, a man came out on the porch wearing a black shirt and a white collar. That was how she met Father Romero and later, Maria. At the thought of Maria, Sofia despaired. What had happened to her, and why couldn't she feel I Am?

She knew Maria must be looking for her, and Sofia talked to I Am. She couldn't feel Him, but she knew He could hear her. He always did. She knew this kind of talking was called praying. Maria had explained it to her. She hadn't told Maria that she already knew how to talk to God and that I Am talked back to her. She sensed Maria couldn't do that and didn't want to make her feel bad because Maria had carefully explained so much to her. Sofia had felt love from Sister Magdalena for the first time she could remember, and now with Maria, she knew what love felt like again. Sofia had sensed the loneliness in Maria, who loved I Am even though she couldn't hear Him. She missed Dog and Mark. Were they all right? She prayed to the Holy Father through his Son and asked the Blessed Mother to pray for them to stay safe.

Please let them find me.

Sofia heard the door open, and several people wearing masks entered the room. She tried to say a soundless hello, but they didn't respond while they unlocked the rolling stretcher. She felt too tired and weak to fight. She remembered the last few days and running in the front yard, and she gave thanks to I Am for those moments and for meeting Maria and Mark and Dog.

Maybe she would see them again.

CHAPTER TWENTY-NINE

Maria flinched and closed her eyes bracing for the blow from Terrence Bradley. There was a grunt and a hard thud, and the pressure on her arm eased. She turned to run but heard a familiar voice.

"Maria," said a voice behind her.

She looked back and couldn't believe her eyes. It was Mark, and he was calling her name. He held his hands out, and she jumped into his arms. Her hands pressed to his back, and she didn't ever want to let go.

"I'm here now," he said.

He was real and strong, and she buried her face in his chest. Mark rested his chin against the top of her head, and after a few moments, she looked around and saw Terrence unconscious on the floor. Behind Mark, Father Romero smiled at her, and behind the pastor, there was a man with a camera. Mark lightly gripped her arms, and she needed to tell him so much, but it would have to wait.

"Maria, I'm so glad you are safe," said Father Romero.

She blushed and said, "Thank you, Father." She gently disengaged from Mark. "Sofia is being held on this floor. We must hurry."

She led them around the corner toward the room where she had last seen Sofia. Maria couldn't fathom how the guard at the nursing station had not heard Terrence go down at Mark's hand. She looked again, and there was no sign of the guard.

They rounded the corner, and Tomás stood over the unmoving sentry.

Maria froze and said, "That man delivered us to Donovan Giulanti."

Tomás looked at her and nodded his acknowledgement.

"I know," said Mark. "He's on our side now."

"I'm sorry," said Tomás. "Donovan lied to me and intends harm to Sofia. I cannot permit that."

Maria looked Tomás up and down and said nothing. There was no time to decide whether she believed the assassin or not. She led the way to the room she remembered Sofia being in, but it was empty, and there was no one at the central desk station.

They made their way to sliding glass doors marked with the word, "Surgery."

Tomás took the lead and glided down the hall and around a corner between operating rooms. There were two dark-clad men in the well lit hallway, each alertly waiting outside an operating room. Tomás held his suppressed pistol tucked behind his leg and walked toward the nearer guard.

The sentries looked startled to see Tomás appear in the hallway but relaxed upon recognizing him. Just as they realized someone should have stopped Tomás outside, the assassin raised his suppressed pistol and shot the guards, one after the other so quickly it sounded like a single hushed sound. Both men crumpled to the floor with a thud, and Father Romero said a prayer for each. The elderly priest muttered that he would have much to confess before this night finished.

Tomás guarded the hallway and their egress while Mark, Father Romero, Maria, and a very wide-eyed Paul, who still shakily pointed a motion action camera, found their way to the nearest operating suite. Opening the door wide enough to peek, Mark saw a small draped form secured to a surgical bed with arms outstretched. A gowned and masked surgeon took a scalpel from a nurse, and another gowned assistant stood ready to assist in the procedure on the patient. Yet another assistant waited by a table supporting a hinged ice chest.

"Stop!" yelled Mark.

He sprang into the operating suite holding his pistol pointed directly at the surgeon.

The surgeon looked surprised but turned his head back down to the operating table, determined to complete his initial incision. Mark thought he would have to shoot him, but in that moment, Maria darted forward between the medical staff and laid her body across Sofia.

"Murderers!" she shouted.

Sofia's torso, covered in surgical drapes, left only her chest exposed. Suddenly, it all made sense to Mark, and he almost pulled the trigger on the surgeon in front of him, but Father Romero gently laid his hand on Mark's right shoulder.

"Wake her up!" commanded Mark.

The surgeon hesitated, but then his shoulders drooped like a man searching for any landmark to find his way home.

No one moved, and Maria cried out, "She's not breathing!"

"You bastards," said Mark. "You didn't need her, just her heart. Is that it? If she dies, you die. Save her now!"

The assistant beside the operating bed reached for an artificial breathing bag and ventilated Sofia. He turned off the anesthetic gas, and her slow heart rate climbed back above a hundred beats per minute. Her skin color warmed from ashen to flushed, and after approximately ten minutes, she started breathing on her own again.

"Oh, thank God," said Paul, his hands trembling but still taking video. He slumped against the operating room wall and wiped one hand against his shirt as sweat dripped from his spent face.

Maria hugged Sofia and murmured small loving words, the kind that mothers whisper to their children and etch into their souls for eternity.

The muscles in Mark's thighs crawled like caterpillars, and he wondered if he could stay standing, but his anger gave him strength. He continued to point his pistol at the surgical team, and each of them looked like they were trying to process what this interruption meant.

Father Romero audibly prayed for Sofia and spoke of his confident trust in God's mercy while he looked at the medical staff standing before Mark's wrath. He prayed aloud for their souls and called on God to guide men and women in their misadventures to His loving grace. One nurse broke down in sobs and collapsed to the floor of the operating suite while the others stood very still with heads bowed trying to find some unknown spot on the floor. Mark couldn't tell if it was from remorse or being discovered, and he interrupted Father Romero.

"Father, we need to get out of here," he said.

Father Romero nodded and went to help Maria lift Sofia off the operating table.

The surgeon had stepped to the side. Out of habit, he still held his gloved hands clasped together to avoid contamination.

"Donovan Giulanti will come for you," said the surgeon. "The other team has already started the procedure on his son." The surgeon nodded toward Sofia. "Without her heart, his boy will die."

Father Romero led the way out of the operating suite into the hallway where Tomás waited. Maria carried Sofia while Paul followed, and Mark kept his pistol trained on the surgical team as he took his exit.

"Donovan Giulanti will kill us and our families," said the surgeon, his eyes sad above his surgical mask.

Mark shook his head and hurled words at the people left in the operating room.

"All of us eventually die," said Mark. "What if the priest is right?"

Mark nodded toward a retreating Father Romero who had turned to help Maria.

"Each of us must choose how to live."

❖

Donovan paced in the surgery waiting area while Vivian sat near a window, looking outside. It had been more than an hour since Lorenzo had been taken back, and by now, the procedure should be well under way. His wife had said nothing more about the girl, and as long as his boy lived, Donovan knew they would never speak of her again.

The confusion surrounding the natural disaster had been fortuitous. Donovan and his followers had virtually taken over the surgery annex. The specialized medical equipment including a heart-lung machine had been flown and delivered, and the hospital administrator had been more than happy to help with emergency privileges given Donovan's generous donation pledge and ability to supply power to the hospital.

One of his lieutenants appeared at the waiting room doorway and approached hesitantly. It was bad news from the look on the man's pale face.

"Well," said Donovan.

The man shuffled back a half step and said, "The girl escaped. I've already alerted our men, and we're searching for her now."

"What?" said Donovan.

He reached down and gripped the back of the chair beside him.

"They took her, sir," said the lieutenant. "There was a priest, and a man, and that nun." The lieutenant stammered. "And they had help from Tomás. Several of the men are down."

Donovan's eyes narrowed.

"You did nothing to stop this?" he asked.

The voices inside his head coalesced into a babble of furious indignation, and he reached out and grasped the lieutenant by his coat collar and shook him until he heard the man's neck snap.

At that moment the building swayed as if the ground was an ocean and waves battered against the walls outside, crashing in great breakers of soil and rock. The window closest to Vivian exploded shards of glass into her like shrapnel, and her scream cut short as she fell backwards. Donovan held his hands out for balance and tried to stay on his feet as he careened in time with the trees outside. He glimpsed Vivian's still and bloody body before the lights went out. Scorched air tasting of grit and ash forced through the shattered window and layered indifferently about the room.

The booming vibrations eased away after another minute leaving near darkness in the waiting room except for the feeble light from an emergency battery powered light fixture in the hallway. Donovan's mind snapped back to his dead lieutenant's words. Then he remembered what the surgeon had told him.

Stepping over the discarded lieutenant's body on the glass-strewn floor, Donovan felt his way directly into the surgical suite. It was deep-mine dark inside the surgery annex except for a couple of battery powered emergency lights scattered about the walls. He checked room after room without visible surgical staff, until finally, he pushed through the door to the last operating room.

Shadows played across the floor and the wall where the emergency lighting tried to penetrate. The room was full of equipment, but there was no living soul in the room. His son lay on the operating table. He had been draped to expose his chest, which had been opened and packed with sponges while his enlarged and pendulous heart lay in a pan that had fallen to the floor alongside an overturned Mayo stand.

Lorenzo was gone.

His boy was no more.

Donovan stood next to his son's corpse and put a hand on his cooling forehead. He had lost his wife and son, and his time in this world amounted to nothing. He couldn't think what to do next as he stood in the shadows, but after a time, his despair give way to a fury that had been building since the night he had offered his all for the life of his son. He felt a thirst creep into his hands, and he clenched his fingers into fists as a great emptiness spread from his chest. He sighed and spoke in the silence.

"I will embrace what is born here today."

Yes, yes, and yes!

The shadows about him rejoiced.

Donovan's thoughts raced in the dark operating theater. The staff had undoubtedly evacuated as soon as their failure became apparent. It mattered not. He had a complete dossier on everyone associated in the care of his son, and they could not hide. He felt the voices feast on his emotions, savoring his agony and his anger, and he reluctantly turned away from what had been his son and traced his way back to the surgery waiting room.

Vivian rested on the soiled and glass strewn floor beneath the shattered window, and he looked again at his wife's last moment in life. He picked up a radio from the dead lieutenant sprawled on the floor and walked down the hall. He almost stumbled over a groaning Terrence Bradley on the floor. Clearly, the older Bradley brother had failed at his task of getting rid of the nun. Donovan drew his pistol and shot Terrence in the head and walked on, barely breaking his stride.

He knew what he needed to do now. He would track down the girl and her rescuers, including Tomás. He keyed the radio and called out commands. None of them would escape this day.

CHAPTER THIRTY

Walter kept discreet watch near the emergency department entrance as more and more confused and wounded souls found their way to the hospital hoping for aid and looking for missing loved ones. He had left Martha sitting beside the sheriff while a unit of packed red blood cells dripped into Roger's intravenous line. The sheriff would be transferred to another hospital for surgery after resuscitation. Between the injured seeking help and the patients and their families trying to evacuate the damaged hospital, this exit offered the best chance if Mark found Sofia and Maria.

Donovan Giulanti's men stood just outside the emergency entrance glass doors, scanning the throng, and Walter saw one of them raise his hand to his ear. The black-coated sentry listened intently, raised his arm, and made a twirling motion with his outstretched and upright index finger. Immediately the adjacent guards snapped to attention and brought weapons to bear from beneath their long black coats, which brought shrieks from those nearby. As more and more people noticed, the crowd pulled away from the doors to gain distance from the gunmen.

Walter tried to think how he could deal with the black coats, as he thought of them, when the ground started shaking again. Violent, undulating waves threatened to throw him off his feet, and the hospital swayed about him. The shuddering building couldn't possibly stay erect, and screams from the people around him echoed the same thought.

The black-coated henchmen sidestepped most of the debris that fell from the exterior of the hospital, but one gunman fell when a brick hit him squarely in the head. Another faltered beneath the panicked people bursting out of the exit. The exiting crowd swept up Walter and left him in the parking lot just outside the emergency department entrance.

Several more trees uprooted about the hospital, and one large maple tree smashed across the loaned industrial generator, which sputtered and coughed and lapsed to halting darkness. The straining earth subsided amid the moans of the newly injured, and both patients and visitors staggered out of the doors including Father Romero and Mark, who was holding Maria and Sofia. Paul emerged behind them, coughing and clutching his camera with white-knuckled hands.

"Where's Tomás?" asked Walter.

He's behind us," said Mark. "He's holding back some of Donovan's men and told us to go ahead. He said he'd catch up."

Walter turned to motion for Felicity, but the van was nowhere to be seen. A tree had split and fallen directly over the van's parking space. The splintered trunk and tree limbs were buried under a mound of brick and masonry.

Paul took the camera away from his face.

"No!" cried Paul, and he started forward. "Felicity!"

Father Romero wrapped his arms around Paul to keep him from rushing into the debris pile.

"Wait, look there," said Walter, pointing to their left.

The van swerved around the corner of the hospital, weaving around knots of survivors with Felicity at the wheel. She pulled up and opened the van sliding door, and one by one, they crowded in. Martin started asking questions while Mark passed a sleeping Sofia to Walter, who climbed in and handed Sofia to Maria while Dog shuffled around inside the van and squeezed in between Maria and Father Romero. Mark turned to look for pursuit and saw Tomás darting out of the hospital waving at them to go as he ran toward them.

Mark jumped aboard and Felicity eased the van away while Tomás ran to catch up. A flood of dark-coated men scurried out of the hospital exit followed by Donovan Giulanti. Tomás had almost reached the van when a gunshot boomed, and he staggered. Beyond Tomás, Mark saw Giulanti holding an outstretched pistol.

Mark grabbed Tomás and pulled him aboard, closing the van sliding door after him.

"Go, go, go!" shouted Mark.

A ping and another ping sounded as gunfire found the van, but nothing penetrated the interior. Felicity dodged the crowd and slalomed around fallen trees which helped to shelter from following gunfire. Veering from the parking lot to Medical Center Drive, she accelerated away from the madness.

Mark had seen Donovan Giulanti's face as they pulled away and knew the man would not let this end. There was nearly full darkness with the dust-laden violet sky and absence of street lights, and Felicity limited her speed on the pockmarked asphalt road to the reach of the van's headlights as she headed out of town toward the nearest highway.

"How is the child?" asked Tomás, holding his left hand over his blood-stained side.

Maria said, "She's not awake, but she's breathing."

"You need a doctor," said Mark to Tomás.

Tomás shrugged his wound away.

"The girl is more important," said the assassin, sinking back in his seat.

Mark thought rapidly. Paducah would be closest, but they couldn't go back the way they had come. He knew Donovan Giulanti would give chase, but the limited visibility should slow any chase vehicles and make it difficult for him to use the helicopter. They could make it to the next largest town with a decent hospital, but could Tomás last that long? He looked paler by the minute.

The road in front of the van lit up, sweeping the darkness aside, and Felicity put one hand in front of her eyes. The light moved back and forth but stayed ahead of their nose more or less.

"It's a searchlight," said Mark.

Donovan had chanced the helicopter after all.

"We need someplace to hide," said Paul.

Felicity nodded, and Martin agreed. Tomás said nothing. Maria held a limp Sofia in her arms and looked hopelessly at Mark. Dog crouched down to maintain position as the van threaded along the broken road.

Father Romero asked, "Is there consecrated ground nearby?"

"Father?" said Mark.

Father Romero had his eyes closed. He opened them and seemed to look far away.

"We will need to be on blessed ground," said Father Romero. "It will make him more vulnerable."

Mark wanted Tomás's opinion, but the man seemed unable to respond. Mark could only think of one patch of holy ground close to them.

"Calvary Cemetery is sanctified ground," he replied. "It is close. Felicity, you can take a right under those trees coming up."

Mark had not been to the cemetery in months. Maddie and Faith had been laid to rest there close to Maddie's parents and near the home and small town she loved. He had an afterthought.

"There are a number of trees," he said. "It will be difficult for a helicopter to land there in darkness."

Felicity looked for the turnoff and checked her mirror when the spotlight from the helicopter veered away for a moment.

"We've got headlights behind us about five hundred yards," she said.

The van passed under some trees, and the turn was close in front of them. They were hidden from the helicopter for a moment.

"Felicity, can you see well enough to take the turn without headlights?" asked Mark.

"Yes," she replied, grasping his intent.

She cut the van's lights and took her foot off the gas pedal letting the van slow to take the turn to the cemetery without braking. She kept the lights off, letting the gloom swallow them. Felicity pulled the van into the cemetery, and under Mark's direction, inched her way to the left on the narrow, winding lane, until at the far back of the ceme-tery, she pulled the van under a copse of trees, shielding any view of them from the air. She set the parking brake and shut off the engine.

They sat in stygian darkness and could see the helicopter search-light on the road half a mile to their right. The stabbing searchlight approached, moving back and forth until it shone on the trees over them. After a time, the helicopter moved off into the night, and the headlights behind did not follow into the cemetery. They could hide here, but for how long? Mark checked Tomás, and the stoic hit man's pulse was weak but present.

Sofia stirred, and Maria gathered her close. Father Romero said prayers of protection for the group and reached over to anoint Sofia with oil and a blessing and did the same for Tomás.

Mark could just make out the Evans family plot in front of them. Maddie and Faith lay there by her parents, and forty feet beyond, a mound of dirt marked a freshly dug grave.

Maria and Sofia clung to him, and their breathing steadied as he watched over them. The silence in the van deepened to light snores in their exhaustion, and Mark thought of the moment he woke up after the accident. Hurting everywhere and almost unable to move, he had listened as Father Romero looked him in the eyes and told him that his world had died. His family lay close to him again, separated by soil and rock and time, and until the last few days, he had wanted to leave this world and catch up to them.

Mark remembered Maria in the kitchen, tending to Sofia, and wondered if Maddie could ever forgive him. What about Faith? His daughter had asked God every night to watch over their family, and now, in the dark, she appeared above the grave and approached, smiling as she watched him holding Sofia.

Mark woke with a start and realized Sofia had crawled into his arms. He leaned over and kissed the little girl on the cheek. Maria had her head on his shoulder, and Dog nosed beside Mark's leg and placed his muzzle on the seat. Sofia woke up and looked at both of them and smiled.

Maria opened tear-filled eyes and raised her head from Mark's shoulder. Sofia reached over to touch Maria's face and opened her mouth to say something but no words emerged. Mark still had his arm around Maria and wanted to pull her to him. He had never felt anything more strongly in his life, but his wife's grave looked at him from beyond the front windscreen, and he hesitated.

Tomás coughed and groaned from his seat. Sofia leaned across Mark and placed her hand on the face of the assassin, who opened his eyes. Sofia closed her eyes for a moment and then smiled at Tomás, who looked at her in wonder. She leaned back and wrapped her arms around Mark again and settled back to sleep.

Mark woke again and checked his watch. The night air had retreated to subdued morning light, and patchy fog covered the ground in shadow. Mark couldn't see it yet, but he felt the looming presence of Apollyon overhead.

Paul said, "I think they've figured out where we are."

Headlights approached along the road about a quarter mile away.

"Should we run?" asked Martin.

The others stirred except for Tomás, who winced in his sleep, but his pulse felt stronger.

Felicity adjusted her seat upright to driving position.

Another set of headlights and then a third joined the vehicles searching the cemetery until they parked in a crescent before them, black on black SUV's blocking any avenue of escape. They heard the helicopter circling, stabbing at the sacrosanct ground with a pencil of brilliant light accenting the predawn morning.

Father Romero finished his unspoken prayer and addressed all of them.

"It is time," he said. "Hold fast, and do not waver, no matter what you see."

CHAPTER THIRTY-ONE

Newly inaugurated Pope Ignatius Ronaldo Ricci waited just inside the balcony above Saint Peter's Square in Rome. White smoke drifted from the chimney above the Sistine Chapel into a somber sky, and Ronaldo prayed for wisdom as he emerged into the modest afternoon light. This announcement was being televised around the world, and he hoped he could honor the memory of his friend Anastasi.

The faithful had gathered through the morning and early afternoon. Feeble rays of light trickled around the expanding shadow of Apollyon, which squeezed the sky as people struggled to speak, gasping for breath between sentences.

The shoulder to shoulder crowd in the square strained to see the new pope, and the unnatural eclipse hemmed the crowd, magnifying their desperation, and in their uncertainty, they prayed for an answer different from what they feared.

Ronaldo thought of Father Romero and his courage years ago. He had word that his friend had recovered and left the hospital, and he gave thanks. He had no doubt that Francisco could stand and face this crowd of onlookers and the near certain death awaiting them all.

Thinking of what they now faced, Ronaldo lost heart for a moment. How could he lead His Church when he felt so inadequate himself? Praying for strength again, he stepped to the balcony railing and faced the crowd which raised their hands as one and repeatedly asked what they should do.

Pope Ronaldo Ricci raised his arms, and the crowd quieted.

"I come to you now when our faith is sorely tested," he began. "It has been my honor to serve in God's Holy Church for the last thirty years, and today, I said farewell to my friend, Pope Anastasi, as he continues his journey to God."

Ronaldo looked out on the men, women, and children in the crowd, who listened to his words, and he hoped he might help them change their fate. He looked down for a moment and searched inside himself for the right words, and when he looked up, he saw a figure atop the obelisk in the center of the square peering back at him.

The elongated shape atop the obelisk smiled at his words and wrapped around the stone monument like a human python, stretching its maws in a yawn of indifference and wagging a mocking tongue.

How did he get up there?

Ronaldo wondered as he continued to speak to the crowd.

"Evil works to hide within and among us, yet the fallen one cannot abide in the light," said Ronaldo. "It is only in secrecy and darkness that evil flourishes."

The man-thing's image darkened until only a shadow remained, and Ronaldo shuddered. Even though the figure had faded in the dim afternoon haze, he knew it certain. Still, he needed to comfort and guide the faithful, and he thought again of Father Romero standing resolute, certain in the promises of Christ.

"I tell you this truth so you may see it is not hopeless," said Ronaldo. "We may ask God in abundant faith to deliver us from this evil that has befallen us. For all who have ears to hear and hearts to beat in love, I ask that you pray with me."

He stretched his arms out over the hushed crowd standing in the penumbra below.

Almost immediately, clouds of dust rumbled up the surrounding streets. The obelisk swayed and started to topple while the crowd scrambled to get out of the way. The stone pavement fractured in a cataclysmic fissure across Saint Peter's Square. The obelisk disappeared into it along with an untold number of panic-stricken observers.

The balcony shook, and Ronaldo gripped the edge of the wall to keep from being thrown to the rippling ground below. He tried to hold on and yelled for the clergy behind him to take cover.

After about forty seconds, the shaking subsided to minor tremors. Ronaldo slowly stood with his hands outstretched over the weeping and moaning crowd to see smoke rising from multiple areas in Rome. Sirens wailed as emergency services began to respond, and after taking a breath, he spoke to the crowd.

"We are opening the doors and will provide help as we can," he said. "Please, pray the Rosary for intercession and say prayers for our deliverance. Believe that it is not too late for us." He made the sign of the cross and said, "In nomine Patris et Filii, et Spiritus Sancti."

Continuing in prayer, Ronaldo looked over the crowd as ambulance crews arrived and tended the wounded about the splintered courtyard. The man-like wraith had disappeared from sight but was never truly gone. Ronaldo raised his hands in supplication and thought again of his friend, Francisco, and prayed that his mission would be successful.

❖

Ari ben Eitan parked his vehicle, a military-painted AIL Storm, outside his sister-in-law's house. She and her husband had built their home into a hillside, and the curving front exterior supported simple lines of stone and concrete covered in stucco. The thick walls and rein-forced door of solid oak and metal manifested how function ruled over style in their lives, and Ari approved. The staged stand-down after the announcement of the rogue planet had allowed him to catch up with his family.

Ari knocked on the door and waited for an answer while he looked up at the dark shadow of Apollyon looming larger by the hour. The unnatural gloom hijacked every sense in the tense quiet all about, and not even a dog barked as each living thing strained to evade the approaching end.

Ari knocked again, and his wife, Avigail, opened the door and rushed out and wrapped her arms around him in relief. His children crowded at the doorway threshold, and his sister-in-law and her husband appeared behind them.

Avigail pulled back and looked at him through tear-filled eyes.

"I was so worried," she said. "I prayed unceasingly for God to bring you back to us."

Ari pulled her close and gave thanks for the thousandth time that he had found such a woman. He had grown up in a non-observant home, and when he realized that Avigail was a child of Yeshua, he had hesitated, but his love for her had been such that he couldn't put her aside. She had never pushed her faith at him, but her daily example and their quiet discussions had caused him to question what he understood about the world in which he lived.

All he knew that was certain was in her arms, and Ari looked up at the end looming overhead and wondered again if there was more just as Avigail had told him. He hoped she was right.

Samuel and Beth had driven all day and night. Exhausted, they found a private campground with available space in Dalhart, Texas. Their campsite had grass, a picnic table, and room for the surplus tent that he had packed in the back of his truck. Samuel knew he needed rest, but in the dim morning light with the rogue planet looming over them, he realized he couldn't sleep. He held Beth's hand and looked at her.

"Are you still okay with this?" he asked.

She nodded.

Beth had spoken only a little through the night, but she hadn't hesitated when he showed up at her house and asked her to come with him. He had explained to her family about his concerns even with a near miss by the rogue planet, but they decided not to leave and didn't want her to go with him either. Beth had hugged her mother and father before taking his arm.

"I believe in him," she said.

She had packed quickly and jumped in the truck while Samuel promised her parents to look after her, and now, she was with him. He got out of the truck and worked at setting up their tent. They couldn't have an open fire in this campground, but he had an old camp stove and some eggs and bacon in the cooler. He set up the stove, and Beth insisted on cooking breakfast. Samuel had nearly ten gallons of stored water in the truck, but he wanted more and hoped to find another container or two.

The family-owned campground had many full-service RV sites, and people gathered outside their rigs, looking up at the approaching menace in the morning sky.

After breakfast, Samuel and Beth sat in the truck and listened to the radio. They heard the new pope's announcement and prayer along with the news of the earthquake in Rome, and at that moment, the ground shook beneath their truck. The tent swayed in front of them in rhythm with the shifting earth, and Beth clenched his hand and prayed. Her words resonated with his yearning heart, and an involuntary tingling spread out to his hands and legs. The bucking ground stilled, and the shouts and screams in the campsite died down. A roaring sound filled the air, and a strong gust of wind blew down their tent.

Could it be a coincidence? Samuel looked up at the sky again. He understood the science, and everything could be explained away as an unfortunate roll of the dice, couldn't it? He only had to look at Beth to understand that miracles existed, and somewhere deep inside, he prayed for something beyond his understanding and a way to keep her safe.

CHAPTER THIRTY-TWO

"Have faith in God, and all things are possible," said Father Romero, looking at each of them in turn.

Mark opened the van sliding door and stepped down. He had come here every day for weeks after the funeral, and then he had come as often as he could, but each time it felt harder. He had tried to understand why, and the only answer he had been able to find was that he was breathing and they were not. This was his first time standing on this ground in almost a year.

He helped Maria out of the van with Sofia, and one-by-one the rest of the group emerged in the pale morning light. Patchy surface fog lingered about, and the grass recoiled with each step spraying shimmering water droplets above the ground, temporarily defying gravity. The air smelled of freshly turned earth and unfinished purpose.

Walter and Paul helped Tomás stagger along until Father Romero stopped just beyond the headstones that marked the last resting place for Maddie and Faith.

The searching helicopter avoided the surrounding trees and landed between headstones thirty meters beyond the freshly opened grave. The rotors slowed, and Mark strained to see beyond the headlights of the vehicles trapping them in the cemetery.

The door to the helicopter slid open. Donovan Giulanti stepped to the ground and stalked around mounded dirt to stand in front of the open grave and face them. Six robust, armed men, dressed in black, exited the blocking SUVs and formed a semicircle behind him.

Maria held her arms around Sofia, and Mark stood beside them. Father Romero stood to the other side of Maria, and Paul and Martin and Felicity waited behind him. Dog made his way close and sat beside Sofia while Tomás stayed upright on the other side of Mark with a supporting hand from Walter.

Donovan Giulanti stood there looking at all of them but scowled as he narrowed his gaze to Mark.

"My son is dead."

"Your son has gone home to God," said Father Romero.

Donovan's face twitched, and his tongue flicked over his lips.

"There is no God or Heaven, and nothing can bring my boy back."

"Why did you have my family killed?" asked Mark.

Maria looked at Mark in surprise.

Donovan smiled in the most casual way and responded.

"You put your nose too close to my affairs," said the big man. "You were not supposed to survive. They died because of you, and I should have had you disappear long ago."

He focused on Sofia and cackled before speaking in an impossibly deep and almost cavernous voice.

"As this world fears its death, I grow in strength."

Father Romero raised his open hand, and Donovan refocused on the priest.

"Are you ill, my son?" asked Father Romero.

Donovan extended his chin up and out to the side, and the glare of the vehicles' headlights gave his face an orange cast. He roared like a jack-o'-lantern come to life.

"I am not your son!"

He writhed before their eyes like Nāga of the netherworld.

Mark asked, "What do you want with Sofia?"

"She was meant to save my boy!" he growled and took a half step forward. "But you took her from me."

Mark stepped in front of Sofia and Maria and pointed up at Apollyon.

"It's over, and none of this will matter in a few more hours," he said.

Donovan extended both shoulders with his palms facing the ground and rose up on his toes. Foam flecked from his mouth, and his voice jarred like the minor bass keys on a piano, discordant and vulgar.

"You are too late," crowed the crime lord. "She cannot stop us in our triumph."

The ground heaved, throwing all of them off their feet as grass and dirt convulsed together. Standing was impossible, and Mark tried to crawl across the shaking ground to Sofia and Maria.

The soil behind Donovan fell away at the open graveside, and orange and yellow flames belched from the newly revealed rent in the earth, blowing embers into the nearest trees and igniting several branches into dancing torches. A stately old pine tree crashed onto one SUV and blocked the cemetery boundary road. Its roots vibrated like viola strings in a ferocious symphony until the tremors eased away.

The group managed to find their feet again, except for Tomás, who sprawled on the ground where he had fallen.

Donovan stood before them, and flames from the newly rent earth wrapped about him and flowed along his outstretched arms to his hands. He yawned in indifference as shadowy filaments enveloped him from head to toe covering his blank face in a mask of gloom.

"I was never vanquished, priest," said something that no longer appeared to be just Donovan Giulanti. "I have fulfilled my purpose this day. The village girl you dispelled me from became the mother of one who might have interfered, but that child hidden from me these years is before us, and we will have her heart just the same."

Donovan pulled a wicked-looking curved knife from his coat.

Mark shuddered at the shadowed face, the same image he remembered from the night of the accident. He strained to move, but somehow his feet had fused to the hallowed ground. He didn't understand, but he couldn't let Donovan take Sofia.

Father Romero stepped forward and intoned with assurance, "From all evil, deliver us, O Lord."

Whatever kept Mark from moving did not affect the old priest, and Donovan's face contorted at the words.

"Stop it, priest," growled Donovan or whatever he had become. "I remember your tricks, and you have no hope here. You will die this day, and no one will remember you as your bones crumble to dust."

Donovan laughed like a group of hyenas converging on a lion's kill.

"God, by your name save me, and by your might defend my cause." Father Romero grew taller and his shoulders squared like a prizefighter. "I command you, unclean spirit, whoever you are, along with all your minions now attacking this servant of God, by the mysteries of the incarnation, passion, resurrection, and the ascension of our Lord Jesus Christ—depart!"

Father Romero thrust out a crucifix and a Bible in his left hand.

The thing called Donovan recoiled as if struck, and the knife wavered as it shook its head and bellowed in frustration. Father Romero's right hand moved gracefully and hurled holy water from a small flask at the thing before them. Skin rippled along its arms and legs like it would burst, and the avatar of Donovan Giulanti stumbled back and clawed at its face amid a cacophony of howls.

Father Romero held up his right hand and said, "I cast you, unclean spirit, along with every satanic power of the enemy, every specter from hell, and all your fell companions in the name of our Lord Jesus Christ."

Donovan dropped the knife and placed both hands to his head. Shaking back and forth, he tried to tear his head from his body.

"Make them stop!" Donovan groaned, his neck muscles pulsing against something unseen. "Please!"

The shadows about Donovan converged, suffusing his face blood red, and a withering darkness swallowed him, blacker than night and triumphant in revelation.

"We are so many," hissed Donovan, his face slack. "and we hunger since the fall."

Donovan collapsed to his knees, and the darkness jumbled about him and gathered into a towering dragon-like creature with horns and clawed wings and slashing fangs. Eyes appeared, far more than any human or animal would have, multiple eyes searching in all directions until the beast opened its jaws and rumbled.

"Strong is your faith, priest, but not stronger than the worst of this world. You are but human and flawed."

Father Romero stood resolute. He held his crucifix outstretched.

"I am a man, but I know your name, Abaddon," he said. "By the power of Our Lord Jesus Christ, I compel you to depart!"

The incarnated brute raised taloned forelimbs, grasping at the sky, and roared above Donovan, who whimpered on his knees. Sweeping back toward the dross-filled flames outlining the chasm in the ground, Abaddon circled the pit, and the taste of rotten eggs fanned toward the group. Mark swallowed the fear in his throat and felt certain he didn't want to go anywhere near that hole in the ground.

The demonic dragon seemed to draw strength from the flaming abyss and turned while stretching out great charred wings and focused on its target once again.

"You don't think this is all an accident, do you?" hissed Abaddon. "You didn't really think I would leave her forever just because a silly priest didn't know to be afraid?"

Pulsing and squirming like a giant shadow box, the incarnate demon cascaded images of a pregnant and terrified young woman, alone and in labor, and then again, the same young woman furtively leaving an infant in a pew at the back of a church.

"She thought she could hide from us even to her death."

The image revolved into a many-faced maelstrom of struggling shadows before revealing a baneful multi-eyed saurian once more.

Bellowing its resolve, Abaddon advanced as fast as a sidewinder toward Father Romero and Sofia until the winged beast towered over the group like every ghost story come to life. The creature of shadows sneered and flexed taloned fingers to crush the life from them.

Father Romero held his crucifix high and said, "You could not hold him. You cannot bind him. You cannot abide him. By the power of Jesus Christ, I command you!"

The brutish brood recoiled from the words at first, but then growled and shook snout to tail shrugging off the command and bore down.

Sofia slipped from Maria and stepped in front of Mark. She held her hands upright in supplication and bowed her head in surrender.

Maria and Mark both shouted, "No!"

They reached for her at the same time, and that is when Dog raced forward and lunged at the threat before any of them could hold the shepherd back.

In that moment, Mark would always remember Sofia's voice.

"Uriel!" she called out.

Dog leaped into the air at the great beast, and time spiraled to a point of brightness that burst into a winged figure of light, iridescent in form and helmeted visor, gleaming sword in hand and shield at the ready.

Startled, the creature reared back in surprise.

"You cannot halt the fate set in motion this day!" shrieked Abaddon.

The spawned creature lunged to disembowel Uriel, and the transformed angelic being brought buckler to bear. Outstretched talons sparked furrows against the shield, and Uriel parried the demon beast, wary of its piercing wings, claws, and rending fangs.

"It is far too late," bellowed Abaddon.

The demon snapped at Uriel's face and swiveled its limber tail like a whip to dismember Uriel, who spun away like a winged Achilles whirling his shimmering sword in an infinite arc of color. Abaddon's tail connected with a nearby pine tree, splintering the trunk and throwing the crown thirty feet off to the right.

Uriel darted in and around the demon monster, trying to draw it away from Sofia and the group. Suddenly, the creature fixed its multitude of eyes on Sofia and waggled its great jaws in frustration.

"We will have our due!" bellowed the demon saurian.

Abaddon spread his charred wings and flung out a train of shadowy figures that encircled Sofia, and each carried a memory from her young life. Here, sitting alone at the orphanage waiting for help that would never come. There, endlessly hoping for her mother or father to return for her, even though she couldn't remember them. And here, realizing that she might perish alone at a young age, and there was nothing she could do about it.

Upon seeing her former crooked self, Sofia averted her eyes and head to her chest, and Abaddon took that moment to charge full tilt with its many eyes focused only on her.

And at that instant, Sofia looked up at the sky and spoke for the second time in her life.

"Your will be done."

She held her ground as the reborn demon horde swarmed for her, and every fettered soul within Abaddon hungered for Sofia's essence and the chance to win favor in the world to come.

At the last second, Uriel darted in front of Sofia and thrust his shining blade of light into the heart of the demon beast, bringing forth a caterwaul of fear and rage. The malevolent horror stumbled back and back to the precipice, its many eyes rolling in disbelief until finally, the demon of many tipped over into the flaming abyss, which gushed molten rock and blue smoke and collapsed in on itself leaving the open grave a pulsating black hole.

The winged apparition named Uriel levitated effortlessly a meter above the grass and turned to face them. Scintillating golden-white light rippled in waves as he smiled at Sofia, and she grinned back. Uriel looked up at the rogue planet with brilliant eyes and raised his gleaming sword which grew brighter and brighter until the cemetery bathed in a golden radiance which penetrated closed eyelids and surrounded them all.

Mark opened his eyes to where Uriel had been but only saw a shimmer of whirling light arcing up to the sky where a brilliant glow effaced one side of Apollyon in a multihued conformation. Tendrils of bright green and blue and shades of violet streaked from behind the rogue planet and across the sky in a massive Aurora Borealis. The headlights of the surrounding vehicles and the rotating beacon on the helicopter extinguished.

A wisp of wind blew any remnants of fog between the surrounding trees into a spiral around the freshly dug earthen crypt, which swallowed any trace of matter that chanced to come near.

There was no longer any sign of Uriel, and Dog lay on his side in the grass. Tomás had risen to one knee, and Father Romero clasped his hands and looked up above. The barest hint of sunlight rimmed one side of Apollyon, and Mark wasn't sure, but he thought the rogue planet had shifted ever so slightly in the sky.

Father Romero quietly mouthed a prayer of thanksgiving. Maria searched for Sofia, who had moved in front of Tomás and placed a hand on his side. Paul stared up at the sky with his arms around Felicity, and Martin shook his camera like something was wrong with it.

Sofia leaned in and spoke to Tomás. Mark could barely hear her saying something about his grandmother, but whatever it was, it brought a wan smile to the man's face.

Mark had forgotten about Donovan and his men, but Walter brought them back into focus.

"Uh-oh," said his friend.

Donovan braced his hand on his raised knee and stood as he shook his slack face and smacked his lips. He brought his fingers up and wiggled them while turning his wrists back and forth. He clenched his hands into fists and thrust his face up at the multicolored sky before looking around. He grunted in frustration. His bodyguards had run off, leaving their unresponsive vehicles as a testament to his failure. Donovan spun about wildly until he spied Sofia, and his shoulders drooped.

"I'm not sure what you did," he said. "But nothing has changed. You will serve your purpose."

Donovan bent over to pick up his knife from the ground. When he straightened back up, he held his pistol in his right hand.

"My family is gone," he said and looked up at the sky again. "Nothing matters anymore."

Father Romero tried to reason with him.

"My son, you don't want to do this," said the priest.

Donovan swayed as he spoke.

"Look above," he said. "There is no right or wrong."

Mark knew there was no sense in talking, but he had to try.

"I'm sorry about your son," he said.

Donovan stared beyond Mark at a future never to come.

"My son is dead," he said. "He is lost to me."

Father Romero said, "He is at peace now."

Donovan swung his hand holding the pistol toward the priest.

"There is no peace," he said. "How can I believe in a God who allowed my son to die?"

"You can't honor your son by killing little girls," said Mark.

Donovan Giulanti turned his full attention to Mark again.

"My son is past caring about honor," he said. "You took him away from me. I brought her here to save my son!" He gestured at Sofia. "Now, it's too late for all of us."

Donovan shrugged his shoulders and glanced up at the doomsday hurtling at them before looking back.

"But I can bring my accounts due before the end," he said. "I brought her here to die, and you will join her. My son is dead because of you, and she still owes me a heart."

Donovan centered his pistol and took steady aim at Sofia.

"No!" screamed Maria, grabbing Sofia and shielding her with her body.

Mark watched it happen in slow motion and feared he would not be quick enough as he leapt for his girls. He saw Donovan's gaze narrow and the tendons slide in his hand as he pulled the trigger three times. Mark even saw the rounds spin in their path toward the girls and watched the bullets slam into his body like hot bricks. He grunted and struggled to get air back into his lungs as he fell to his hands and knees in front of Maria.

Donovan's face masked in fury as he aimed again. Only this time, Mark couldn't stop it. He wanted to tell Maria to hide behind him but didn't have the wind to speak.

Please God, let it be me and not them.

A suppressed gunshot sounded close at hand, and Donovan looked surprised as a bloom of red blossomed on his shirt. He stumbled but ignored the wound in his obsession to finish his task, and he stepped toward Maria and Sofia with murder in his eyes.

Tomás staggered to the front with his pistol outstretched, and Donovan aimed and fired at the assassin. Tomás shrugged off one gunshot wound after another and returned fire. In a haze, Mark saw Donovan falter under several clustered wounds to his torso, and then Tomás was on him, driving the big man back until they were at the edge of the open grave which beckoned like nothing else on this planet, a living, breathing nothingness which would not be denied. Donovan dug in his heels and grappled with the assassin, who leveraged Donovan's arms and pushed forward relentlessly.

Tomás cried out, "Grandmother, I did it!"

Donovan's eyes widened, and his mouth contorted in a silent scream as Tomás heaved once more and both of them tumbled into the crypt. The surrounding mound of dirt oscillated and collapsed into the open grave in rhythm with the planet's keening death song until only undisturbed grass remained.

Mark lay on the cold ground and sensed Maria and Sofia beside him as Father Romero anointed his forehead and prayed. Staring up at the covered sky, the rogue planet expanded in blackness to the edges of his vision. He had protected Sofia, but only for a few hours, and he sank into the grass and the earth beneath, brown and gray and black. The musty scent of dirt filled his nose and mouth, and he breathed it in to mix with his soul, and after a while, the pain ebbed away, leaving only light and peace.

Mark opened his eyes and looked up. There was no impending disaster, just wispy cotton candy clouds in an otherwise azure sky. Vivid green trees swayed gently in the breeze around him, and he stood on a worn path of short grass beside a white wooden picket fence.

There was a gate there, and somehow he knew if he walked through that gate, he could stay forever. He considered doing just that and saw someone approaching. He strained to see and almost fell. Madelyn and Faith walked toward him hand in hand, smiling and laughing together.

"Always late to the party, babe," said Maddie.

She had loved to tease when he got lost in his work and forgot everything else around him. How he wished he could live every one of those moments again.

"Is this Heaven?" he asked.

Faith stood there grinning at him with that same crooked grin she always gave when he was slow on the uptake. She loved to be one step ahead of him.

"It is now, Dad. He told us we'd see you soon."

Mark wanted to ask who He was, but Maddie reached over the

fence and brushed at the front of his shirt. The blood and gore from the bullet impacts disappeared. He had his family again, and he felt whole. Wherever this was, it felt like Heaven to him.

"I'm sorry," he said. "I'm so sorry."

"It wasn't your fault," said Maddie. "We were all tired, but you were right. Donovan Giulanti tried to have you killed, and there wasn't anything you could have done."

Maddie looked at him, waiting, her eyes full of love.

Mark asked, "I can stay here with you?"

They were standing with the gate between them.

"Yes," said Maddie.

Faith stood there grinning, waiting for him to understand. She always had a way of making him feel he was one idea behind, even when he wasn't.

He should just open the gate and cross through the fence. Didn't he deserve to be happy with his family? Mark placed a hand on the gate, but he kept seeing Maria and Sofia and Walter and even Roger.

"What about my friends?" he asked.

Maddie and Faith stood there waiting for him to admit what he didn't want to say.

"I can't leave them now."

"They need you," said Maddie.

"She loves you," said Faith.

His daughter reached across the picket fence to pat his chest, and Mark felt a stabbing fire like a broken rib with each breath or cough.

"But I can't let you go again," he said, his breath catching. "I can't bear it."

Maddie and Faith waved to him from the other side.

"We love you," said both of them, smiling. "We will see you again."

Their voices trailed off, and Mark opened his eyes to see the headstones of his wife and daughter behind an owl-eyed Paul, who knelt a short distance away and peered around Father Romero.

Mark's chest grated with each inhalation, and the ground pushed against his back. Maria knelt beside his head with her hands on either side of his face. He forced a shallow breath in and out. It hurt. He looked over and saw Sofia smiling on his left. She had her hand on his chest, and he reached up and brushed her face with his fingers.

"Welcome back," said Walter with a smile that wrapped around his face.

Martin looked up and down and straight ahead and pried at his camera while muttering softly. Paul shook his head while Felicity fell to her knees beside him with her hands clasped and fingers interlaced.

"I can't believe it's real," said Paul. "It's all true."

Mark touched his chest which ached like one enormous bruise, but there were no holes. He looked at Sofia, and she grinned.

Above Maria, Mark saw only half the outline of the rogue planet. It had moved in the sky noticeably from left to right. Maria rubbed his temples, and it felt good. He focused on that for a moment.

A tongue licked his face, slobbering wet and warm. It was Dog.

CHAPTER THIRTY-THREE

Mark sat in a rocking chair on his front porch and listened to the emergency crank radio retrieved from his safe. It still worked unlike many other devices powered by electricity, and they could sometimes catch a short broadcast or a bit of music from one of the few stations still on the air.

Walter had already been by to check in and complain about the coffee and tease his girls, as he called them. Mark thought his old friend said it just so he would get hugs from them, and he couldn't blame him.

Maria had brought Mark a blanket for his shoulders, but the clear day already felt warmer with full sunshine. The rogue planet had missed the Earth by eighty thousand miles. There had been further earthquakes and volcanic eruptions and flooding and loss of life, but somehow the Earth and the Moon still orbited each other and the Sun. Three weeks later, Mark looked up at the bright blue sky and felt grateful every day.

The music on the radio faded in and out, which had been the norm since Apollyon. The broadcast gave way to a news interview regarding the recent close call for the planet and the speculation by a young amateur scientist that a coronal mass ejection from the Sun struck directly at Earth and would have decimated the planet except for Apollyon, which was between the Sun and the Earth and took the brunt of the Sun's plasma burst.

"The heating at the back side of the rogue planet exposed pockets of gas and increased the velocity of Apollyon just enough to pass in front of the Earth."

Samuel Branchwater was being interviewed from a location in Texas as part of a team headed up by Professor Barry Michaels, former science advisor to the president. The professor had come out to stand with Samuel and explained that the plasma burst from the Sun had been more powerful than any in recorded history.

"Professor, what do you think?" asked one reporter. "Will we see Apollyon again like some comets?"

"I think we are more fortunate than we know," said the professor. "The rogue planet is on a trajectory with enough velocity to take it out of our solar system. I think young Samuel is on the right path with his theory, and I expect great things from him in the future." Professor Michaels added that the Sun's plasma burst would have fried the planet to a crisp were it not for the interposition of Apollyon. "As it is, we'll be dealing with the damage from the electromagnetic pulse for some time."

"But Professor, wouldn't it be impossibly coincidental for all this to happen in just this way?" asked one reporter.

"Depends on who's doing the driving," said Professor Michaels.

Mark said exactly the same thing at exactly the same time, and shivers ran down his spine.

"What did you say?" asked Maria, walking out onto the porch.

She always seemed to hear him, even when the doors were closed, like she knew what he was thinking, but he would never admit that. She came out to the front porch to enjoy the view and sat in the chair next to him.

"I was listening to the news and agreeing that we're more fortunate than we know," he said.

There was a gleeful shout, and Sofia raced around the house, her long brown hair flying behind her. Dog bounded after her, careful not to trip her up. Was that shepherd laughing? Mark glanced over at

Maria. He knew she heard him, and he tried to think of what to say next.

"Roger and Martha are coming by this afternoon," she said. "He wants to ask for your help when you feel up to it."

She had her poker face on.

Mark waited for her to say more, but she seemed content to rock in silence next to him. The sheriff had survived his gunshot wound and convalesced under the care of Martha, who would not let him out of her sight.

"Is there something else?" he asked.

Maria crossed her legs. She was wearing sneakers with low-cut sports socks. He didn't know why that was suddenly so fascinating, and he felt his heart beat faster.

"Father Romero sent a letter," she said.

Mark knew she was concerned about when to return to the convent. He'd been careful about what he said after they returned to the farm, and she had stayed with him while he healed. The farmhouse walls needed patching, but Maria had forbidden him getting anywhere near a ladder. His chest still felt like one big strained muscle with any exertion like now when his breathing quickened. He thought of Maddie and Faith again and knew he needed to say something. Courage, man, he thought.

Maria sighed, uncrossed her legs, and started to stand.

"Maria?"

Mark rubbed at his face, which felt warm. He'd managed to say her name, but his tongue felt like a piece of framing wood.

"Yes?"

"What did Father Romero have to say?"

Mark kind of blurted out the words, and he looked down at the porch and winced. He really wanted to know what his friend said, but there was so much more he needed to say.

Maria sat back down and said, "He wanted to know if we were all right and if we needed anything. He wants to check on Sofia and hopes to come and see her in a few weeks."

Mark nodded. Transportation had changed drastically with the damage from Apollyon, and it had not been easy for Father Romero to make his way back to his parish. Sofia's status was still uncertain, and Mark couldn't bear to think of her separated from him or Maria.

"What are you thinking?" he asked.

"I'm not sure what to do," she said. "I have asked God what his plan is for me."

"And?"

Mark saw her hesitation, and when she didn't answer right away, he rallied his courage.

"Do you think God could allow you to stay here with us?" he asked.

Maria seemed unable to respond and looked at him, her exquisite brown eyes full of mystery, longing, and a promise that pulled him to her.

Mark reached over and placed his hand on hers.

"We would be lost without you."

She bowed her head, and a tear ran down her face.

Mark held her hand and half-stumbled to one knee in front of her.

Please God, let me say this well.

"I want you to stay as my wife and Sofia's mother for the rest of our lives. Do you think God could let you do that?"

She seemed frozen like she struggled to believe his words.

"Maria, I love you," he said. "I want you, and I need you. Please be my wife."

He focused on her face. He could feel Maddie and Faith urging him on, and Faith's words kept ringing in his ears.

They need you too, Dad.

He felt the silence and sensed that Sofia and Dog were watching from the front yard. He saw Maria's face flash to them and could see their reflection in her tear-filled eyes. They were both smiling.

Maria bowed her head for a moment and then looked at him, her eyes shining.

"Yes, I will marry you, Mark Lawson."

She caught her breath at the end of her reply and nodded her head up and down.

Sofia shouted, "Yaaaah!"

Dog barked excitedly.

Mark stood, and Maria came to him with a slight pressure from his hands. He wrapped his arms around her while she looked up at him, and gently, tenderly, he found her lips with his. The universe slowed, measured only by her beating heart, and his soul reached out to hers until they paced together, not two but one. She pulled him close, and he quickly warmed to the task at hand. Then, he felt young hands hugging both of them, and Dog wedged in to reinforce the family rule of no hugging without the dog.

Sofia raised her arms to be held, and Mark picked her up, holding her with his right arm. His chest only hurt a little. She kissed him on his cheek and kissed Maria on her cheek. Both of them kissed her back, and she giggled. They swayed, dancing to music that sprang forth from the radio like magic before fading out.

Mark slowly sat back down on the chair with Maria on his left knee and Sofia on his right. He breathed in the sweet grass-scented air and the reality of a second chance. Faith was right. Each person has their gifts. Maddie and Faith could love without limits, and Sofia could heal and see angels. He was a blessed man.

-The End-

ACKNOWLEDGMENTS

I would like to thank Jack, Phillip, Rachel, and Stephanie for their comments and feedback while beta-reading versions of this novel in progress. Thank you to Sara DeGonia for her work as editor. Finally, thank you to Les@GermanCreative for her cover design.

ABOUT THE AUTHOR

Lawrence Simpson is an emerging author of fiction. This is his fifth novel. He is retired and enjoys writing, flying, and camping.

For more books and updates:
www.LawrenceSimpsonWrites.com